WHISPERS IN
AUTUMN

WHISPERS IN AUTUMN

TRISHA LEIGH

For Anthony, who was the first person to tell me this story had merit, and who has been a treasured part of my life—even when I've done nothing to deserve him.

1.

Before my eyelids crack open I know I've traveled again.

The oppressive, terrifying certainty that I no longer exist is a dead giveaway. The familiarity of the sensation does nothing to dull the roaring panic as sweat rolls off me and a scream begs to erupt from my heaving chest.

Breathe, Althea. You still exist.

My heart rate slows as it responds to the calming voice of reason in my head. It sounds like me, only prettier and definitely calmer. At least part of my brain possesses some clarity.

It's early morning. It always is. The sound of movement on the floor below forces my fists to unclench, releasing the garish orange comforter wrinkled inside them. Last night I fell asleep at the Hammonds' house, where the bedding is green and spring is creeping toward an end. I never get used to starting over like this, but as my travels grow more frequent, a kind of numbness settles in as my feet find their way out from under the heavy down and settle into the slippers beside the bed.

As if I never left.

I shuffle across the thick brown carpet and kneel on the padded window seat to peer outside. The trees are bright splotches against the vivid blue sky—some crimson, others a sunny yellow—with a few fiery oranges scattered about. Their bold colors verify my suspicions.

It's autumn now.

My breath fogs up the glass, obscuring the view. Despite my best efforts, water wells up in my eyes. This is still Earth, I remind myself. The only world I've ever known. It just looks different than it did yesterday.

Spring was short for me this time, a mere three or four weeks. I haven't been yanked out of a season that fast in years. Even without control over my season hops, part of me never gives up hope that someday it will stop. That I will stay in one place, find a way to fit in.

It's no use, though. The years have taught me that hope is a worthless dream.

I gnaw on my fingertips and assemble the facts of this life in my mind. Autumn means Connecticut and that means the Morgans.

Althea Morgan. That's the autumn me.

The name rolls around in my head a few times in an attempt to make it stick. It usually takes a few days before it does.

"Thea, darling! Come and get some breakfast! Opening block starts in less than an hour!"

A sigh begins deep inside and burbles up until it spills out in a heavy *whoosh*. Mr. Morgan doesn't need to inform me what time I'm required to be settled at my desk, ready to listen to fruitless lectures. It hasn't changed in ten years.

Not ready to face the breakfast scene, I head for the shower instead, still chanting my name under my breath. The cleansing room contains a frilly robe, some makeup I'll hardly wear, a toothbrush, and some fluffy orange towels. All items that belong to me but aren't mine.

Without needing to check, I know similar provisions hang in the closet and are stuffed in the dark oak furniture. In my worst moments I want to rip everything to shreds. On traveling days it's hard to summon the energy.

Under the stream of hot water, the scent of jasmine fills my nose. All my showers, in all my houses, are stocked with the same homemade shampoo. I asked my winter mother why she made it for me one time and earned a strange look but no answer. The fragrance clings to me whether I wash my hair or not, and is one of the most constant things in my life, though I've never smelled the flower itself.

It only blooms in the summer. The one season I've never seen.

I press my forehead against the cold white tile and try to stop shivering. The struggle to shake off the traveling knocks me to my knees on the slippery floor. Nagging fear that the shower is imagined, that the orange comforter and the autumn leaves are part of a dream, chokes off my air supply. I'm sure I'm truly gone this time, hidden forever in the black emptiness between seasons. The pain from the scalding water against my face, the sight of blood where the pink razor nicks my skin, both offer a trembling belief that my body exists here—now—at the Morgans'.

Going to sleep one place, with a certain family, and waking up in another life often tips me sideways for the first couple of hours. I don't recall the traveling, but rather the endless dark void of the process. As though my body dissolves into a million pieces, and no matter how many times it happens, my brain frets I won't get put back together.

The familiarity of my morning ritual helps as I stand in front of the mirror and conquer the tangles in my sopping red hair. Next, I cover my damp body with jeans and a long-sleeved T-shirt, dry my hair and then brush my teeth. Ready to face the day, I leave the cleansing room, cross to the bedroom door, and push it closed.

My locket works loose from beneath the shirt collar, dropping into my palm as I flop down onto the mussed bed. This necklace alone joins me on my strange travels.

A jeweled four-pointed star, no bigger than my thumbnail, dangles off the end of a gold chain so delicate it could snap with almost no effort at all. Gold flecks litter the surface of the reflective black jewel. I pry it open with practiced care and pull out the tiny folded square of paper lodged inside. Rereading it on travel days has become a ritual.

Althea,
You feel different because you are Something Else, a Dissident. But you are not the only one. There are more, and you will find each other when it is necessary. In the meantime, trust no one.
Ko

Who Ko is and why he scrunched this note inside my necklace are vexing mysteries. The word *Dissident* doesn't exist on Earth, at least not in any of the textbooks presented to me during my preparatory phase, though it clearly means I'm not like everyone else. If the note weren't addressed to me, I would assume it's a mistake.

But my name *is* on it, and I *am* different.

My fingers refold the paper as it had been before, the only way it will settle back inside the small locket. Reading the note helps me feel less alone, even though that's what I am. It reminds me to bury the differences hiding inside me. After all these years, concealing them is second nature. It used to be hard when I was small, when I still believed people would hear me if I shouted loud enough—before I accepted I am like a shadow, something people see but acknowledge as a mere trick of the eye. Whatever hides the real me from the world helps safeguard my secrets. It also ensures my solitude.

"Thea! Ten-minute warning!"

Irritation skips through me at the nickname. All my parents insist on using one version or another. I broke the Hammonds of the habit when I spent three consecutive years with them in Portland, Oregon— minus summers, of course. They've gone back to calling me Allie now.

The cold kitchen waits at the bottom of the stairs, on the left through a doorway. I slide into my seat across the round table from Mr. Morgan and force a smile in response to his. There's nothing remarkable about him, nothing that would cause someone to remember his face. His hair and eyes are exactly the same shade of sandy brown as the bushy mustache that sits on his upper lip.

"Good morning. Have some pancakes. You'll need to be out the door in eight minutes."

Neither of them notices I've been away. It's a mystery, what they believe about my absences. I can't remember how much time has passed since I last lived under their roof. I stare down at my plate. It feels like it's been a while.

Mr. Morgan turns his attention back to his breakfast, finishing off a stack of cranberry pancakes doused in honey. The cranberry pancakes are one of the better things about the Morgans. It's one of their markers, the little nuances separating one family from the next, like the frilly clothes and the tendency to decorate in shades of orange and brown. It could be worse. The Clarks, my winter family, love to cook with chickpeas.

The thought of spring and the Hammonds' gooey, homemade cinnamon rolls jams a lump into my throat. I push the memory away and scarf three pancakes and two pieces of turkey bacon, then down a glass of orange juice before standing up and carrying the plate to the sink. I eat out of habit, and because it's expected.

What's *normal.*

Mrs. Morgan washes the dishes by hand, a white, lace-edged apron protecting her calf-length dress. I slide an arm around her slender waist and kiss her cheek as a stray piece of graying hair tickles my neck. My lips smile as my stomach heaves and the cranberry pancakes threaten to take a curtain call. I plant a matching kiss on Mr. Morgan before heading out of the kitchen toward the front door.

Two shelves and a table full of family photos flank the path through the living room. The pictures featuring my face are all set against autumn backdrops. The Morgans never mention it or act like it's weird. I don't think they know I leave.

A backpack waits on a hook next to the front door, worn and smelling vaguely of stale sweat. The canvas bag weighs nearly nothing; it contains only identification and extra pencils. Everything else will be waiting in opening block. I might have left the backpack on its hook last night, after Cell.

If I'd been here last night.

The clock on the wall clicks to eight-fifteen and I step out onto the porch, where crisp, cool autumn air infiltrates my lungs. The sun is out, its rays lukewarm instead of hot, the way they were yesterday in the Portland springtime. The temperature hovers around sixty degrees. Pleasant, some might say. It's a bit chilly for me, and I think for a split second about going back inside to grab a sweater.

Up and down the street, doors open and children step outside the exact same time. A boy who looks to be my age two doors down, a little girl farther up the block. Our feet hit the sidewalk together. Mine lead toward Upper Cell, where I'll begin the last year of my preparatory phase. Not that it makes a difference. I have no one to miss when we Ascend to adulthood, no friends at Danbury Preparatory Cell.

I haven't got friends anywhere.

2.

Danbury Prep is a replica of my other Cells, from the redbrick exterior covering its two stories to the perfectly manicured lawn. We've studied biology on repeat for years, until understanding how each individual cell is an identical match to the next and together they create something greater—an organism— is second nature. In the same way, the Cells we attend make up the preparatory phase of development. Primer Cell begins at age five, followed by Intermediate Cell, and finally Upper Cell. Ascension after the last year— the Terminal year—takes place between our sixteen and seventeenth nataldays.

The sight of this particular Cell brews apprehension in my center. My pace doesn't falter, because being tardy is not Acceptable, but the terrifying weight of my perceived invisibility returns with a vengeance. Students laugh and talk with one another, ignoring me as they amble toward their opening block. Sweat breaks out on my forehead and my stomach twists. I wait to disappear into the crushing black nothingness of travel.

Then some giggling younger girls toss odd looks my direction, their acknowledgment unwinding the tension from my neck and shoulders. Even though I am insubstantial to them, I am not invisible. My peers see me. They just don't *see* me. Not well enough to respond properly, to befriend me, to ask me to sit at their eatery tables.

As though somewhere deep inside they know I'm a Dissident, and have a built-in instinct to avoid me. They often watch me through befuddled eyes, as though trying to figure me out. Because each human, like each molecule in a cell, is supposed to be indistinguishable from the rest, and I am not.

I am *not*.

It took over a year to make friends with Val and Monica the time I stayed put in Portland with the Hammonds. They grew used to the strangeness I haul around like an extra appendage, even teased me about it. Now that I don't stay for long, they look through me like everyone else.

That's the hardest part of going back.

Today a pasted-on grin allows me to blend in, if not be welcomed. My schedule is always the same, and since my Cells are identical, knowing where to go isn't a problem. I make my way through the quiet halls to algebra.

The swell of kids at the door moves aside, and I head to the rear of the square colorless room. Notepads and textbooks lay atop the clammy metal desks. The lights dim twice in quick succession, letting us know block is about to begin. As they dim a third time they remain that way, and the big screen in the front of the room flickers to life. Beside it, a lone portrait adorns the bare white walls. One hangs in every classroom, each depicting one of the four leaders of the Others.

The Others are our government, our royalty, our absolute rulers. Since they arrived on Earth they've decreed what is Acceptable, who is Broken, who we Partner with, what our Career will be. Every major choice in our lives is decided by them. They are better than us. Smarter, stronger, more powerful.

At least, that's what we're taught. I have no reason to doubt them, besides the pricks of wrongness their appearance scatters across my skin.

The picture in the algebra room depicts the Other known as Air. The perfect blond-haired man, all chiseled jaw and sharp cheekbones, stares down at us from the wall. His inhospitable gaze, completely black but for a pinpoint of intense blue at the center, reminds us they are watching.

Always.

We do not see Others often, at least not in person, but they see us. They've installed cameras everywhere, and adults interact with them via the Network on a regular basis. Their presence is felt among humans in the form of awe and deference. As far as I can tell, no one fears them. Except me.

The Monitor appears on the display screen and pulls my gaze from Air's intense black one. The bespectacled man looks more like a mole in an earth science textbook than a human, with his small, beady eyes and twitching nose. He takes attendance and we raise our hands one at a time to announce our presence. I've never witnessed an absence.

He begins the lecture and everyone starts taking notes. There's no good reason for this, since it's the same material we've covered three times before. The Upper Cell subjects and lectures don't change in all four years. It's clear to me we're not here to learn, not any longer, but more as a way to keep us controlled and supervised until the Others decide how we can best serve them as adults. None of my Cellmates seem to notice the repetition. Or mind. Their eyes lock on the Monitor, glancing down every couple of moments to jot down some notes with interested half-smiles.

After listening to him drone on for a half an hour, in which I count all seventy-two squares on his ugly plaid shirt and decide his eyes are exactly the color of dead grass, it's time to move on. Calculus is next, followed by astronomy, lunch, more astronomy, exercise, physics, and then chemistry. Our math and science skills are ingrained by now, but few Careers put them to good use.

Cold dismay pours through me when lunch block arrives. No one sits alone in the eatery, and the tables are assigned by year. Usually we split up by gender, too, but that's not a rule. For a second I think Val's waving her arms at me, a seat saved next to her, but this is Danbury, Connecticut not Portland, Oregon. Even if it were Portland, Val wouldn't save me a seat.

Not anymore.

I force a smile and locate an empty seat at a table full of other Terminals, or Terms, as we're called for short. The girls scoot away from me as I settle into a hard chair. It's subtle, as any discord is not Acceptable, and they all do it at once as though they can't help it. Their faces reflect brief confusion, like they don't understand why either, but settle into contented smiles in the blink of an eye. The lump reappears in my throat and I work on swallowing. I should be used to it, but my outcast status hits hard the first day at a new Cell.

Instead of dwelling on the aching discomfort of being snubbed, I pretend interest in the portraits on the wall. In the eatery, pictures of the four Other leaders hang together. Air. Water. Fire. Earth.

The Elements.

There are many Others but only four Elements. They are Other, but more powerful, more beautiful. And exceedingly rare. Each generation, four Others are marked with a secret brand. They become the Elements and wield the power to control that for which they are named.

The four scowl down from their portraits, unhappy and disgruntled. All men, save one. Fire is a woman with hair as deep red as my own, but it sprouts from her head in a wild tangle of curls, where mine hangs thick and straight. The blistering contempt in her face shoots a flame-tipped arrow of foreboding through my center.

Lunch consists of identical bowls of salad covered with fruit, chicken, and an oil-based dressing. I pay dutiful interest to my food and half listen to the chatter fluttering about the table. A brunette with crooked teeth and a big nose jabbers louder than the rest, then a tiny girl interrupts. Her inky hair curls away from her head in loose ringlets, and watching them bounce enthralls me for several seconds as she speaks.

"I hope I end up with an Administration placement. I love working for the Others."

The brunette smiles, but it doesn't reach her empty eyes. "You're a shoo-in after helping in the Administrative Center for four years."

Most people have more than one talent, but when they're given a Career, people are always happy about it. Which isn't odd, considering people are always happy. No human on Earth is anything but serene, content, pleased. Except me.

But according to Ko, I am Something Else. Dissident.

The subject changes abruptly when a girl with hair so blond it's almost white puts down her fork. "Has anyone been asked to the Gathering this weekend?"

Heads around my table shake from side to side. The blond girl's smile stretches her cheeks wide, and the tall brunette's mouth drops open, face reflecting delighted shock. "Brittany, someone asked you, I can see it on your face. How come you're just now telling us?"

"It happened on my way to lunch. Greg asked me."

Oohs and ahhs and congratulations abound, which I can't echo sincerely without knowing who Greg is. Their talk about Careers, the Gathering, and boys fades into the background as lunch disappears into my not-hungry stomach. Conversations are pretty much the same everywhere. Since we possess a limited number of topics, it's not difficult to guess what will be discussed. Occasionally schoolwork, sometimes the Summer Celebration or the movie we watched last weekend.

Every once in a while someone will attend a Partnering ceremony, or a death pyre, but those are rare.

The Gathering, unique to the last year, will provide plenty of fodder for gossip this autumn. It will take place in a few days, intended to promote voluntary Partnering. If we're going to choose our own Partner, we have to declare intentions before summer.

Vines of panic coil around my heart as fear, icy and hot, clenches in my stomach. The thought of Partnering, so appealing and exciting to most girls, never triggers positive feelings in me. After our preparatory phase is complete and we're Partnered adults, we're not allowed in public except during once a month designated outings. All work is done through the Network. Our *lives* are lived through the Network.

If I Partner, will he be like my parade of changing parents? Will I travel between Iowa, Portland, and Danbury, a new Partner in each place, none of them noticing when I come and go?

The idea of being cooped up with a boy who looks right through me, working for the Others all day and then sitting in front of mindless movies all night, is enough to bring hysterical water to my eyes. I've never seen anyone else react this way and I blink it back, keeping my gaze trained on my empty salad bowl. No one notices anyway.

Trust no one.

The words from my note leap into my mind. They imply no one should know about me, about my travels, how I have feelings that aren't always good.

I'll have to Partner to keep my secret. I know that.

But knowing doesn't stop every last piece of me from screaming in resistance. Invisible bonds pin me in place, cramming me into a mold that I don't fit into.

Don't be silly, Althea. You belong here. You need to calm down.

I brush the hair away from my sweaty forehead and rest my palms face up in my lap where they'll be safe. The bell rings and we get up from the table, a robotic staff coming behind us to clear our dishes and trash. I trail the herd out of the room, still working to control my unpleasant thoughts, hiding the struggle behind a manufactured smile. My smiles require effort; everyone else looks as though reasons exist to lift their lips in happiness.

Those reasons are as elusive today as they've always been.

The rest of the day passes in a blur, but listening to the same lectures for a fourth time doesn't require much attention. My peers seem genuinely interested in learning about molecules, equations, planet histories, and the like all over again. They smile at one another in the hallways, a spring in their steps.

My feet drag through the door to chemistry, the end block of my day. A boy sits in the back corner, near where I plan to settle, and something about him piques my interest. His dark blond hair is long enough that it curls a bit at the tips. His eyes focus on the dark, empty screen in the front as he waits for the Monitor to appear. They're blue, a blue so brilliant it's like looking at the sky. The same shade of blue I see in the mirror.

The lights dim the first time as I take a seat next to him and open my notebook. This Monitor is easy to remember, a woman who looks about ten years older than us and is passionate about chemistry. She doesn't reprimand us when we don't understand, not exactly.

Her smile, though, it wavers a bit. She fascinates me.

I've seen another smile waver like that, but just one. The memory nudges against the walls I've erected around it, whispering through the cracks.

A Monitor in Portland asked me to clean her room after Cell that last spring in Portland. The way she accepted my presence made my blood sing with genuine pleasure; it lulled me into a place of comfort.

That comfort betrayed me. Naturally.

Even now, remembering what I said quickens my heart and floods my cheeks with heat.

Sometimes it scares me, the way the Others keep us separated. I wish you could come and Monitor us in person.

The mistake, the blatant admission of wishing for life to be different, hit me even before the sentence fell from my lips. Horrified, I waited for her to turn me in, to tell the Others about the girl who doesn't trust them. The girl who fears them.

She didn't. Instead she dismissed me. But her smile. . .it wobbled.

I traveled that night. My own stupidity cost me my friends, the Hammonds, and the life I'd been allowed to build during those seasons in Portland. I've never forgotten what I am again, never made the mistake of imagining that I belong.

The boy next to me shifts in his seat, leaning down to get a new pencil out of his battered bag and jarring me out of my reverie. His head ends up near my right elbow as he rummages, and the change in position sends a gust of air my direction. The permeating, distinctive smell of pine threatens to overwhelm me. It's not unpleasant, just forceful, and a slow breath helps me acclimate.

When he straightens up and catches me watching him, a blush creeps across his pale cheeks. He turns his attention back to the screen, nearly knocking a notepad off the desk in his haste.

I refocus on the Monitor as well, not wanting to earn any unwanted attention, but continue to sneak looks at my new neighbor. It's nagging me now, the idea that something is wrong about him. Then it hits me like a punch in the gut.

He isn't smiling.

3.

Pine Boy, whose name is actually Lucas—thank you, pointless attendance roster—hustles away after chemistry without a word. I wander out at a more measured pace, not anxious for the open time after Cell. Everyone over the age of thirteen has an hour to waste before going home. My Cellmates will end up at one of the three public establishments in town: the pizza parlor, the bowling alley, or the park. They never extend an invitation for me to join them, but I probably wouldn't accept anyway. It's just another chance to give away my secrets.

Consequently, my free hour is most often spent wandering alone around town. The day gets colder as the sun sinks toward the horizon and I curse my haste to leave the Morgans' without a sweater this morning. Maybe Air would relax with the autumn chill thing if I asked nicely. His dead, pitiless gaze pops into my mind's eye and I shiver.

Maybe not.

Today my meandering leads me to the park. A brisk wind continues to blow, stirring up the colorful leaves and swirling them across the sidewalk. The breeze pierces through my thin shirtsleeves and attacks my skin, raising goose bumps along my arms. I check my watch but there are still forty-five minutes to survive before going "home" is an option.

The inner park is a large clearing filled with toys for little kids. This time of year sunflowers shoot up above the waist-high grass past the clearing, their bright yellow faces and velvety brown noses mocking my gray spirits. A thin grove of trees scatter beyond the flowers, less than twenty deep from the end of the field to the boundary separating us from the Wilds. For the moment their dramatic leaves brighten the drab afternoon.

A group of teenagers spin on a merry-go-round meant for much smaller children, but the cover offered by the trees allows me to give them a wide berth. I stroll as far as permitted, all the way to the city limit. An electric fence surrounds the park and I resist the urge to run my hand over the boundary to test its power. A silly thought, I know.

My mind wanders as I gaze through the wire fence, woven tight to keep the predators out. The forest is dense, and though leaves rustle and branches tremble, the plant life hides whatever lurks. A shudder starts in my shoulders and makes its way down through my toes.

Animals.

Evil creatures that would maim, rip, and kill humans without a second thought. If that doesn't work, their diseases will do the trick. When the Others came to our planet they erected the twenty-foot boundary to ensure our safety. Farther out a net hangs, stopping about six feet from the earth to prevent the flying creatures from getting in. The Others walk in the Wilds sometimes. Humans never do. It's not Acceptable to leave the safety of town, not that anyone would.

There's no reason to believe the Others would lie about our inability to survive without their protection. They've taken care of us since coming to this planet, guarding us against attack, providing for us, ensuring our happiness. But lately my ingrained fear of the animals struggles against jealousy. Not because I want to be out there with them, but because I envy their freedom.

The trees shimmying in the breeze are mostly oak and maple, lacking both the scent and lush green of a grove of pines. The thought of pine trees reminds me of the unsmiling boy in my chemistry block. Focusing on that mystery is far more interesting than moping about being cold.

The events of the day replay like scenes from a movie, the questions surrounding the boy burrowing under my skin. It might be the season, the new Cell year, or my unexpected arrival just this morning, but I can't shake the feeling that something significant is about to happen.

Another silly thought. Nothing changes in this world.

A glance at my watch reveals a mere ten minutes until curfew. I'm not sure what would happen if I were late, seeing how I've never had the guts to try it. Instead of summoning the courage to flout the rules, I step into a jog.

Around the corner of the Morgans' street, the sight of a boy lying on his back two houses down, staring up at the sky, stops me short. The mop of blond curls and dingy red backpack tell me it's Pine Boy. That he lives nearby is a surprise, though I don't know why. I can't even remember the last time I lived in Danbury, and people employed in certain Careers do relocate from time to time.

He sits up and sees me standing here gawking at him and makes an effort to appear happy. The corners of his mouth look like they would fall down if he let them, like they're being pushed up and held instead of lifting of their own accord. Having spent years manufacturing my own smile, spotting another fake one is surprisingly easy.

As I draw closer, the swirling air lands on my tongue, eliciting a cough at the sharp taste of pine. Maybe he woke too late to shower this morning and overdid it on the cologne. Our gazes fuse until an uneven spot on the sidewalk forces my eyes forward again. Fog grows inside my mind as he mutters something under his breath and heads inside.

When our eyes locked it felt as though the world ceased to be. Like the opposite of the crushing emptiness of my traveling nightmares, where the world still is but I am not. Just now, staring at this strange boy, it felt as though only the two of us exist.

The premonition that change waits on the fringes of my world returns in a rush. I'm suddenly certain that the appearance of this boy is part of whatever's coming.

I crash through the Morgans' front door as the clock chimes five, struggling to catch my breath and get it together before Mr. Morgan looks up from his paper. The normalcy of the scene helps. Each day after work Mr. Morgan changes out of his dress pants and tie, exchanging them for faded khakis and a white polo. Running water and clanging pots mean Mrs. Morgan is fluttering about the kitchen making dinner. Without laying eyes on her I know she's wearing a floral print dress covered by the same feminine apron she had on this morning. Mrs. Morgan doesn't believe in wearing pants. The closet here boasts more dresses and skirts than my other two combined and I'm lucky she acquires jeans for me at all.

With a deep inhale I push the corners of my own mouth up, the effort bringing back the memory of the boy's smile as I hang my bag by the door.

"Hi, Mr.. . .Dad. I'm home."

He glances at the clock, flicks a glance my direction, then returns his eyes to the paper. "Hi, honey. Better go get changed and start on your homework. The pot roast will be delivered any minute."

I try sneaking past the kitchen with a tossed hello to Mrs. Morgan but she calls me back, greeting me with a hug. She mashes potatoes on the stove, and the smell of bubbling corn casserole wafts from the oven. This mother's cooking stands out, but they all only prepare side dishes. The Others dress, sanitize, and deliver all our animal proteins.

"I know you need to get changed, but come tell me how it feels to be a Terminal!" Mrs. Morgan beams at me like it's an accomplishment, when all I've done is age.

"Great, Mom."

"How are your friends? Is everyone excited about the Gathering?"

That one question, combined with the churning feelings stirred up by the day, rattles me. My palms heat up. "Yes. Excited. I'm going to change now."

The bedroom, orange and brown and sterile and *not mine,* brings the reality of my bizarre life crashing down.

Of course she would assume I have friends and that we discuss the most anticipated event of the autumn, of the last year. That's what Term girls do when they stay in one place. I hate forcing myself to look happy every day when my insides are tied up in knots. I hate being different. Not for the first time, I hate Ko for leaving me with just a stupid note. He has no idea how hard it is to not have anyone to talk to. To be alone. To have people look *through* me, never *at* me. It terrifies me that he might be lying, that I alone am a Dissident.

That there are no more like me, whatever I am.

With no one around to see, water falls from my eyes and spills down my cheeks unchecked. I throw myself onto the thick bedding and curl up into a ball. Memories of the years spent with the Hammonds stab into my skin like pins, pricking me with loss so deep it aches in every pore.

Within seconds, sweat plasters my thick hair to my forehead and the back of my neck. The T-shirt, too flimsy outdoors, clings to my skin as I struggle to rip it off, to release the heat. Free of the shirt, I clutch the comforter until an acrid, smoky scent rises around me and I snatch my hands away. The orange cloth smolders around the edges of my blackened, charred handprints. I dampen the blistering embers with my shirt.

Calm down, Althea. Get control of yourself. It's the only way to make it stop.

This has happened before, in the moments when I fail to staunch the flow of despair. One more way I'm not right, another sliver to bury. Several deep breaths bring back a tenuous control, but the room hovers at least twenty degrees hotter than it should be when a knock sounds at the door.

"Thea, honey? Dinner's ready."

Before I can answer, the doorknob twists and the lightweight wood swings inward. Panic surges even as my expression struggles toward neutral. I twist my face away from Mrs. Morgan to hide the water, rubbing it into my cheeks. If she were my mother—my real one— I imagine I would run and bury my puffy face in her apron and let her tell me everything will be fine.

But she's not. And it won't be.

Her deep brown eyes widen as she waves a delicate hand in front of her face, creating a breeze. "Goodness! Why is it so warm in here?"

She glances my way and I see myself through her eyes, sitting on the bed in nothing but my sensible bra and jeans, sweat running off of me in rivers. But she makes no comment, instead walking to the bay window and turning the crank. It opens wide, cool air racking my sticky body with chills. Keeping a smile in place is harder through chattering teeth.

Mrs. Morgan pats my head before pausing in the doorway. "I'll turn in a trouble ticket about our heater. Perhaps something has gone awry. At any rate, dear, finish changing into proper clothes and come downstairs. The roast has just arrived."

She turns and leaves the room, closing the door behind her. I jump up and cross to the window in a flash, pulling it shut. The room settles into a tolerant temperature a few minutes later, signaling the end of my episode. I should have had my meltdown at the park earlier; then I wouldn't have been so cold all afternoon.

There's no way for me to change who I am, only to hide who I am. Chafing acceptance trickles over me as I peel off my jeans and slip into a thin black sweater and a purple skirt that swings about my knees.

Mrs. Morgan believes in dressing for dinner.

4.

This is the third Saturday of the month, which means a Family Outing.

The Others allow adults in public for an hour in the morning, primarily to get fresh air. All my parents exercise every day on the treadmill in the den, but they seem to appreciate the hike outside once a month. The Morgans and I don hideous, matching orange tracksuits and step out onto the porch at nine o'clock. Mr. Morgan stretches his thighs as front doors open and houses spit more tracksuit-clad people into the morning up and down the block. At nine-oh-five, we all walk to the street.

All of the towns I live in are laid out the same, in a series of rings. Cell, the pizza parlor, and the bowling alley sit in the center. Five loops outside those are streets filled with identical, two-story residences. The park wraps around the outermost edge, a buffer between us and the Wilds. The Saturday Outings begin at Cell and travel along Main Street, the only road that leads directly from the center of the city to the boundary.

We parade from our homes and gather at the Cell in complete silence. At exactly nine-twenty we spill onto Main Street. I spot the pine-scented boy and his parents the same moment he sees me, raising his eyebrows in a silent hello. An odd combination of pleasure and trepidation fight for my attention, but neither wins and I eventually distract myself by studying the rest of the group. To my right, the girl with the black curls, the one who wants to work in Administration, bounces next to two petite, adult copies of her. A couple of younger children skip next to one another in perfect synchronization.

The day dawned crisp and breezy, and even though the sun has risen, frosty dew slicks dying blades of grass. The morning is as quiet as the humans moving through it, save the occasional scuff of a sneaker or a swallowed cough. Closer to the boundary we might hear birds singing or animals scratching up breakfast, but not this far inside the city.

A typical Family Outing lasts about an hour, from nine until ten. Brunch deliveries wait in the kitchens upon our return, and then we watch the afternoon movie together. As we near the boundary today, though, the people at the front of our hiking brigade slow to a stop. I crane my neck, straining to glimpse what has caught their attention. When I do, my stomach plummets into my shoes.

A group of Wardens stand at attention in front of the boundary.

I've witnessed Wardens in person just four times. I remember them all with clarity; they were the scariest days of my life. I count them quickly. Eight Wardens. I've never seen so many in one place before. Never seen more than two, actually, the number sent out to collect the Broken. They flank a large video screen they've hung on the fence. Off to one side sits a white plastic table that holds a punch bowl, some blocks of pale pink rock, and several jugs of what looks like water.

The Wardens are the enforcement arm of the Others' government, but aside from their tan uniforms with shiny black accents, they look the same as the rest of their race; tall, blond, and beautiful to the point of not appearing real. Unlike the Elements, they have no blue pinpoints interrupting their glossy, black gaze. No whites like a human eye, no pupil or iris. Just an endless void. The effect makes them appear sightless, but they're not.

They shouldn't be here now. No one is Broken. But no one speaks or questions them, even though I don't think the Others informed anyone of this alteration. We all simply wait.

Once everyone has entered the park, a Warden clears his throat. "There will be a brief video presentation regarding this change to your monthly Outing, and afterward we invite the Terminal students to join us for a drink celebrating our presence among you in your final year at Cell."

His beautiful voice pours into my ears like a sweet coating of honey, but the sight of him embeds a throbbing ache behind my eyes. Looking directly at the Others causes a jabbing pain deep in my brain, like needles being slammed through my forehead. Perhaps because our mere human minds can't process their superior existence.

That is what they would have us believe.

Most of my fellow humans stare at the ground or into the Wilds—no one maintains direct eye contact with the Wardens. My heart spasms and clenches, a sense of foreboding wriggling past my boredom as the screen flickers to life.

Our Cell Administrator slides into his office chair on the screen, even though he should be on the Outing, not at Cell on a Sunday. I focus on holding my head still, refusing to let it whip around to look for him because everyone else remains motionless. And the

Wardens aren't interested in the screen. Their black-hole eyes train on the crowd, watching for. . .what?

The Administrator's round belly barely fits behind his desk, and he works to smooth his tie into place. Serenity paints his familiar, fleshy face as he smiles and nods into the camera. "Good morning. As you've noticed, the Others have dispatched Wardens to Danbury. Their purpose here is to observe and conduct interviews with the Terminal class, which will begin tomorrow. The sessions will be held one student at a time during chemistry, one block each week until completion. The Others wish for me to convey their appreciation for your cooperation in this matter. Thank you."

The screen goes black. Sweat dampens the back of my neck, spinning chills down my arms in the clammy morning. They're going to talk to us alone. Just the Terminals. Why? Since chemistry is my end block, the seventh of my day, I have seven weeks to figure out how I'm going to keep my secrets while alone in a room with a Warden. Or more than one.

After all these years, fooling the kids at school and my fake parents is second nature, but something tells me the Others won't be affected by my semi-invisibility.

The Wardens march to the table. One stands behind the cut-glass punch bowl, a plastic dipper in his hand. "If you would all gather around, we'll begin serving you in a moment."

He doesn't elaborate on what we'll be served. My legs don't want to follow the direction to gather, even though there's no choice. I can't refuse, not while my Cellmates shamble obediently closer to the table, forming a loose line. I manage to find a place, nearly bumping into a boy I don't recognize. His glossy black hair hangs over one almond-shaped eye and he offers a half smile as he motions me in front of him.

He's a Barbarus, an uncommon thing here in Danbury. We've been instructed that even though the Barbarus look different on the outside, inside they're like the rest of us. They even differ in appearance from one another. Some have funny-shaped eyes, some a kind of light brown skin or noses that seem too big for their faces. Since they don't teach us about what existed before the Others came, we don't know about the origin of the Barbarus, but only a handful remain on Earth.

Even though a few attend my Cell in Portland, when I turn to thank him breath catches in my throat. The boy's complexion appears yellow in the dappled autumn sunlight, and he's barely taller than I am. The

42

slanted eyes, the jet-black hair, and short stature all align with my knowledge of this particular human variation. But his eyes are wrong. They're a clear sky blue when they should be dark brown.

It takes a moment to recover, but habit pastes a fake smile on my lips while my brain catches up. "Uh, thanks."

"You're welcome."

I turn around. At the table, two Wardens grab the pinkish lumps and set to crushing them under their hands. The Others prepare food and deliver drinks for us every day, but I've never seen the process. Either the substance is soft or the Wardens are strong; perhaps the truth is a little of both. Soon piles of pink dust scatter the white tabletop. A breeze blows some of the particles into the faces of the Terms nearest the table. They giggle, swiping dust off one another's shoulders and shaking it out of their hair, trading their laughter for violent sneezes after a moment or two.

The majority of the pink substance dissolves in the jugs, coloring the clear water as the Wardens shake them and then begin to pour rations into tiny plastic cups. The first of my Cellmates, a tall girl with a long brown ponytail, accepts the gift and drinks it down in two gulps before rejoining her parents. The next two are boys, one blond and one a redhead like me. The line moves forward slowly, but too fast for my pounding heart. This development scares me, although as with the fear I have of the Others, I can't put a finger on the reason.

Except that I don't want to be observed or interviewed or noticed at all. Not by the Others.

I spot Pine Boy—Lucas—four or five people ahead when he turns, scanning the faces of the kids behind him. Our eyes meet, and for a split second I see my fears reflected on his pale face. Then he spins around again, stepping ahead as the line moves.

The novelty of this exercise makes it hard to breathe. Trusting no one, hiding in plain sight, I depend on the familiar ins and outs of the days on Earth. Without them, how will I know how to act Acceptable?

"What do you suppose they're looking for in Danbury? And why just the Term class?"

The Barbarus boy's voice slithers over my shoulder in a whisper. I shrug, dying to talk with someone but unwilling to display any hesitation while the Wardens scrutinize the moving line. The boy's questions border on suspicious, and tangle with the similar emotion in my gut. It's weird to hear an innate distrust of the Others in a voice not my own.

Trust no one.

That definitely includes a strange Barbarus who appears the same morning as the Wardens.

The sight of the first nosebleed pulls my attention from the new boy. The second, third, and fourth jerk my stomach into knots. It's not as though I've never seen one before. People take ill. There are Healers and nosebleeds aren't serious.

But all of the Terms with blood dripping from their noses have already swallowed their offerings.

The affected kids wipe absently at the red flow and don't seem to be in pain, a kind of bemused expression on their faces as they await further instruction.

A gurgle rises in my throat, a desire to point out the problem, but not a single person utters a word. Not the kids' parents, not their friends. But the Wardens notice, and less than five minutes later two more of them arrive in a rider. The Others mode of transportation glints black from front to rear, hovering three feet off the grass on four spinning disks, whirring quietly.

The newest Wardens guide the bleeding Terms through the open rider doors, slamming them shut with distinct finality.

No one says a word then either.

Parents wait for their Terms to finish partaking, talking contentedly among themselves. Little children bend and pick at blades of grass, tossing them at one another or braiding them into wreaths. *The kids in the rider are going to a Healer,* I tell myself. They're not being taken away. They're not Broken.

I swallow once, then again, but the fear climbing up my throat refuses to dissipate. The line plods forward, and as we move, more anomalies make it impossible to breathe without gulping air.

The girl who had been at the front of the line, the one with the brown ponytail, rubs itchy eyes until her hands come away bloody.

A thin crimson ribbon trails from the redheaded boy's lips after he coughs.

They both disappear into the rider.

The Wardens behind the table ignore their growing collection of bloody Terms, passing out cup after cup of pink liquid. My Cellmates still don't pause before draining their celebratory gift, and as I creep closer to having to do the same, it comforts me that the rest of the Terms appear unaffected.

I realize then that the kids in the rider are the ones who breathed in the pink dust as it blew into their faces.

The Barbarus boy says nothing further, leaving me to believe I imagined the disquiet in his voice moments before. Sweat trickles down my back as Lucas drinks and joins his parents at the entrance of the park. His face no longer reflects worry, but remains ashen. Uneasiness claws at my lungs, shredding them as though there's no oxygen in this entire world. What the Barbarus said about the Others dispatching the Wardens to observe our class in particular, rings in my ears like a warning. If they're looking for something, and the interviews are designed to help them find it, perhaps the pink drink is also a test. Are the kids in the rider failing or passing?

They're failing. As much as I want to believe they'll be okay, it's hard. I've never known a single person who got into a rider to return. Ever.

It's my turn. The Wardens, apparently tired of this entire process, hand me my cup and pass out the remaining doses to the Barbarus and three girls behind him all at once.

"That will be all. You may return to your homes."

None of the Wardens leave, continuing to watch, perhaps in case any more of us start gushing blood onto our tracksuits.

"Bottoms up." The Barbarus boy tips his pink concoction past his lips and tosses the cup into a waste receptacle.

He waits, watching me with as much interest as the Wardens, and it's obvious I'm not getting out of this new ritual. Mr. and Mrs. Morgan appear, stepping to my side with warm smiles.

"Oh, Thea dear, do drink that. It was so kind of the Others to think of you at the outset of your last year." Mrs. Morgan pats my arm, nudging my hand toward my face.

It's now or never. Even hesitating as long as I have could be a warning to the Wardens that I don't trust them as blindly as everyone else. The Barbarus stares with a grin that glints in his eyes. Mr. Morgan's stomach growls, and I know he's anxious for brunch. From the corner of my eye, I watch Lucas and his parents hurry out of the park.

The liquid tastes like water despite its pinkness, but it's warm instead of cool like I expect. I toss the cup and smile at my fake parents. "Let's go home. I'm hungry." I turn to say goodbye to the Barbarus, but he's already moving away. I crane my neck, looking for his parents, but don't see them.

The Morgans and I trek back through town alongside the rest of Danbury, chatting with the neighbors while Mrs. Morgan coos over their baby boy. I feel lucky to have escaped injury and detection this morning, but then, as we turn onto the Morgans' street, I start to sweat. It's residual panic, I think at first, but then the heat trapped inside me bulges uncomfortably. It rises up and out with an uncontrollable strength. It's escaped my restraint on many occasions, but never with this kind of force. Never so powerful it makes me feel explosive, as though it's trying to melt me from the inside.

As soon as we enter the house, I mumble that I've got to use the wasteroom and make a beeline for the mirror. My cheeks are flushed bright red. Sweat drizzles from the hair around my forehead. I breathe in through my nose and blow out through my mouth as my limbs shake so badly it knocks me to the floor. The white tiles burn my knees as if they are blocks of ice.

The heat has to go somewhere. My body can't hold it.

Instinct propels me across the floor to the toilet. I submerge my hands in the water and stop pushing the power back down inside me.

I don't feel better until every last drop of water has boiled away.

5.

The next morning—the day of the Gathering— yawns as bright as the day before, the temperature holding steady for early fall in Connecticut. I couldn't be more pleased about the nice weather, and I say a quick wish for my next travel to take me back to the spring. Winter is coming, otherwise known as the bane of my existence.

Much like my required attendance at tonight's Gathering.

Deciding what to wear is a necessary evil. The clothes hanging in the closet offer plenty of options, thanks to Mrs. Morgan's penchant for pretty things, and I grab a dress at random. I don't have a date but am expected to make myself attractive. Or as attractive as a shadow person can be, at any rate.

Now that the Wardens are in town, I have to try even harder to do everything right.

I didn't leave the house this morning, not even during the allowed weekend hour. Little noises made me jump and I've worn a rut in my bedroom carpet checking out the window. I expected to see Wardens racing to haul me away each time, yet they haven't come.

During Sunday Sharing, when my "parents" asked about my life, I told them I'm looking forward to exams, and to finding a Partner at the Gathering, because that's what normal Term girls talk about during the last year.

My autumn parents smiled as though it pleased them, their only daughter taking an interest in her future. Some people the Morgans' ages have siblings, more than one child born to the same couple, but it doesn't happen anymore. Now the Others have declared having more than one baby Unacceptable. Unless the first child is Broken.

The Wardens take babies and children who are Broken, who are sick, don't act normal, or don't look right. I have no doubt that they'll come for me one day.

The deep navy material of the dress makes my eyes stand out and it's snug in all the right places. I have to admit it makes me feel a little bit pretty. Mrs. Morgan insists on styling my hair, so my deep red locks now hang in fat curls down my back, the sides secured under a headband. My hair's too thick to hold the style for long and will relax into waves before the Gathering even begins, but the attention is nice. I even give in to her prodding and apply a little makeup before grabbing a bag and heading out. Like five days a week at Cell isn't enough.

The transformation in the eatery is stunning. Instead of the sterile, white-tiled environment we eat in every day, this new one is nothing less than elegant. The floors are wooden, the walls painted a deep caramel color, and every inch of the room reflects the season. Trees that look as real as the ones outside seem to reach off the walls, thin branches dripping radiant leaves toward the floor. Painted sunflowers and fall flora stand in between them, separated by long tables slathered with food. The three video screens are lit, as usual, and the Monitors watch over the proceedings with proud, glowing smiles.

Students shuffle between the tables, talking and laughing with one another, though it's quieter than a typical lunch block. Some mingle, but the majority isn't any more comfortable with the opposite sex tonight than during Cell hours. The girls chatter in hushed tones among themselves and the boys stand in silence and stuff their faces. I sidle up to the largest cluster of girls, allowing myself a moment to wonder how Val and Monica are getting along on this night; whether they're going alone, what they're wearing, if they're excited.

Only a moment, though.

I hover around the edges of the groups, wanting nothing more than to blend in. Conversations swirl through the air; they fall on my ears but don't penetrate. Instead, my eyes search the room for the pine-scented boy.

Since that first day in Danbury, pretty much all my spare time has been spent seeking his face. I've tried to stop, but I guess I really don't want to. The memory of his pale face at the Outing yesterday hovers in my memory, and the small part of me that isn't scared of being discovered or of trusting someone—the same part that misses having another human to talk to, to touch, to know—hopes he's different because he's like me.

Without warning my eyes collide with his across the room; a cool, blue flame meeting a white-hot one for a split second until we both look away. Our gazes wander back and his smile drops from his lips, swapped for curiosity and anxiety.

I tear my eyes away and pick up a glass of punch, readjusting my own expression. My face flames, the cup like an ice cube inside my superheated hand. Dread burrows under my confusion over Lucas as the sides of the cup slump inward. The melted plastic sticks to my palm, but I dislodge it with a few furtive shakes above the waste receptacle. It lands atop assorted items, walls goopy and misshapen. Real smooth.

The tone of the murmurings shifts, jittery laughter turning to hushed whispers. My heart trips into stutters, and this time not because of a too-familiar pair of blue eyes.

There, stepping through the entrance to the eatery, are the Wardens.

Even though their presence isn't a surprise after yesterday, the actual sight of them is as shocking as always. They ignore us and march to the nearest video screen to consult with our chaperones. Everyone watches, wide-eyed but not displeased, while I slink closer to eavesdrop.

The Monitor in charge, a rail-thin bald man who instructs calculus, offers a greeting. "Welcome to Danbury, Wardens. All of the Terminals have arrived. Please make yourselves at home and let us know if we can provide any additional assistance."

The Warden in front, a tall, muscular man nods. I've been staring at him for longer than I should, and a stabbing ache swells behind my eyes. I've never been so close to an Other before, and when my eyes demand relief and slide away, I notice a raised red mark just under his left ear. A scar of some sort.

My jaw drops. Its pattern mirrors the shape of my locket.

The room wobbles as my body sways and threatens to topple. I manage to stay on my feet and keep my hands clasped in front of me. My body temperature rises so high that anything I brush against could burst into flames. Which might not work in my favor.

"Thank you. We're here to follow up on some reports we're received." The Warden turns and surveys the room, obviously with no intention of offering clarification.

I haven't a clue what reports he's talking about or why they're observing us, but fear cannonballs into my belly. Again I worry that attempting to trick a Warden during a one-on-one conversation is a recipe for disaster. I can't be alone with them.

The Wardens disperse, moving about the room. The mood in the eatery returns to the previous nervous excitement, with the addition of some awe-filled staring at our observers. My Cellmates display no concern, even though the Others who are here searching for something—or someone—*take* people. Even though they took six of our Cellmates just yesterday, six kids not attending their first Gathering, as far as I can tell.

Without thinking, I steal toward the door. Disappearing is the single focus of my mind, every thought of staying composed driven out by alarm. The part of my brain that usually calms me in moments of panic screams at me to run. They can't see me like this, amped up and sweaty, failing to appear as calm and happy as my peers.

It feels as though hours pass before I slip out of the eatery and into the empty hall. The black boxes mounted on either side of the door take note of my exit, little red lights illuminated and staring. The creepy feeling of being watched raises the hairs along my arms and the back of my neck. The Others record everything, but no one could be watching every camera at every moment. . .I don't think. At least the wasterooms are out here and we're allowed to use them. Leaving shouldn't raise any suspicions.

Two Wardens step around the far corner. The mere sight of them threatens to knock me over but I continue without collapsing, passing them and turning the corner toward the girls' wasteroom. Instead of entering I scurry to the end of the hall.

Up or down?

Making a snap decision, I head down the stairs.

Venturing away from where I'm supposed to be could be a mistake, but every instinct forces me as far from the Wardens as possible.

If hiding is the wrong choice, it's too late to regret it now. Decision made.

A metal door labeled "Maintenance" catches my eye and the knob turns easily in my hand. The room belches musty air and a massive cobweb splays across my face before my eyes adjust to the dark.

There's no time to recover from the first shock or even wipe the sticky wisps from my nose and mouth before strong hands reach out from the darkness. One arm encircles my waist as the other clamps down over my mouth.

They're both freezing. The cold bites my skin, making it feel windburned. A scream wells up in my throat with nowhere to go, and sweat streams out of every pore as I struggle against the viselike hold. My captor's chilly breath tickles my ear and I lean away from his lips with renewed determination. Anguish floods my veins.

I'm going to die. And no one will even notice.

"Stop squirming." He grunts as my hip bone digs into his upper thigh. "I'm not going to hurt you. I didn't want you to make a ruckus when you saw me. I'm going to let you go now. Don't scream."

I don't recognize the voice, not that I expect to. The hand over my mouth lifts ever so slightly. Like he's testing me. I will myself to stay quiet, to earn some trust. When he turns me loose I spin away on shaky legs, whirling to confront him. My defensive posture eases due to plain shock.

Pine Boy.

He's smiling now and not forcing it. "You look surprised. Me, too. I had this crazy idea that a dark basement room would keep me safe from jasmine-scented girls I've been trying to avoid."

My glare arrives without warning, no second thought given to letting my real emotions show. "Why are you avoiding me? And what are you doing down here in the first place?"

He doesn't answer either question, and instead wipes his palms on his pants and then studies them. The scalded red skin is visible even in the dim light. "Man, are you sick or something? You're on fire."

"No, I just. . .you grabbed me. I was scared!"

He shrugs and lets the subject drop, wandering over to sit on a waist-high steel pipe. Since he's not going to kill me, at least not right away, I take a better look around the room. It's filled wall to wall with desks, chairs, and scrap material, along with other unrecognizable clutter.

"So, why do you smell like that?"

His voice startles me. I'm so intent on my surroundings I've almost forgotten I'm not alone. "Why do you care?"

Nagging distrust and years of conditioning stop me from telling him to take a whiff of himself sometime before he lectures me.

"It's sort of nice, actually, but if it's perfume you could scale it back. Almost knocked me out of my chair in chem the other day. It reminds me of summer in Georgia."

"Did you used to live in Georgia?" I catch his eye and see fear for a split second before it makes way for studied neutrality.

"Just visited once. For my grandmother's death pyre."

"Oh." I roam down one of the aisles, finding it easier to breathe out of his sight. Our interaction feels honest and it scares me more than a little. I'm so desperate for a connection I'm not being careful enough. It would be best to get out of here, away from him. My brain accepts and rebels against this simultaneously.

Taking a brief moment to regroup helps me calm down but it doesn't help me figure out what's going on or what he's doing down here. Or why it's so easy to talk to him.

Trust no one.

The warning likely applies to handsome, talkative boys hiding in basements for no good reason. I need to tread carefully, even if he does seem different. Maybe I just want him to be someone like me so badly I'm seeing things that aren't there.

Movement catches my eye. I squint, edging toward it with more curiosity than caution.

Until I make out what it is that's moving.

6.

I stumble, tripping over several plastic crates and landing hard on my rear end. Pieces of metal and other unidentified objects skitter and bounce across the concrete floor, making a racket loud enough to be heard in the next town, never mind upstairs. I scramble backward on my butt in an attempt to put distance between me and the animal. Lucas is gone, escaped because of the noise or perhaps because of what's in the back of the room.

There's a fish back there. In a bowl.

Someone is keeping a live animal right here in the Cell, exposing all of us to unknown diseases. Hysteria rises as I press a hand to my mouth and suck air through my fingers. Maybe the fish can't hurt us like some bigger animals, the ones with rows of teeth, but still. Animals of any kind are not allowed inside the boundary.

I have to get out of here. Need supersedes caution—I scoot out the door and down the hall, looking back and forth and wondering which way the boy would have gone. Not back upstairs. Not home before curfew. I sprint up the stairs. My luck holds, and no Wardens appear to bar my path out the front door. The biting autumn air aches in my ears with each sharp inhale, forcing me to a stop after a few minutes. There isn't much occasion to sprint in my world.

A figure darts out from beside a house and runs at me. I freeze to the spot, a scream gathering in my lungs but whooshing out in a gurgle when his face comes into view at the last second.

It's him. Again.

"What are you doing standing in the middle of the street? Are you crazy? Why aren't you back at the Gathering?"

The questions come fast, hushed but in an unhappy tone I've never heard before except in my own head. For a minute, the struggle to form answers stuns me and I don't fight as he drags me back with him into the shadows.

This is odd, considering.

Traipsing around someone's yard when you're supposed to be at a Gathering is not Acceptable. Nothing about me is Acceptable, though, and I'm tired of pretending to be like everyone else, of doing what I'm supposed to. This boy is the first person, besides the young chemistry Monitor with the quivery smile, who might be different.

I want to find out why.

Standing in the dark between twin houses, my white tennis shoes growing moist from the dewy grass, I fix him with a stare. "You're supposed to be at the Gathering, too. Why aren't you?"

He looks as if he's considering giving me an answer but decides against it. Instead he cocks his head to one side and offers a genuine smile. A deep dimple appears in his right cheek. "What's your name, nosy? Or should I call you Jasmine?"

I frown, refusing to drop his gaze. He knows my name—we've had five days of blocks together. "Only if I can call you Pine."

Worry flashes across his fair features but he hides it away. The teasing tone sounds forced now. "I'll tell you mine if you tell me yours. Promise."

His coaxing wins me over and I play along. "Althea."

He sticks out a hand. It looks soft and warm, but I know from experience it's not. Then again, most people feel colder than me, especially when I'm worked up.

"Lucas."

We shake hands like adults, mine trembling from the chill clinging to his. The smile falls from my face as the memory of the fish in the basement storage room barges to the forefront.

His tentative smile turns puzzled. "What is it?"

"That room in the Cell basement has a fish in it. Who could have put it there? Do you think they're trying to get us all sick?"

Dread bubbles as the images of what could happen dance through my imagination.

His smile returns and he chuckles. I wonder if he has a death wish or something. He's definitely nuts, wandering out here at night and hiding from the Wardens. Probably Broken, or on the edge of it.

I don't stop to wonder what it says about me that I'm doing the same thing.

"That's Fils. He's mine. And he doesn't have diseases."

My mouth falls open so hard it makes my jaw ache. I close it just as roughly, my teeth clacking together. "What do you mean, he's *yours*? *You're* keeping a fish in the Cell? Have you gone completely banana balls? Wait, what do you mean his name is Fils? How do you know his name?"

He snorts as if it's the dumbest question he's ever heard. "Because I named him. He can't talk so I guess he didn't have a name before that. I wanted to call him something."

"What's Fils mean? I've never heard that word before."

Lucas shrugs, a light pink blossoming on his pale cheeks. He avoids my eyes as he mumbles an answer. "I don't know what it means. I hear the word in my dreams sometimes."

The way he says *dreams* recalls the strange ones that occasionally visit me. More like memories, they don't come often enough, leaving me wistful and clinging to tendrils as I wake, like Lucas sounds now. The faces of the people in them are blurry, fleeting, but make me feel loved and something more. . .like how I imagine a real home would feel.

The longing on Lucas's face makes my heart ache. The instinct to comfort him comes out of nowhere; I have to fist my hands to keep from reaching out. "How did you get a fish, exactly? And how do you know Fils isn't making you sick?"

"I caught him in a pond. I've had him five years and I'm still alive. I've touched him, fed him, and cleaned out his bowl. I'm fine."

"How is that even possible? Who taught you how to take care of him?"

"I just figured it out. It's not that hard."

Lucas's logic rings true but a lifetime of fear isn't going to disappear because some handsome new boy says it should. "Well, you do what you want. You shouldn't be keeping it at Cell, though."

His eyes widen, darting back and forth as he presses a finger to his lips. We draw deeper into the shadows beside the quiet house, my back pressed against his chest. It's firmer than it looks. My heartbeat quickens when his arm winds around my waist.

Wardens—two this time—tread heavily down the street sweeping flashlights in an arc. I hold my breath, body vibrating as Lucas sucks his in as well. If my heart weren't pounding from terror it would be struggling with such nearness to a boy—to another human being, really. His peculiar scent mingles with my own odd fragrance, creating a not entirely unpleasant mixture that hovers around us in a cloud. I fervently hope it doesn't extend to the sidewalk because if the Wardens smell it, they will investigate. The combination is thick and unusual, created by two scents that would never rub against each other in nature.

The Wardens pass, the pool of yellow from their lights falling about ten feet short of our hiding place. They continue down the street but neither of us moves until the street has been silent for at least five minutes. Lucas exhales and lets me loose. I sag against him for a moment before turning. Our eyes meet, full of questions neither of us is willing to answer. Or even ask. He might be wondering if I'm going to report the fish. After the close call, I know I'm rethinking my need to find out more about him. He may already have witnessed too much.

"We'd better get home." Lucas glances down at his watch. "It's after nine. The Gathering is over."

I missed my Gathering. I wish I could care. I don't care about anything except not getting caught and carted off by the Others. I cared about the Hammonds once. About Val and Monica.

Caring only makes it harder.

Lucas and I head down the sidewalk together. A moment later we come across a group of kids and attach ourselves to the rear. I move in silence, their talk bouncing over me until the word *Gathering* snaps me to attention. A dark-haired boy walks next to Brittany, holding her hand. Greg, probably.

Greg talks too loud. "Did you guys see the new kid tonight?

A short, squat boy answers, laughing. "Yes! It'll be exciting to have a Barbarus at Cell."

I hadn't noticed the new boy at Cell tonight, but apparently everyone else did. My Cellmates laugh, excited about the beginning of our last year. They shoot interested looks toward Lucas and me, and for the first time something besides confusion paints my Cellmates' faces as they attempt to make sense of my presence. It looks like. . .curiosity? After a moment, understanding dawns.

They wonder if Lucas and I are courting.

I reach a hand up to touch my cheeks. They're on fire, burning my palm before I snatch it away. Lucas glances at me, his icy blue eyes lighting with interest as he takes in my face. No doubt it's an interesting shade, but he's smart enough not to comment.

The evening is cool and a slight breeze tosses leaves to and fro. Even so, the walk isn't unpleasant. By the time we reach the Morgans' street we're alone again, everyone else having turned off at their respective streets or houses. Uneasiness wraps around me as we slow to a stop in front of his house.

He raises a finger as though he's going to touch my cheek. I bat it away. This is terrible. I don't want any part of courting, and people thinking we are will earn too much attention. "Look, I don't understand why you're out wandering around or hiding from the Wardens, but I think we should stay away from each other."

I say it because my mind insists he's some kind of trouble. What I *want* is the opposite.

He looks down at his feet. "If you change your mind, maybe we could meet in the park during open hour tomorrow. I saw you wandering by yourself near the boundary every day last week."

My mind races over my afternoons, searching for anything I might have done that would raise suspicion. "You saw me? How?"

"I like to climb trees. You never look up, you know."

The thought of Lucas watching me stroll about without my knowledge makes me both embarrassed and angry. "I don't think so. I don't need any extra attention, and you and your fish and your hiding in the shadows is bound to get one or both of us in trouble."

"What do you mean, any *extra* attention?"

One evening alone with another person and my secret's all but painted on my forehead. Running from the Wardens, frowning at him, saying right out loud I don't want to catch the Wardens' eyes. I force a smile, cursing my loose lips and ignoring the beads of sweat breaking out on my palms. "Did I say extra? I just meant attention. With the Wardens in town and everything. Good night."

Lucas grabs my wrist and holds on tight, stopping me from heading to the Morgans'. His fingers tighten and my skin chafes as I try to twist free, his frigid touch relieving the burning panic for a moment. A wild look flashes in his eyes and he leans in until our noses almost touch.

My breath catches as our eyes meet, a shocking anticipation mingling with fear. I push away from him, heart thrashing, but he only leans closer. I freeze, closing my eyes against whatever is coming next.

Words emerge from his pale lips in a whisper, expelling breath frostier than the breeze winding about us. "Think about it, Althea. There's a good chance one or both of us is going to get into trouble anyway."

He releases me and walks in a measured pace up his driveway and into the front door of the brick house without a backward glance. The porch light winks off like clockwork as soon as the door clicks shut behind him.

My legs tremble, wobbling at the knees from the fright, from the implied threat. I should move, get to the Morgans' before I'm late. With the Wardens in town, plus my slipping out of the Gathering early and all but confessing my abnormalities to Lucas, I shouldn't do anything else to make myself worth watching.

The dark windows of his house proffer no answers. Nothing about him makes sense. Nothing. My inability to read him, his insistence on acting like he doesn't know he's not normal frightens me more than anything else.

A minute later I enter the Morgans' two-story brick house—identical to Lucas's—and lean back against the closed door. The clock on the wall clicks to nine-fifteen and through the window I see our porch light extinguish, plunging the world into darkness.

7.

Monday arrives and another day forces me out of bed, into the shower, down for breakfast, and out the front door. Revulsion tumbles through me at the sight of two Wardens posted outside the entrance to the Cell, but I somehow manage to pass by without cringing. The algebra Monitor has fifty-seven squares on his shirt today; they're larger than last week and red. Everything else is the same except for the Warden who surveys the room from the doorway every ten minutes. Oh, and the Barbarus—Deshi—settles into my first block. None of the kids who disappeared at the Outing are present, and though I never knew their names, the Monitors don't record any absences.

It's as if they were never here.

It's not as if the Wardens taking away the Broken is new; I've even seen it a couple of times. But those people were obviously irreparable. An old lady who died next door. A misshapen baby. Not perfectly healthy Terms with simple nosebleeds.

I push the events of the last two days out of my head, deciding to focus on the fact that I survived. In the eatery, a shudder rolls through my body at the memory of the disease-infested fish swimming around downstairs. Lucas's words blow through my mind like a blast of winter wind. If he told the truth, if he's had the fish all this time with no ill effects, what could it mean?

It could mean the Others lie to us.

I've never considered it until recently, never had a reason to doubt that they act in the best interest of the humans under their rule. But if they lied about fish, they could be lying about *all* the animals. And if they're not all dangerous, then why build the boundaries?

I stop the train of thought before it charges out of hand. The opinion of one possibly Broken boy isn't enough proof to send me down that path. Where it might end scares me too much.

Five Wardens police lunch block, not bothering to hide their blatant eavesdropping. I plop down at the same table as last week, where the girls are at least used to my presence if not comfortable with it. Brittany swoons over Greg holding her hand at the Gathering while the rest listen with open-mouthed smiles. I urge my stomach to eat, but it refuses to cooperate.

A hush falls over the table, much like it did at Sunday's Gathering, but this time when I look up the girls aren't looking at the invading Wardens. They're looking at me.

Or rather, behind me.

Spinning around in my seat, knocking my milk carton off the table in the process, my eyes meet Lucas's as the now-familiar pine scent washes over me. The girls must smell it, too, but no one comments.

Instead they all sit there, not one of them bothering to close their slack jaws. The milk soaks through my pants, cold and sticky against my skin. I pick up my napkin, pressing it to the wet spot while I wonder what Lucas thinks he's doing. There might not be rules about mixing in the eatery, but girls and boys separate by their own preference.

An easy smile parts his lips, oozes charm all over the place. "Afternoon, ladies."

Without waiting for an invitation, he swings a chair from the nearest table and wedges it between mine and the girl's next to me. My brain searches for her name, the tiny girl with the bouncy black curls.

Leah, I think.

She studies Lucas, her lips tilted up in a friendly smile. He drops his salad, fork, and drink on the table and sits, then stuffs a bite of lettuce into his mouth and washes it down with a swig of milk as though he hasn't a care in the world. The grin never leaves his face and I suspect he's enjoying himself. Embarrassing me.

Making a scene. Shouldering his way into my life when I clearly asked him to stay out of it.

I kick him under the table. His smile stretches wider.

I realize one of the girls is addressing me. It's Sarah, her wide blue eyes flickering with curiosity. "Hey, you. Are you going to introduce us to your friend?"

A Warden saunters behind her head. He pauses to listen.

"Wha. . .oh. Sure. This is Lucas. Lucas, this is everybody."

None of the girls has ever voluntarily spoken to me. Between that and the staring Warden I'm too shell-shocked to think about eating. The girls resume chatting and feeding their faces as though having a boy at our table happens every day. My heart slows as the Warden moves away from us. Lucas chews beside me, and when he's sure everyone's attention is elsewhere he kicks me back. I keep smiling.

If he can do it, so can I.

"Wild about the Wardens showing up and the interviews and everything. I bet that's never happened at another Gathering before." Lucas's tone is hushed, conspiratorial.

Sarah, the tall, mouthy girl, leans forward onto her elbows. Her dirt brown hair spills over her shoulder, the tips swirling in her leftover salad dressing. "Until Sunday. My dad works as Liaison and he told me the Wardens were dispatched to the Gatherings in *four* cities last weekend."

I nearly choke on my tongue as he winks at her.

"Really? Did he say why?"

"No one knows. I mean, except the Wardens and whoever sent them." Sarah notices that her hair is getting oily and leans back, patting the ends dry with her napkin.

I lick my lips and swallow a couple of times before my tongue works. "Which cities?"

Lucas shoots me a surprised look.

Sarah squeezes her eyes shut and taps a finger on her pursed lips. "Hmmm. Atlanta, Des Moines. . .and Portland. I'm pretty sure."

My heart stops beating and everything disappears. The eatery. The girls. The Wardens. I taste blood and realize I've bitten the inside of my cheek. Those are *my* cities, at least three of them are. In the spring I plant gardens with the Hammonds in Portland. Bitter, miserable winters with the Clarks in Des Moines. It's always autumn in Danbury, at least when I'm here. I've never been to Atlanta, but I've also never had a summer. Not only are the Wardens observing Terms, they're targeting the cities I travel between.

It doesn't mean anything. They aren't looking for me. They can't be.

The black spots in my vision dissolve slowly and the sound of ragged breathing fills the air. Lucas jabs me in the leg and I realize it's me. The voices around the table fall silent as the girls stare, vague vexation marring their perfect expressions.

I force a bite of salad into my mouth. Our table has caught the Wardens' attention again.

Lucas nudges my hips with his on our way out of the eatery and the girls poke one another and point. He seems determined to confirm everyone's suspicions as far as our courting is concerned, and a warm fountain spurts in my chest without warning, a mixture of pleasure and annoyance.

He grins as though he can see my thoughts. "See you in chem."

Before I decide on an appropriate response, he saunters off down the hall. The group of girls surrounds me, their huge smiles inviting me to believe things could be different. In spite of the past, of all I know to be true, part of me basks in their interest in my life.

"So are you two courting? Have you declared intentions?" Sarah, ever nosy, walks beside me down the hall.

"No, no. We're just friends right now." I don't know why I add the last part. Maybe I just want them to keep talking to me.

They look a little disappointed, but hope hovers around the edges. The blonde, Brittany, shrugs with a wide smile. "Well, I think Greg will ask me soon. Maybe we'll both be courting before the Autumn Mixer. That would be fun!"

"Maybe." The opportunity to ask about the interviews, which began today and fester in the back of my mind like an open sore, is too good to pass up. "So do any of you have chemistry for opening block?"

Their smiles turn disinterested in the blink of an eye. I glance around, making sure no Wardens are listening in on our conversation.

After a moment Brittany answers. "I do."

"What did the Wardens ask during your interview?"

She stops, cocking her head to one side with a baffled smile. "You know, it's the funniest thing. I can't even remember!"

The girls laugh at her forgetfulness, and their voices trail off as they disappear around the corner. For the moment, I'm alone in the hall. The corners of my mouth fall and I massage my cheeks where they ache.

I might kill Lucas for sitting with us at lunch and making a scene. I'm sure the Wardens didn't miss that. Then again, he did squeeze that information out of Sarah. No small feat. He could be an ally. After all he didn't turn me in even with all the Unacceptable behavior Sunday night.

Of course, I didn't turn *him* in either.

I push down the hope swelling in my chest. It's enough that he's not out to get me. I glance down at the faint red streaks still circling my wrist, the product of his rough grip, and wonder why I'm so sure he's not. Just because he has the ability to charm everyone, myself included, doesn't mean he's not hiding something.

By the time chemistry rolls around I'm sick and tired of the excited whispers about my possible courting. Being ignored is much less bothersome, but it seems my anonymity has escaped me at the worst possible moment. I've managed to shed my see-through existence just when the Wardens arrive. It figures.

Lucas is back in the seat next to mine. We smile at each other, but neither of us means it. The amiable mood that captured him at lunch has abandoned ship. I haven't made any decisions regarding him except that he's trouble, any way you slice it.

He glances at me and then away, and I think I see dark veins shooting through the whites of his eyes. Before I can get him to look at me again, Leah twists around in her chair a couple of rows up. At first, remembering her outgoing smile at lunch, I wonder if she wants to be friends with him.

That's before I get a good look at her expression.

A small, disingenuous smile plays on her lips. My gaze travels down her arms to meet a series of bruises. Purpling splotches dot her upper arms, wrapping around the skinny flesh like a wreath. I avert my eyes when reading her face becomes painful. She stares daggers at Lucas, her expression dripping with malice. Like she wants to hurt him. Smiling the whole time.

She spins around when the Monitor appears on the screen and I nudge Lucas with the toe of my sneaker. He refuses to meet my questioning stare.

I've never seen anyone with an expression like Leah's. Ever.

*

Halfway through block the Monitor has a coughing fit. When she takes a drink of water, Lucas's hand darts over my desk. A piece of paper drifts down until it rests unassumingly on top of my notes.

After the next Warden check I nudge the note open with my pencil, fighting the natural frown

80

begging to overtake my mouth. I read it in bits, keeping an eye on the video screen.

Allie—
Meet me at the park, by the boundary.

Peeking at both the Monitor and the rest of the class, I scribble a response.

Lucas—
No. And don't call me Allie.

I toss the note in his lap when no one's looking, my heart stuttering when a Warden comes in and stands in the doorway seconds later. I return my attention to the lecture, feeling his hard-edged, painful gaze on me.

He stays through the rest of the block, which ends after another exhausting twenty minutes, then leaves before we trickle out. A note slips from under my pad of paper and falls to the floor as I gather my things. I retrieve it and read, curious despite my reservations.

Althea—

Please. I've found out more about the Wardens' appearance in Danbury.

I grind my teeth down, my jaw tight. He's dangling a carrot, one he no doubt picked up on after my questions about the cities that are being included in the interviews. I'm not going. It's probably a trick.

The words from Ko's letter scroll through my mind, a different sentence standing out for the first time. *There are more. You will find each other when it is necessary.*

It could mean Lucas is like me. Then again, he could just as easily not be like me. Ko neglected to expand on how to identify the "more" when the elusive time comes. Seems like a pretty important detail to omit.

In the end, the decision to meet Lucas makes itself. I can't read him, and I'm not ready to trust him, but I have to do something. The Wardens are here; they're everywhere I go. If Lucas knows anything at all, I need to know it, too.

*

The hike out to the park is shorter than usual, different. I move quicker with someone waiting for me on the other end. A strange fluttering begins in my gut and sets my knees trembling. No one has met me after Cell in four years; it's a simple sign of friendship normal kids take for granted. My eyes sweep back and forth along the boundary, but after my first pass Lucas hasn't arrived.

Then he lands in front of me and I fall on my butt for the second time since I've met him.

I get up, dusting off my jeans and avoiding the laughter in his eyes. His blond curls blow a bit in the breeze, giving him a carefree appearance. He's so serious at Cell and when he's hiding from the Wardens. Rightly so. Here, with no one watching, his shoulders relax and his smile bursts forth instead of stretching across thin lips, displaying the deep dimple in one cheek. The wall in his gaze, though, the one he uses to separates me from his thoughts, is as impregnable as ever.

The dirty look I've been holding inside since lunch clamors to get out. Instead I smile, unwilling to give him one more reason to suspect anything's off about me, and glance up at the huge tree he jumped out of. "Seriously? Did you have to tackle me from above?"

"I didn't tackle you, Thea. It's not my fault you're so uptight."

"Don't call me Thea."

"Don't call me Allie. Don't call me Thea," he mimics. I want to punch him square in his just-right nose. "What shall I call you, then, hmm?"

"Althea. My name. Didn't you say you had something to tell me?"

"Let's walk."

Lucas leads the way to the boundary and we settle into a measured pace that takes us in a loop around the park. He pulls me to a stop after several wasted minutes. The nearest security camera is a ways off. No Wardens around either.

"Well?"

"I heard something when I passed the Administrative Center this afternoon. The video screen was on and someone was in there."

"Who?"

"I didn't see his face. I missed the beginning of the conversation, but I know all ten Wardens stayed behind. They set up two posts—one in the Cell and one in the Wilds. They're looking for something. Or someone. I'm not sure."

My stomach sinks, even though I've figured as much. "What are they looking for?"

Please don't say a girl who has feelings and lights things on fire.

"All I heard him say was that the Prime Other. . ." Lucas trails off and straightens up, his eyes focusing over my left shoulder. An easy smile steals onto his face.

Someone's behind me. I swallow hard, sure they overheard us.

A strange, musical voice breaks the quiet afternoon. "Hi. Am I interrupting?"

I spin around, words of welcome sticking in my throat at the sight of Deshi's face.

Lucas steps forward, coming to my rescue. He frowns at me while his face is turned away from the newcomer, eyes urging me to get hold of myself. "Of course not. What's your name, man?"

The Barbarus grasps Lucas's hand in a firm shake. He puts me off, and though I can't identify exactly why, it's not simply his novel appearance. It's those eyes, along with an arrogance that hovers in the air around him.

"Deshi."

"I'm Lucas. This is Althea." His voice wraps around my name, like the way he says it can protect me.

Deshi doesn't seem to notice; he just nods. The silence grows uncomfortable and sweat dampens my underarms. I wish I'd never come to the park.

"So, what are you two doing out here by yourselves?" It's an odd question, vaguely suspicious like the ones on Saturday at the Outing, but not unfriendly.

Lucas shifts away from me before answering. "Just out walking. Enjoying the weather."

"Bit cool, isn't it?" Deshi looks at me as he asks, his smile not quite soothing the worry in my gut.

"It's fine." I try to keep the irritation out of my voice.

He glances down at his watch. "Well, time to go. Maybe we could all hang out sometime."

Deshi brushes past us and disappears into the trees as the smell in his wake makes my eyes water. I freeze. Dirt, wet grass, rain. He smells like lying facedown in the spring grass. It's powerful. Like my smell.

"Weird dude."

"Yeah. . ." I turn to Lucas, search his face for the answers he seems determined not to give me. I'm trapped between the hope that maybe I've found more people like me and the threat of exposing my true self at the worst possible moment.

I'm under attack.

From the Wardens and their observance. From Lucas and his friendly, albeit pushy, manner. Now from Deshi, who has my eyes and smells like spring but makes me want to run and hide with his too-friendly, offhand questions.

"Lucas, why were you hiding in the basement Sunday instead of at the Gathering?"

"I wasn't hiding. I was just checking on Fils."

"Oh."

Lucas looks at me, eyes full of his own questions, but I shrug. My gut tells me he *was* hiding down there, but I can't prove it. Without more to go on, there's no advantage to giving him more ammunition. I don't trust him, or Deshi.

"Did you know everyone thinks we're courting?"

The random question startles me, traps words in my throat. Our showing up together after the Gathering and then Lucas joining me at lunch today would raise anyone's eyebrows. I grind my teeth together. This is Lucas's fault, and the added stress infuriates me. "So?"

"So I think we should go to the Autumn Mixer together. Everyone will think it's weird if we don't."

Helpless irritation numbs my brain as I search for an answer. I'm going to the mixer, of course. We all are. There are two during the last year of the preparatory phase. The Autumn Mixer will be to the bowling alley. In the spring, a pizza date. "Why do you care what people think?"

He looks away, staring out into the Wilds instead of at me. "I don't really. The Wardens are looking for something, though. I don't want them to decide I'm worth watching. After last weekend, I guess I assumed you felt the same way."

He's right, but either way will earn us more attention. Voluntary Partnering isn't common; it will make us a focal point. Then again, not going together when we're expected to could be even worse. Once people choose Partners they never change their minds.

Our eyes meet and I nod. He smiles, the one I've come to recognize as genuine. A strange but pleasant tickle flushes me with heat. It's probably normal to feel excitement over having a date to the mixer, no matter who he is or why he asks.

After all, trusting him and using him to blend in are two different things.

"I guess I'd better get to the. . .get home. It's almost curfew. See you tomorrow."

I turn my back on him and retrace our steps along the boundary, heading back toward the park entrance alone. On Main Street, a few of my Cellmates appear and we march home together.

Lucas, and now Deshi, complicates my life almost more than the Wardens. Until last week, each day pretty much went like the next. Sure, I wasn't happy. I never fit in and knew inside I would never be like everyone else. Now, though, the blaring changes make my nerves jangle, each one twanging in variance with the next. Sparring with Lucas adds clanging alarms to the din; the knowledge of whether they are meant to be beacons or warnings eludes me. I've got to put space between us, stop sneaking around and play by the rules. Ko's rules. *My* rules.

Lucas hollers my name once, but I ignore him.

For today, that is my decision.

8.

I almost get used to Deshi and Lucas hovering around the edges of my life over the next couple of days, and the Wardens popping in and out of every block.

Almost.

The Terms who aren't me adjust to the Wardens' presence faster than they do Deshi's. It's not that he's a Barbarus; the guy just makes everyone uncomfortable. My Cellmates react to him a little like they do me, with confusion and a preference to avoid him. He sits at crowded eatery tables and barges into conversations, asks tons of questions, and doesn't pick up on hints. He talks to the girls more than boys—and to me more than anyone.

He watches, too. He's good at disguising it, but I notice.

We've begun the second week of interviews, but no one talks about them. Not a word breathed in the halls, no gossip at lunch, even though Sarah, the loud girl with the blue eyes, disappeared after hers this morning. Her presence was easily missed in the eatery, the conversation around our table lacking without her willingness to lead, but no one mentioned it. I finally asked if anyone knew where she was after confirming she hadn't decided to sit at a different table.

Leah informed me in a rather bored tone that Sarah never returned from her interview.

The conversation turned to the upcoming Mixer. They all laughed and smiled as though their friend Sarah would not be missed, but an hour later ice still chills my veins. As I sit in astronomy block, I think about how Sarah is not the first one to be taken during this process. A handsome blond boy with straight, white teeth went missing last Friday.

Astronomy is the Others' favorite subject, one we sit through for two hours a day instead of one, both before and after lunch. They love to teach us about their history, and we certainly know more about the Others' past than our own. Which isn't hard, considering we're taught nothing of the human past. Today we've gone over a map of the solar system, memorizing planet and species names, which are still active and which have been eliminated. The Others come from a planet named Deasupra, and they drill its specifics into our memories even though it no longer exists. A war destroyed their home, which is why they inhabit ours.

Leah distracts me when she leans to her right and flags down Greg's attention. Greg's been hanging around our table in the eatery since he and Brittany began their official courtship with a Parental Sanction. It's the first step in voluntary Partnering, to have dinner with each other's parents and register intentions with the Others. Greg's a nice enough guy, a little obnoxious at times.

Now he angles his head toward Leah to catch her words. They're loud enough to carry the few rows back to me.

"Have you noticed how many of their previous host planets are listed under the eliminated chart?"

It's all of them. All the planets the Others inhabited before Earth no longer exist.

Leah pauses, and when she continues, a forced playfulness tints her words. "You should ask the Monitor about it—and about what's going to happen to us."

No. No, you shouldn't ask that, Greg.

Leah hasn't been the same since the day she showed up in chemistry with those bruises. In fact, she's been acting. . .inhuman, somehow. It's a good thing she has seventh block chemistry, because the way she's behaving, she'll never survive the interviews. I can't for the life of me figure out what she's up to now.

Deshi sits two desks to my left and observes the conversation as well, a faint smile playing on his thin lips. He's watching the Monitor but the slight tilt of his head, the faraway look in his eyes, says he's listening to Leah.

Apprehension squeezes my lungs as Greg's hand shoots up. The Monitor calls on him. I press my eyes closed, silently urging him to think twice. We don't ask questions. We certainly don't second-guess what the Others have taught us our whole lives.

His rich, laughing baritone assaults my ears and my airway nearly collapses. "So, what do the Others do to the planets they occupy? Kill everyone?"

Greg laughs but no one joins in. Leah sits back in her chair, arms folded across her chest as she stares at the screen, awaiting the answer.

The Monitor's brow folds up, puzzlement scrunching his smooth skin. "Gregory, that question is outside my training. But don't be ridiculous. The Others do not kill their hosts. Look at how good they have been to the inhabitants of Earth. I suggest you remember that before you speak out again."

Greg, properly chastised, shoots a quizzical smile toward Leah, who ignores him. The excitement is over before it began, and at least no Warden witnessed the aberration. Still, the Monitor will most likely report the incident. The cold smile on Deshi's face raises the hairs along the back of my neck. He looks as though Greg's outburst has somehow made his day.

We move outside for physical exercise, Greg's strange question apparently forgotten by everyone but me. Each day is the same; we walk one mile and then jog another at a measured pace before returning inside. We are to stay healthy, to improve the quality of our lives.

Whatever that means.

We girls amble about ten paces behind the boys, who jockey with one another for position. A small, playful scuffle breaks out. The next moments happen in an instant as two boys stumble backward. Deshi's shiny black hair flashes in the sun at the same moment that the second boy trips. He tumbles to the ground, all awkward angles, near the tree line. The boys stop and gather around when he doesn't move. We hasten to catch up, then join them in gaping at the scene.

Greg lies on his back, eyes closed and head sagging to one side. His chin rests near his collar and blood pools around the back of his head. The culprit is a jagged rock, part of a small garden along the path, half buried in the ankle-length grass. The ground soaks up puddles of blood and the blades of brown grass mat together. The squishy-looking insides of Greg's head ooze from the split in his skull.

Everyone moves back, their eyes wide with uncertainty but not fear. If anything, they're mesmerized by the sight. Silence permeates the moment and I press a hand to my mouth, swallowing hard. My thoughts march in a slow-motion parade. Those are Greg's brains. On the ground. Ten minutes ago he was perfectly normal. He laughed and talked too loud and said stupid things in astronomy.

He said stupid things in astronomy.

The moments before the accident explode in my mind's eye and trigger a suspicion that Deshi pushed Greg. The way he watched the scene in astronomy with barely restrained glee, the way their feet and hands tangled before Greg fell.

Bile sloshes in my gut as the thought turns solid and puts down roots. Things like this don't happen on Earth, not under the Others. People don't hurt one another.

I decide I'm imagining it, and pull my eyes away from Greg's ruined body.

I've never seen anyone get hurt before, nothing worse than a scraped knee or bumped head as a child. Well, except that one broken bone. I don't like to think about that.

I struggle with my expression, too aware of Deshi's eyes and the fact that Greg's injury isn't affecting anyone else. A strong arm supports me by the waist and I don't have to turn to know who's behind me. His scent is as recognizable as his face.

Without thinking twice I droop back into his chest, working hard to control my reaction to the sickening sight. Lucas holds me up for several minutes as deep breaths help me relax. Pushing away from him and daring to open my eyes, I see my fellow students have turned away from Greg's injured body, all talking at once and arguing about what to do next.

"We can't leave him here. Exercise is almost over."

"Someone should go in and tell the Administrator what happened."

"What's the Administrator going to do? We should get a Healer."

"None of the Healers can help. Look at him. He's Broken." Deshi, the owner of that last voice, stands away from the crowd and leans against a tree with his feet crossed at the ankle. He studies his fingernails and heaves a sigh. "Come on, I'm just saying what you're all thinking. The Healers don't deal with injuries this bad."

The way he says it sends nausea rolling through me. Like he couldn't care less. Then again, no one else cares either. Deshi is an enigma, acting friendly or even coconspiratorial one minute, then blissfully accepting of the status quo the next.

The cluster nods along with him, turns their backs on the injured boy, and jog toward the building. Deshi raises an eyebrow when neither Lucas nor I move. "You coming?"

"Someone should tell the Administrator what happened. I'll go." Lucas speaks up with a smooth, confident smile.

After studying us for a moment with a piercing gaze, Deshi follows the pack inside.

"Go on, Althea. You don't have to wait. You've made it clear staying away from me is a priority." Lucas trains his eyes on the distance. On nothing at all. His voice dismisses me, but instead I shift closer to him.

For some reason I can't put my finger on, the thought of leaving his side brings on unstoppable waves of panic. Lucas may not be a Dissident like me, but he makes me feel safe. Right now, with the Wardens watching our every move, kids disappearing from Cell, and a boy with splattered brains lying on the ground at my feet, I'll take it.

I studiously ignore Greg's splayed body. Impatience creeps in at Lucas's unwillingness to make a move. Getting out of here, away from the. . .from Greg, is a top priority in my book. "Well? Shouldn't we go in and tell the Administrator? I mean, Greg might need help."

"I don't think anyone can help him."

Unlike Deshi, Lucas sounds sorry to say those words. Steeling myself, I glance down, concentrating on Greg's chest rather than the gaping wound in his head. It's almost okay that way; I don't have to see the blood. After a moment his chest moves, ever so slightly. Shallow.

"He's breathing, Lucas. We should go get someone right now." My hand darts out and slips into his, tugging him toward the Cell. The strange mixture of my superheated skin and his frigid palm no longer sends shivers down my spine, instead offering comfort borne of growing familiarity. Maybe even friendship. He doesn't resist, though he glances more than once over his shoulder.

"What are you looking at?"

"Huh?"

"Why do you keep looking back and forth between the trees and the Cell?"

"I'm waiting to see if they'll come on their own."

"Who?"

His fingers tighten around mine as he smiles down at me. For a second I forget the question. Okay, maybe more than one second. The world tilts, as though I've fallen into his dimple. My chest is tight and uncomfortable, and the solid reality of his voice anchors me in the moment.

"The Wardens, of course. The Others say they're always watching, and ten Wardens are wandering around town. How come they aren't here?"

Like his insistence that the fish isn't deadly, the question implies that the Others might lie. That suggestion makes his words treasonous, blasphemous, and downright crazy. But the lingering idea that Greg's outburst in astronomy had something to do with his demise won't go away, and hearing Lucas voice a similar sentiment snaps me out of my winter-scented dreamland and dumps me back into real life.

No one talks that way. But I think that way.

People don't question the Others. They rule us, maintain a pleasant society, employ us, but they are *not* us. They are Other.

"Lucas." The word escapes my lungs in a gasp and I can't help but shoot a paranoid glance around the empty field. "What are you saying? That the Others would lie? You can't say that."

"I know. I'm sorry. I don't know where that came from." Lucas's cheeks flush pink and he refuses to meet my gaze.

We walk into Cell in silence, our wet tennis shoes squeaking on the hard floors as we enter, the sound echoing off the empty walls. The Administrative Center is in the middle of the building, enclosed entirely by glass. Lucas drops my hand as we approach the doors.

"Let me do the talking. I still wish you'd just go to block," he mutters under his breath without looking at me.

I don't budge, earning a sigh. Though my outside fakes serenity, inside I'm shaking. I've never been to the center of any of my Cells, never met an Administrator. As far as I know, hardly anyone has met one in person. There isn't any reason to come to the Administrator's office unless you're an Apprentice, and there's only one per year. Ours is Leah.

I wipe sweaty, slick palms on my jeans and straighten my back as Lucas pushes the red button next to the floor-to-ceiling glass doors and waits for them to open. Resisting the urge to clean the perspiration off my brow takes massive effort when the camera over the door swivels our direction. Lucas appears calm, as if he barges into uncharted waters on a daily basis.

Maybe he does, what do I know?

The doors slide open in complete silence, one retreating left and the other right. Nothing greets us but a breeze that lifts stray pieces of crimson hair about my face. I secure them behind my ears as the story

Lucas told in the park the other day assaults my memory and twists my heart into knots.

He said he overheard that conversation in the Administrative Center by walking past, but he must have lied. The glass is too thick to hear anything. But why would he lie to me?

My mind searches for alternatives, ways his story could possibly be true. There simply aren't any, unless he can hear through walls or the conversation took place elsewhere. I try hard, because I want to come up with a plausible option, but there isn't one. I want to run and hide, but at the moment running isn't an option. I can't go anywhere without making a scene, and there is no way I'm letting Lucas goad me into exposing myself.

I step as far away from him as possible without leaving the room, not missing the fast, questioning look he shoots my direction. We pass through another doorway and our footsteps fall silent as we stride onto a deep purple carpet. The room is empty except for the video screen, which takes up the entire wall to our left. It blinks on and we wait for the Administrator to appear. He slides into the chair waiting behind a desk, having to squeeze to accommodate his stomach again. A brief look of surprise passes over his face when he sees us.

"Shouldn't the two of you be in your blocks?"

My mouth goes dry and my tongue cleaves to the roof of my mouth.

Luckily, Lucas doesn't seem to be dealing with the same issues. "Yes, sir. It's just. . .one of the students fell outside during exercise. He's cracked his head pretty good and he's not getting up. We thought someone should know."

The Administrator fidgets while the news sinks in, his exact reaction hard to pinpoint. A bit troubled, perhaps confused. He's not displeased, exactly, just a bit out of sorts. This isn't an everyday occurrence. Before he can answer, the smaller, private screen on his desk lights up and beeps. His eyes flit to the desktop display. "You may go, children. I will deal with the boy."

A disembodied voice squawks from his video screen before we shuffle from the room. It sounds like a woman. The only Others I've ever seen in person are Wardens, and they're all men. I assumed Fire represented the single exception, though now that I think about it I see it's silly. There must be women.

"Not to worry, Administrator. Everything is fine. The boy is Broken, and a girl—your Apprentice—is also being taken for refreshing due to the incident reported after their astronomy lesson. Wardens have been dispatched to collect them."

I gasp involuntarily, prompting Lucas to grab my hand again and tug me out of the office. Once alone, I yank my hand free and walk ahead of him down the hall, trying to make sense of what we heard. The term *refreshing* is brand new to me, but they must be talking about Leah. It doesn't make sense; she was fine when we left the field.

Unless them taking her has more to do with what happened in astronomy than what transpired outside.

Lucas jogs to catch up, stopping beside me to stare out the second-story window, which offers an unobstructed view of the exercise field. I hardly notice he's there, his lies and presence temporarily forgotten.

Greg is where we left him.

A large black rider pulls up to the edge of the grass, hovering right above the ground, its spinning disks a blur of movement. It gleams even though the day is overcast. Two Wardens hop out, slam the front doors shut, and lift the rear hatch before going to Greg. They wear their standard tan uniforms, complete with black hats, belts, and boots. Even from here their beauty dazzles and I squint to relieve some of the eyestrain.

Always men, always handsome, and never with a trace of imperfection. No bent noses or crooked teeth. No wrinkles. Not a freckle. It's too far to make out whether these Wardens have the star-shaped mark on their necks.

It's often crossed my mind, the obvious question that if I'm different—*Dissident*—does that mean I'm not human? And if I'm not. . .what am I? I'm nowhere near perfect enough to be Other, but the fact that I feel *everything* doesn't make a great case for my humanity either. I glance sideways at Lucas, studying him while he watches the scene below. It doesn't hurt to look at him but he resembles the Wardens. He is sort of beautiful.

I turn back to the windows before he catches me staring.

The Wardens reach Greg's body and position themselves at his head and feet. Without care or concern they bend down, one twisting his fingers through Greg's longish brown hair, the second snatching up a foot, and hoist him roughly off the ground. They make their way back to the black rider and pitch Greg's body inside the rear hatch.

I wince, feeling the hard bounce in my bones as if they'd tossed me. Lucas reaches for me but I scoot out of range.

One of the Wardens stationed at our Cell leads Leah outside and ushers her into the rider's backseat. Within minutes the scene returns to normal as the rider pulls out and disappears down the street. Whether Leah will return from this refreshing, whether she'll be the same if she does, is a mystery.

We'll never see Greg again, though. That much I know.

9.

"**W**here are you going?"

"Block." Lucas isn't picking up on my hints right now, which is odd because I'm sure they're saying *stop following me.*

"What'd I do?"

"Nothing. I just need to get to my block. So do you."

He stops walking. About time.

As chemistry looms, my overwrought brain hasn't come up with any plausible way to avoid him, but I get out of talking by slinking into the room at the last second and keeping my eyes on the Monitor. Questions, none of which have anything to do with chem, prod my mind until my brain feels bruised. My feelings regarding Lucas conflict at every intersection.

Sometimes, like in the field, Lucas seems a little bit like me. Or, at the very least, close to being a friend. But then there's the fact that he's hiding an animal, he doesn't smile all the time, and the Wardens seem to make him as nervous as they make me. The bottom line is that I learned years ago not to be tricked into getting comfortable, and I'm nowhere near ready to trust him. Now that he lied about overhearing the conversation in the Administrator's office, I'm farther away than ever.

As soon as the day is over I grab my things and fly out of the room, down the hall, and through the front doors. I've had years of practice disappearing for the hour after Cell, and tagging along with my Cellmates to the pizza parlor is as good a way as any. Lucas, and probably Deshi, will expect me to go to the park alone and I have no desire to see either of them.

The next forty minutes pass quickly; gossip about whether or not Leah will return, along with the events of astronomy, fill most of the time. No one asks for my version and I don't offer an opinion. Nobody even mentions Greg falling in exercise. I do hear about a second blond boy, Jack, not returning from his Warden interview. That makes nine kids gone since the Wardens arrived, counting the six they took at the Outing. Ten if I include Leah.

Eleven if I include Greg.

Five weeks until my number is called. If only people remembered what happened in the interviews, perhaps I could find a way to prepare. But the more questions I ask, the less likely I'll continue to blend in with my Cellmates, and I need the anonymity they offer more than ever. I don't push and no one else seems the slightest bit interested in the Wardens' purpose here or the fact that they're focused on our year in particular.

Lucas is waiting on the Morgans' street, standing smack in the middle of the sidewalk with his arms folded across his chest. Despite the requisite smile, he doesn't look pleased at my earlier disappearing act. "What's going on, Althea?"

"Nothing. Nothing is going on."

An unfamiliar, chafing feeling rattles inside me. It must be anger, but it's been so long since I've experienced the feeling toward a live person it takes me a while to place it. I want to scream, to let it out, but I know that's not the best idea. The rage pours out toward Lucas even though expressing any emotion other than contentment is not Acceptable.

In fact, acting unpleasant never happens. Not because people are scared of the Others. Because as far as I know, no one experiences feelings other than pleasure, happiness, and the occasional instance of excitement.

Except me.

Looking at Lucas's face, I reconsider the assumption.

"Well, something must be going on, because you're definitely avoiding me."

My anger bubbles over. "Maybe because you're a liar, Lucas! A big. . .fat. . .liar."

He takes a step toward me. His face turns a splotchy crimson, and in that instant, reason burrows past fury and fear takes a seat. We're alone on an empty street. He grabbed me before, hard enough to leave a mark.

He stops his advance a couple of feet away and I relax a smidgen.

"Really, a liar? What did I lie about exactly?"

"About overhearing that conversation in the Administrator's office, that's what."

"What are you talking about?" Despite his belligerent tone, his cheeks pale.

"You know exactly what I'm talking about. To get into the office we rang a buzzer, passed inspection by the camera, *and* went through a second door—a thick, wooden one—to talk to the Administrator. Just how did you manage to hear through all that?"

"I. . .well, it's not what you think!"

"I don't know what to think, Lucas. All I know is unless you have secret superhearing or something, there is no way you 'accidentally overhead' anything." The rage bleeds out as fast as it took over, leaving exhaustion in its wake. It turns out fighting takes a lot out of a person.

We watch each other, breath coming in similar erratic patterns. I refuse to let his gaze wander from mine. I've had it with all the double-talk, the running around, and, most of all, the secrets. Hiding secrets of my own is difficult enough; there's no room for Lucas's as well.

"Listen, Althea. I did lie to you, but I didn't make up what I heard, I swear."

His bright, sky-colored eyes beg me to understand but don't offer me a reason. Past experience insists I can't give in to the desire to trust him without risking everything, without being carted away Broken myself.

I shake my head, ponytail swishing back and forth. A shiver works its way across my skin as the cold air brushes my bare neck. I pull my sweater tight around me. He's waiting, and curfew is bearing down on us. "Then tell me the truth."

"Believe me, there's nothing I want more than someone to trust, but. . ."

My breath catches in my throat. "Someone to trust?"

Waiting for his response nearly kills me. It's the same thing I've searched for since I learned to read that stupid note. Something that's never truly been mine, not even during those three years at the Hammonds'. If only I could get a read on him, find a reason to follow my instinctive pull toward him, maybe I could let my guard down.

His face closes up, leaving me on the wrong side of a slammed door. "I can't tell you."

The words crush me. He might as well be standing on top of my chest instead of talking to me from several feet away. Lucas's eyes convey fear bordering on desperation so intense I look away. They mirror the feelings fighting for my attention.

"Why? Why not?"

"I just. . .I just can't. I'm sorry."

Lucas heads next door, leaving me alone on the street. I may as well be the only person on Earth. It takes a full five minutes to convince myself he's not coming back.

After the brief respite granted by Lucas's presence, the solitude is unbearable. It's made everything worse instead of better. We've spent just a few moments together, but after having him talk to me at Cell, wait for me after, tease me about my name, returning to the silence is torture.

Miserable to the point of physically shaking, refusing to listen to the voice of reason assuring me that not trusting Lucas is the right thing, I hide along the side of the Morgans' house. No one is around to see, and it feels surprisingly good to give in to the water

111

for a moment. It winds down my cheeks and drips off my chin. A drop lands on my hand and I lick it off.

Curfew lurks minutes away, so I gather myself and walk around front, part of me hoping Lucas will be loitering outside. The street looms empty in the twilight, turning that hope to ash.

A figure waits on the Morgans' steps, short legs stretched out in front of him. The sight of Deshi clenches my stomach as nerves buzz in my ears. There's nowhere to go, but the desire to run tempts me anyhow.

He stands as I approach. "Hey, Thea."

I don't bother correcting him. "Hi."

"I've been waiting for you."

I tilt my head, asking a silent why as one horrible possibility after another rushes through my mind.

"I know it's almost curfew, so I'll get right to the point. Will you go to the Autumn Mixer with me?"

Deshi smiles a little bit shyly, making me feel almost guilty for avoiding him when he seems to need a friend as badly as I do. But as much as I'd like to get out of the date with Lucas, going with Deshi would be worse. Just standing here talking to him sends my heart into a race with my lungs. And not in a good way.

"I, um. Well, Lucas already asked me."

Deshi steps down from the porch and walks toward me, stopping only inches away. He stares at me, *through* me, before offering a rueful grin. He reaches up to brush my hair back behind my shoulder, making my skin crawl. I resist the urge to retreat, smiling with what I hope is apology and not repugnance.

"The rumors are true, then," he murmurs. "How interesting. Well, see you tomorrow."

He leaves me to suck in the chilly air and try to compose myself. Something isn't right about Deshi. He smiles all the time. He acts normal, except for the occasional off-kilter musing. The way he watches, though. The way he makes me feel cold. An indefinable and alien quality runs underneath his normal exterior.

I haven't forgotten his arrival in Danbury coincided with the Wardens'.

Whether it means he's working for them, or if he simply recognizes a difference in me akin to his own, one thing feels true—he's dangerous.

10.

I wish for the millionth time there was a way to ditch the mixer tonight.

Since we're rarely allowed out after five p.m.—a rule that goes for adults as well as children—the Mixers an exception and therefore exciting for everyone involved. Even though we fought, Lucas's company is welcome after existing in almost complete silence these past days.

We don't have to be friends. I haven't forgotten the lie or his refusal to come clean about it. But maybe spending the evening together will give me a chance to learn whether he's like me or just simply crazy.

It takes longer than normal for me to get ready; I'm finishing up just as a knock comes at the door. My hair cascades down my back instead of hanging in its typical ponytail. Mrs. Morgan even curled it again. Checking the mirror one last time, I feel good about my light blue dress, white cardigan, and canvas tennis shoes. I descend the stairs hauling my anxiety along as an unwelcome burden.

The Morgans and Lucas stand in the foyer looking uncomfortable; my stomach flip-flops at the sight of them. They're all shifting feet, smiling at one another in silence as they shake hands. The scent of the au gratin potatoes we had for dinner hangs in the air. The foyer light makes Lucas appear to be under a spotlight, the subject of an interrogation, and the image might amuse me if we weren't so close to being subjected to that very thing.

Mr. Morgan catches sight of me, his eyes lighting up. "Thea, you look beautiful! Have a good time. I'll expect you home no later than nine."

He kisses my cheek and shuffles back into the living room to watch tonight's inane, Other-produced movie. Mrs. Morgan gives me a tight hug, then pecks my date on the cheek before joining her Partner, leaving Lucas and me alone.

Lucas raises his eyebrows. "How come he can call you Thea?" He waves a hand and shakes his head before I can answer. "Never mind. It doesn't matter. You do look pretty, you know."

I scrunch up my nose as if the compliment disgusts me, even though it definitely does not. "You don't have to say that. They can't hear you."

"I mean it." Lucas grabs my hand and pulls me out the door.

He doesn't drop it as we walk into town, not even when two Wardens pass us on their patrol. I think about pulling away, but people do think we're courting. I want to bring up the argument we had the other day, but the simple phrase *I'm still angry with you for lying* sticks in my throat. No one gets angry. People don't fight. Even though I shouted at him and he knows I was mad, there's a good chance he's forgotten or explained it away. That's how people deal with me when I act wrong. They simply look past it.

Except Lucas has never once looked through me, around me, like everyone else. Deep down I know he hasn't forgotten our argument. Whether Lucas is a Dissident, too, or simply a strange, lonely, Broken human boy, he's as different as I am.

He still holds on tight to my hand as we enter the bowling alley ten minutes later. It's hard to tell if his hand is even cold anymore—mine may have warmed it up. I guess he's taking this whole act pretty seriously. After all, he only asked me here because people *think* we're courting, not because we are.

Our Cellmates buzz about, a few pausing to point and whisper as we enter. Discomfort wraps around me and I concentrate on not sweating. Lucas squeezes my hand as though he can feel it.

He shrugs at my questioning glance. "You get warmer when you're nervous. Don't pay attention to them. They're excited for us."

It's true, I decide as my eyes slide over their faces. Their expressions reveal good-natured envy, and longing, but also giant smiles. Even Brittany, here alone after Greg Broke, grins from ear to ear. After a few moments they stop looking.

No one bowls yet; most just mill around, unsure what to do. Five Wardens are scattered evenly around the room so they won't miss a thing. Lucas tugs me right over to the middle lane, settles me on the cushioned bench, and walks away to get us shoes. The building is older than any of the town's houses or the Cell, and it smells like sweat and feet, among other things. The sound of our voices, hard-soled shoes clicking on the wood floor, and the thunks of heavy balls hitting the trays echo off the concrete walls as our Cellmates settle in for the evening activity.

Lucas returns with two pairs of shoes and two balls, which he dumps on the motorized belt next to our lane. "The pink one is yours."

"How come I get the pink one? Just because I'm a girl?"

"You want the blue one?" His cheeks color and I almost feel badly for teasing him.

He really is handsome. Lucas's chest spreads into sturdy shoulders, arms that I suspect would make me feel protected from the whole rest of the world. He's taller than me, maybe by as much as four or five inches, and those blond curls give him a playful, open appearance that begs to be trusted.

"I'm joking, Lucas. It's fine. I like pink." I catch his eye and smile.

His face breaks into a heart-stopping smile and I forget to wonder anything. "You got me. Know how to play?"

"I haven't for years. None of my parents like it very much."

"None of your parents?"

Man. The slip happened without me realizing it. He makes me too comfortable, and this mistake drags up that horrendous memory of the Monitor in Portland, the one I turned quivery after I talked about the Others while cleaning her room after Cell.

I take my cue from Lucas, the way he acts like everything he says or does is normal, even when it isn't. "I meant neither of my parents. Neither of my parents likes to bowl."

"Do you guys have room for a few more?" It's Brittany, and I've never been so happy to see her porcelain doll face.

Lucas's eyes linger on mine for another second before he answers her. "Of course. The lane holds six."

She nods and skips off, presumably to get a ball and more people. I sit behind the computer, making a valiant effort to figure out how to enter our names. It's a good excuse to keep my face turned away from Lucas, too. The computer is foreign and old-fashioned and I give up after several minutes, my mind not able to focus on the task at hand. Instead I watch my Cellmates as they begin to play.

Another voice, smooth and confident and familiar, interrupts. "Room for one more?"

Deshi. Again.

I don't respond and Lucas intervenes. "Sure, of course, Desh."

"Thanks. I'll grab a ball."

He swaggers to the racks of bowling balls. The bright lights illuminate the strange gold, or maybe bronze, color of his skin. Not like a tan, though. More yellowish.

A pinch releases me from my trance.

"Ow!" Rubbing the inside of my upper arm, I glare up at Lucas.

"You're staring. It's rude. Get up; you don't know how to work that thing."

Obeying stings because he's right. He slides into the seat and starts punching buttons. Our names, along with Deshi's and Brittany's, appear on the screen.

Brittany returns, Leah and another blond girl I don't know trailing behind her.

The sight of Leah stuns me. I don't know when she got back from her refreshing but this is the first I've seen her. She seems the same, not better or worse. I stare as she leans close to Lucas, looking over his shoulder as he types their names into the computer. Her chest rubs against his shoulder blade and he stiffens. She retreats a bit, that strange nonsmile painting her lips. From what I overhear, her personality still teeters a bit off-center, her tone of voice leaning toward accusation more often than not. Whatever the Others did to her, it doesn't appear to have changed anything.

Deshi returns, strutting by me and stirring up the air. His rich, wet-earth scent wriggles into my mouth and nose, depositing a deluge of questions along with it. I can't get over the smell of him and search his face again for anything kindred. Nothing.

Lucas walks up and puts a hand on my shoulder, watching as Deshi drops his heavy ball onto the belt.

If anyone harbors doubts about our courting, they won't after tonight. Knowing whatever's between Lucas and me is just for show should make tonight easier. But it turns out it makes enduring his forced affection even worse. I don't want to think about why.

I'm up first, so I stand and pick up the pink ball, extricating myself from Lucas's touch. The ball feels awkward in my hands; it's been years since I've bowled. Concentrating, or trying to, I manage to knock over a few pins. After my second throw all but one pin lie prone on the polished wood. Hitting them feels good. I've felt like smashing something for days.

Leah goes next, shouldering me hard on her way to the lane. I stumble and fall onto the cushioned bench.

She smiles, and I swear venom drips from her teeth. "Oops. Sorry, Morgan."

Right.

Deshi's name displays next. His grace steals my attention as forcefully as it did the first day I met him. He moves with smooth purpose, as though his feet hardly touch the ground, and knocks down all ten pins on the first try. My brain tries to make sense of Deshi, to reconcile all that I know and suspect, while more of our Cellmates roll their balls down the polished wood lanes. He's very friendly. People are more used to him now, but he's not really one of them.

So why does he twist my nerves into pretzels?

It's partly the way he smells—that powerful scent that recalls the way I smell like jasmine all the time and Lucas smells like pine. More than that, it's the way both

121

he and Lucas question the Others without acting as though it's strange to question them.

When I return to the benches after my second turn, only having knocked down six pins this time, Deshi and Lucas sit together behind the computer, talking.

Deshi's smug, serene voice slices through the bowling alley noise like a knife through butter. "From Iowa. Yeah. My parents relocated because of their Careers."

He takes a deep breath through his nose, a small smile floating around his lips. Does he smell Lucas's pine scent? Is he sitting there wondering if *we* are the promised "more" from his own note from Ko, perhaps Dissidents like him? We are similar in some ways, Deshi, Lucas, and I. Our eyes, for one. Our inability to completely fit in, or to make friends at Cell. It's crossed my mind more than once during these couple of autumn weeks that they could both be working with the Others trying to find me, or someone like me.

Or they could be Broken, and so could I.

Even though their conversation sounds innocuous, Lucas's rigid posture and the way his eyes continually seek mine transmit a palpable aggravation, pushing my own anxiety into a steady climb. Our hands brush, causing an uncomfortable sensation to travel up my arm. My skin is too hot and his may as well be made of ice. I suddenly wonder what would happen if our skin lingered together too long when I'm keyed up. Would I melt him?

Too many questions, not enough answers. This is becoming the story of my life and it's *not* okay. It's never been okay, but for the first time I feel exposed. The note, lying to everyone, hiding my fits of water or anger, has all seemed a bit abstract until the Wardens showed up in Danbury, looking for something. Someone. Until Lucas smelled like winter and really saw me, until Deshi showed up and maybe Broke Greg.

I've clung to a childhood fantasy that because Ko wrote me that note, he's been watching over me, ready to send me spinning into a new season if any danger gets too close, but it's time to let go of that idea. I have no safety net. If Ko has been pulling the strings on my existence until now, he's lost control this autumn.

If I'm going to survive the Wardens' interviews, I'll have to figure out how to do it myself.

The evening stumbles on, interrupted by our meal—another treat. Fried chicken and potatoes. We aren't usually allowed to eat fried food, and the flavor explodes in my mouth, crunchy and savory. Everyone else chews delightedly, exclaiming over our special night and that we should thank the Others for such a wonderful meal. Focusing on the food distracts me for twenty minutes or so, but when it's gone, all I can think about is the need to put distance between myself and the boys. Watching the clock becomes my favorite pastime.

Lucas's polite talk, banter, and sweet glances my direction convinces everyone he's relaxed and enjoying the mixer, but not me.

He and Deshi spend most of the evening with their heads bent together, murmuring too low to be heard through the rest of the din, amplifying my paranoia that they're plotting against me. The second the clock hits eight-thirty Lucas stands up, grabs my pink ball and his blue one, and returns them to their shelves. The rest of the Terms are slower to respond to the time, since we have another half an hour before we're required to be home.

Helping me to my feet, Lucas clears his throat and announces, "See everyone at Cell."

"What's the hurry?" Leah asks, still oddly aggressive.

"Yes, Lucas. What's the hurry? Want Althea all to yourself for a few minutes, perhaps to do a little *talking*?" Deshi smiles at his own suggestion, but a fleeting challenge lights his eyes.

Through our clasped hands, Lucas trembles as his face goes white. "No. I promised her dad we wouldn't be late, is all. See you."

He bites off the words and hauls me out the door so fast I have to trot to keep up. After we turn a corner he stops, sucking in ragged, deep breaths. I wait, a little dumbfounded.

He casts his eyes at the ground. "Sorry," he mumbles.

"For what?"

"Losing it back there. I don't like talking to Deshi."

He could be trying to trick me, but his words feel honest, like most of our conversations. All but one, the one that stops me from taking a chance. Still, relief washes through me at his confession—he senses the off quality in Deshi as well.

"I know what you mean. It's like he thinks he's better than us."

Lucas doesn't answer, just drops my hand and starts toward home. I take care to leave space between us, because even though my pulse has returned to normal, cold air still blasts off Lucas. I want to know more about why Deshi bothers him, if he notices the Barbarus's odor or thinks anything of it, but he probably won't tell me.

We pass the rest of the way back to the Morgans' in silence. Lucas trudges next to me all the way onto the porch, where his face is half hidden between the bright glow of the porch light and the deepening night shadows. His eyes glitter with a desire so fierce I look away.

He grabs my hands. "I wish we could be friends. Can't we?"

Every cell in my body wants to say yes. I have to clamp my lips shut to keep the assent from escaping, but the memory of his untruth withers the word on my tongue. It seems safer to go back to my solitude, even though it's a miserable state, because at least that way no one can figure out my secrets. So I don't say anything and we stare at each other for a long time. I wonder what he's thinking, wish he would tell me.

Finally he leans in, hesitates for a split second, then brushes his cool lips across my warm cheek. A pleasant shudder rolls down from my shoulders and curls my toes, leaving warm, seeping heat in their wake. That combined with the walls in between us squeeze my heart so hard it can hardly beat.

"Good night, Althea. I'll see you at Cell." Lucas drops my hands, his defeated air trampling the mood.

He slumps down the front steps, onto the sidewalk, and all the way to his front door. He never looks back but he knows I'm watching. It's easy to see in the way his shoulders hunch up as though they can protect him from my gaze. My intestines twist into knots and for once the sweat forming over my body has nothing to do with an internal loss of control.

Lucas did it. With his nearness. With his lips. With that look in his eyes, the one that makes me feel like I'm looking into my own.

I can't change my mind about him, no matter how desperate I am to trust someone, to finally have an ally in life. I understand the defeat in his posture. As much as I want to talk to him and hold nothing back—to share sorrow, and pain, and anger—letting my guard down isn't smart.

That's why *I* feel desperate and defeated. I don't know why *he* does.

I try for some normalcy and attempt to relax while brushing my teeth, changing my clothes, and crawling under the comforter, but it doesn't bring me any answers. That his reasons mirror my own is too much to hope for, but what else could be behind his inhuman, myriad emotions baffles me. I wonder again if he's Broken and somehow manages to keep it hidden. It's hard to imagine no one else ever notices he's not always happy. I know from experience how hard a thing it is to hide, especially as a child. Sighing, I force

127

my eyes closed and try to tempt sleep. Lucas might be thinking about me, too.

Inside where no one, not even me, can squash it. . .I hope he is.

11.

My emotional state falls into deeper unrest over the next several days. The leftover nervousness from the mixer, combined with the certainty that I'll be taken after my interview in less than a month, fill my mind and spill over into the rest of me. It results in an increased obsession with questioning everything I've ever been told. Despite the fact that the Others live apart from us, I've never second-guessed their truthfulness. They're frighteningly unfeeling and even cruel, but why would they need to lie?

I waste hours worrying over what to do about Lucas and Deshi. I observe the change in Leah, quietly severe and frightening. Two more Term girls are taken away during the third week of interviews. Greg's empty seat in astronomy boils my blood. The more I think about the day he Broke, the more certain I am that Deshi hurt him on purpose.

There must be a way to find out what's going on. My need to take action, to find out what's going on this autumn generates an idea. I could eavesdrop on a Warden interview. If only I knew what they wanted, what they were looking for, I could figure out how to make sure they don't think I've got it.

It's the most dangerous idea I've ever had, and getting caught would cement my presence in their minds. On the other hand, I'm so incredibly tired of playing these questions on an endless loop but being too afraid to try to find out the answers to what makes me so different. The logistics of how to listen in and not get caught are still rattling around in my mind.

Today I scoot in the Morgans' door and participate in the evening ritual. Dinner is roast duck, rice, and zucchini. Mrs. Morgan's rice, potatoes, and vegetables are seasoned to perfection, as always. The Others' duck, shipped out of a regional factory, tastes bland in comparison. My autumn parents don't notice anything amiss about my attitude, which is good.

And bad.

A storm builds in my belly, filling it so that choking down dinner is a monumental task. I try to shake it off, focusing on the Morgans' conversation instead.

"Yes, I saw them today when I was cleaning the curtains in the front room. Two Wardens. Walked straight into the house next door." Mrs. Morgan utters the observation with the same tone she uses to call me to dinner or comment on Mr. Morgan's shirt and tie combination in the morning.

My jaw freezes in mid-chew as Mr. Morgan responds.

"Coming to register the new baby, no doubt."

The Others register every baby once it survives its first year. I've never seen the process in person, but we're told registering consists of a simple medical procedure and the issuing of identification.

Mrs. Morgan nods, sawing off a piece of duck and swirling it around in the sweet, hot mustard on her plate. "When we saw the little guy—Roark—at this month's Outing I thought his face was too flat, his ears too small. Something is funny about the way his eyes are slanted, too. At any rate, the Wardens took Roark when they left."

"Yes. Broken, sure as the day is long. Too bad." Mr. Morgan doesn't sound like he thinks it's too bad. He sounds like he'd rather be eating than having this conversation.

Without warning, the storm inside me breaks loose. A million grievances built up over sixteen years. The Broken baby next door. The Morgans' casual discussion of the news. Simmering resentment over Lucas and his lies, wild fear over Deshi's attention. Leah. Greg. The Wardens. The interviews.

131

Shoving the chair back so hard it topples, I loom over the table as the Morgans gape at me with baffled expressions. Anger escapes my tenuous hold, rocketing straight out of my mouth. "What is wrong with you people? Don't you get that the neighbors had their child taken away? Their *child!*"

The last words shriek from my lips, scraping my throat raw and causing Mrs. Morgan to slide a few feet away from the table. Her eyes meet mine and I hold onto her gaze, willing her to understand.

Why does the child have to go away? Don't you notice when I go away? Do you miss me at all?

I push these thoughts at her, all the questions I've ever wanted to ask. They scream in my mind, directed at the poor woman who, in all fairness, has never done anything but take care of me.

To my utter astonishment her eyes focus on me, really *focus*, for the first time.

Instead of her normal, pleasant demeanor, fright slithers onto her face. Uncertainty joins it moments later, and she stands and backs away.

"Who…who are you?" She points at me, her hand trembling, and then looks at her Partner. "Who is she? Why is she here? She's not ours!"

Mr. Morgan returns her stare, quizzical but not disturbed, and remains silent. Whatever's happening isn't affecting him. Just her. A closer look reveals pain etched in her every wrinkle.

Certainty that my outburst has done something more than simply shock her sneaks in, but I push it away. It's impossible. I don't even know what's happening.

All I know is I have to fix this. Fix her.

"What? Of course I'm yours."

My feeble attempt to calm the situation achieves nothing and Mrs. Morgan's panic shoots up faster than a dandelion in the springtime. She presses against the door leading to the backyard. Her hand snakes behind her, scrabbling for the knob.

You can't let her leave.

Cognitive ability returns with that one clear, simple command. Mrs. Morgan somehow knows I'm a Dissident, and she can't run all over Danbury screaming about it.

My own panic rises, emotions flailing haplessly as I search for a solution. The temperature in the kitchen climbs toward unbearable. Steam rises out of the water-filled pots in the sink and fogs up the windows. Custard, simmering on the stove, starts to boil.

Do something. Anything!

"Dad! Stop her, she needs a Healer!"

My voice spurs Mr. Morgan into action and he crosses the small kitchen in three steps, grabbing his Partner by the arm. He speaks in a soothing voice, the fixed smile never leaving his face. "Now, Angie, calm down. I don't know what's wrong, but we're going to get you fixed up."

Their eyes lock, hers huge and incredulous. "Fixed up? I don't want to be fixed up. I want to be free! What's the matter with you? Can't you see what they've done? What's happened to everyone?"

Each shouted word pushes Mr. Morgan farther away. His hands cover his ears as he falls back into his chair at the dinner table where he gawks at his Partner. She scans the room in an unceasing circle, making me worry her eyeballs might fall out of her head. The thought of hurting her closes my throat, but my choices ooze away like sap down a tree trunk. She shrinks away as I approach, as though she's hoping to disappear right through the door.

I don't know what I'm going to do. All I know is she has to shut up.

Without any idea of how to accomplish this, I reach out and grab her shoulders as tight as I dare. She meets my eyes, terror widening her pupils until all I see is black.

"You know what they've done, don't you? What are you?" She whispers the words so softly there's no way Mr. Morgan hears. For a moment I'm too stunned to move. The need to question her overtakes my fear, but then Mr. Morgan gets up from his chair again, moving toward us with uncertain steps. Before he gets close enough to ask what I'm doing or what she's saying, I shove her.

Hard.

12.

The crack of her head against the door makes me sick, and my hands fall from her shoulders. Mrs. Morgan's eyes roll back in her head and flutter shut as she slumps to the floor at my feet.

Mr. Morgan stares over my shoulder, looking down at his Partner with his mouth hanging open. "What happened?"

He'd seen the entire thing. Hadn't he?

"She, um, collapsed. Get her to the couch. I'll call the Healer."

He scoops Mrs. Morgan off the floor and disappears into the living room. Disbelief crowds my mind as the back door holds me upright. I knocked someone out. My fake mother, no less. Giggles threaten to erupt, out of place and inappropriate. I'm probably in the process of Breaking.

Stalling any longer will do nothing except arouse suspicion. The communication console is in the den, down the dimly lit hall behind the third door on the left. A standard fifty-two-inch screen hangs suspended on the wall to my right. Mr. Morgan's desk sits across from it, a twenty-inch model mounted to the top. The

136

large screen is for connecting with his work supervisors. Mr. Morgan works in Travel. His days have to be boring, given that few people travel except the Others, and they don't need people like Mr. Morgan. They come and go as they please.

The smaller screen on the desk is for contacting the Others. Healers are human, but we aren't allowed direct communication with one another. We have to go through *them*.

There's a red button on the lower right-hand side of the screen that connects me to an operator of sorts. I push it, and after a second an Other pops up, sitting behind a large desk. His blond hair is grown out past his ears and shines like the sun is pouring onto it. The empty, glinting black gaze threatens to swallow me whole.

I avert my gaze, his stunning features sparking a sharp, persistent ache behind my eyes. I look to the side of the screen so I can see him, but not directly.

His voice matches his expression. Exquisite but bored. "Yes, how can I help?"

My features rearrange into a pleasant expression. "My mother collapsed. We need a Healer."

"Very well." He taps a few buttons on the screen in front of him. "One has been dispatched. Estimated arrival time: three and a half minutes. Good day."

He clicks another button without waiting for a response and the screen goes black. Lingering in the darkness for a minute helps me calm down, but my skin heats up again when the front door buzzes.

I drag myself out of the den and back toward the living room. Mrs. Morgan lies on the couch with Mr. Morgan kneeling on the floor beside her. His face betrays keen interest but no worry, lacks even a touch of concern. Even an evening this out of the ordinary can't get under his skin.

A middle-aged man, presumably the Healer, hovers over them both. "Can you tell me what happened?"

Standing in the shadowy hallway, my presence still undetected, I hold my breath and wait. My legs ache with unspent energy, ready to take off running at the first whiff of trouble.

Mr. Morgan rubs his face, the first chink in his armor since the episode began. "She. . .well, we were eating dinner. Then she started shouting funny things and went to the back door like she was going to run outside. Then our daughter, Thea. . .Thea, where are you?"

I slink forward, still with a clear path to the front door.

"Ah, there you are. Anyhow, Thea suggested we needed a Healer because of how Angie looked—her eyes were rolling around and wild. Then she just fell down on the floor. I carried her in here and Thea went to call you."

Utter disbelief pours through me at Mr. Morgan's version of the story. He didn't even mention my outburst. The air around me, previously sticky and hot, drops a few degrees. Something thick and oily drips in globs between my fingers. When I jerk my hand off the wall, its imprint remains melted into the paint.

Oops. Good thing the hallway is dark.

The Healer's eyebrows, thick and reddish brown like his hair, scrunch together. He rubs his generous waistline with one hand and considers this information. He places a hand on Mrs. Morgan's chest, then touches her forehead. "Go grab a wet towel, please, girl?"

I don't want to go, but I don't refuse. Enough rules have been broken for one night. And this way I can rinse the white paint off my hand.

The kitchen light is still on, the scene a blaring reminder of what transpired. Feeling guilty, I right my chair and return it to its place at the table. I grab Mrs. Morgan's from where it's scooted near the door and reposition it as well. The custard burns on the stove with an acrid, sweeter-than-candy smell. I dump it in the sink and fill the pot with water. The rags are in a

139

drawer by the stove. I wet one down, fold it, and return to the living room.

The Healer takes it from me and places it on Mrs. Morgan's forehead while I resume my post by the front door. My mind races, attempting to make some sort of sense out of what's happening. How after all these years Mrs. Morgan finally *saw* me, recognized me for what I am—whatever that is.

The Healer looks thoughtful, his jewel green eyes studying his patient. "I believe, based on what you told me, that your Partner is going to be fine. Her vital signs are strong but she meets several criteria. I'm going to have to take her with me for observation."

"Criteria? What criteria?" My mouth races ahead of my brain. Luckily, the Healer doesn't seem to think it's odd.

"If an injury or illness has certain symptoms I'm required to have the Regional Healer examine her before she returns to her life."

"What's a Regional Healer?"

His eyes narrow on mine. "Why do you ask?"

"Oh, um. I'm about to get a Career at the end of the year and I'm interested in healing, that's all."

He laughs, loosening my anxiety a bit.

"Don't set your sights on being a Regional Healer, girl. He is Other." He turns to Mr. Morgan. "Where is the communicator?"

"Down the hall. Thea will show you."

I retrace my earlier steps as the Healer's words echo in my mind. *The Regional Healer is Other.* He might be able to tell what really happened to Mrs. Morgan.

I do my best to stay calm with the Healer trailing me into the den. After he sits behind the desk, he waits for me to leave the room before turning on the device. I linger outside the door, hoping to overhear the conversation.

The same voice that greeted me spouts out a moment later. "Yes, how can I help?"

"There is an illness here that needs to be reviewed by the Regional Healer. Please send transport." The Healer's voice booms confidently, even though he probably doesn't have to do this often. The term Regional Healer is new to me. One more thing they never told us about.

"Describe criteria met." The voice remains flat and unimpressed by the staggering events of my evening. Imagining the handsome face doesn't hurt like looking at it does.

"Talking oddly. Attempting to run away." The Healer ticks the insane events off like a list of homework.

"That is Acceptable. Transport is on its way. Estimated arrival time: four minutes and twenty-seven seconds. Good day."

The sound of the Healer's muted footsteps approaching the door gets me moving. I sprint down the hall and shut myself in the wasteroom before he walks past. The sound of my erratic breathing fills the dark silence until I hear rider doors slam shut outside.

Back in the living room, two Others march through the open front door, some sort of bed suspended between them. The sight of the technology catches me off guard; it's not something the Others share with us. Seeing it stretches the gulf between our species so wide that their side is no longer visible from mine. The fluffy-looking mattress floats waist-high beside the couch, proving their superiority without a word.

The Others stand at each end, not dressed like any Wardens I've ever seen. The realization stops me short. Besides Wardens, I've never seen Others in person. These two wear identical white shirts with short sleeves, pants, and pristine white sneakers. Besides their clothing, though, they look the same. Longish golden hair. Black eyes. Symmetrical features. Intimidating. Painful.

My gaze slides to their necks. It's there. The mark shaped like the star of my locket.

They lift Mrs. Morgan, one grabbing her head, the second scooping up her feet. It takes me back to the afternoon when the Wardens did the same to Greg's body. These two take more care with Mrs. Morgan as they settle her among the bed's white folds. Leather straps, invisible until now, snake up and secure her feet, hands, and forehead without help. One of the Others flicks his long, tanned finger and the cot floats toward the door. The Healer acts like he's seen this before, but Mr. Morgan's eyes are as wide as mine.

As one Other follows the cot outside, the second turns to Mr. Morgan. "You and your daughter will come with us."

13.

Mr. Morgan nods and stands without a hitch. I have no idea what to do. To hesitate will make it clear they should be suspicious of me. To go with them could mean being found out. They don't wait, expecting me to follow without protest, since everyone does what they say.

The Other ushers Mr. Morgan out the door and turns back, watching me through keen eyes. My brain urges my feet to step forward and my face to remain blank. Neutral is all that's manageable right now, which must be Acceptable at a time like this.

If only he would move. The doorway grows narrower as I approach, constricting the path past him. He won't miss the heat pouring off me or the swirling scent of jasmine.

A quick, focused attempt at calming down does little good. I walk the remaining half of the room and the heat in my face and palms, where it's always the worst, heightens. The smell I can't help, can't turn off. Hopefully he'll assume what Lucas did—that the fragrance is some sort of perfume.

I draw in a breath and hold it as our bodies draw near enough to touch. My mind screams in panic, and the odd voice that doesn't sound quite like my own spreads words of comfort through my head.

He's waiting for you to pass. He did the same thing with Mr. Morgan. Stay cool. Literally.

It works, or at least he doesn't knock me down and drag me away. I hug my side of the door frame to avoid touching him. A breeze blows his shiny blond hair back a bit, the close-up sight of the scar battering my frayed senses.

The cool night air ruffles my sweaty hair, a welcome respite from the stuffy, oppressive house. My lungs pull in great gulps as I head toward the rider hovering at the curb. Without years of practice controlling my expression I'd be a goner already. A few short moments alone with Others for the first time in my life and I've already noticed how they see me. They don't look through me. I don't confuse them.

It's terrifying.

Sixteen years on Earth and riders are still a rare sight, even considering they've been in Danbury twice already this autumn. The sight of the transports normally tighten my chest, and the idea that I'm about to get inside one makes me feel ready to explode. The Others' impatience at my uncertainty outside the open door wraps around my body like a glove. Realizing how a normal person would act in this situation makes it that much harder, since it goes against my every instinct.

They would trust the Others.

I take a deep breath, plant a foot on a little bar six inches off the ground, and leap inside. The Other slams the door behind me, then crawls into the front seat beside the driver. I wedge into the smallest of spots between Mr. Morgan and the Healer, my hips smashed against theirs and my arms crossed in front of me.

Across from where Mr. Morgan, the Healer, and I crowd on a bench, Mrs. Morgan lies immobile on her floating bed. In separate seats facing forward, the two Others operate the controls. They each have a set in front of them and it appears they both play a role in making the transport go.

As soon as the door clicks shut the rider takes off. At first it's not too impressive. I'm more focused on trying to keep the temperature inside the cramped space from broiling everyone than on the view, or the mechanism of the transport. Keeping control gets harder as our rider approaches the boundary and slows down, rolling to a stop a few feet from the electric fence. From my spot in the middle, facing front, the entire scene is crystal clear.

I wish it weren't.

When we pull to a stop, the Warden sitting on the left side swings his door open and climbs out. He walks up to the boundary, then makes a sharp left into the trees. After about twenty seconds a gate opens in the fence. I'd never have guessed it was there if it hadn't happened right in front of my eyes.

The Other climbs back into the rider and we pull forward through the gate. It closes behind us, trapping us in the Wilds. Trees of all shapes, types, and colors surround the rider as we move along. Our speed increases outside the boundary, the world blurring until nothing is distinguishable.

An attack of claustrophobia hits me as we slip farther and farther from the familiar and enter a place I know I'm not meant to be. I'm sure we're all about to suffocate in the tight quarters, and panic rolls over me in waves. It washes out of me as heat and before long, the rider is sweltering.

First the Healer, who's a bit heavyset, starts fanning his face.

Then a sheen of sweat appears on Mr. Morgan's tall forehead.

By the time the Others feel the heat wave, I've lost control. My panicked attempts to rein it in, to staunch the fear, only make the rider hotter. The driver glances toward his counterpart and I strain to make out his words. I think he says, "Too many bodies in here."

Without warning a window in the roof cracks open and autumn air rushes through the transport. Sweet relief courses through my body, causing my knees to go weak and tingly. It's short-lived, though, as the rider eases to a stop.

The doors open and the Others stand, waiting. "Please get out."

We oblige. After all, they did say please. The Others have impeccable manners.

We all do.

The night is opaque, oppressive even, as I step out of the transport and squint. Mr. Morgan climbs out behind me, followed by the Healer. One of the Others beckons the floating bed with one long finger and it also obeys his command to exit the rider. My eyes start to adjust to the darkness, and I glimpse the outline of a tall building towering above us. It's as black as the surrounding night, but moonbeams glint off its surface. The structure reaches so high it's impossible to make out the number of floors in the milky moonlight.

Perhaps I couldn't see the top even if it were day.

One Other starts into the building, where the doors slide apart like the ones at the Administrator's office. We all follow, and without checking, I know the second Other brings up the rear. Though my mind races at breakneck speed, it doesn't land on how to get out of this nightmare. Instead I follow the Other in the lead, docile and obedient. Choices stumble through my head, even though my gut says nothing can help me now. I could fall down and pretend to be ill, too. I could run. I could stay and play along, praying they don't notice anything odd.

Right.

Running is not an option. They've driven us outside the boundary. The location is unfamiliar and the sheer number of animals between here and town ensures I'd never get back alive. And if I did, they'd be waiting. Acting hurt or sick would get me Broken for real.

Playing along is the best choice. The Others have no reason to expect a fight, no reason to suspect someone like me exists. People report the Broken, if that's even what I am. The Others don't spend much time considering humans any kind of threat. They don't spend much time considering us at all, as far as I can tell.

At the end of the lengthy hallway, along which we've passed not a single door, the Other stops in front of a solid wall. I'm convinced we're walking straight into a tomb—fitting since we'll probably never walk out of this place alive. He presses his hand into the material, leaving an imprint behind, and within seconds the wall starts to go transparent. I blink, and the wall is still gone. We walk through the gap into a huge room. If this is a tomb, it's big enough for everyone in Danbury.

The room is vast and intimidating; the ceiling could be non-existent and the walls to the left and right are barely visible from where we stand. Dozens of tables, piled high with tubes, metal boxes, glass jars, and more vaguely menacing machines, clutter the floor. None of it is recognizable. It's dusty and unused, and somehow old compared to the rider and the building and that floating bed.

For some reason the sight of it ramps up my fear enough that I worry about my hands lighting something on fire.

The Others lead us through the tables, keeping to a path that winds its way among them. We reach the back of the room and stop at a glossy black desk littered with notebooks. Two flat screens sit back-to-back, one facing us, the second turned toward the chair.

The Other seated at the desk is a woman dressed in business attire. Another first for me on this night of unprecedented events.

Maybe this is an actual nightmare. Perhaps I'm about to wake up in Iowa at the Clarks', and it'll be winter. Squeezing my eyes shut, I give it a try. When I peek again, the blazing beauty of the female is the only thing in my range of vision. Pain stabs behind my eyes. Her star mark is redder than the men's.

She speaks in a voice as intoxicating as her face. "Please enter your names."

The screen facing us lights up, glowing a soft blue and illuminating the Healer's paunchy features. An entry bar appears. He states his name and the letters type across the screen. The computer accepts his declaration, replacing his name with another blank bar. Mr. Morgan follows the Healer's example, then it's my turn.

The name Althea Morgan might not even be real. I hold my breath but no alarm sounds.

The Other beckons us through a door behind the seated woman, scanning a pale blue beam across our eyes as we pause beside him. We file past in the same orderly fashion we've displayed thus far. The lights are dimmer back here. The ceiling remains out of view but these walls are closer together. The claustrophobia from the rider returns and I blink sweat out of my eyes.

Three floating cots span the room, the only furniture except for a table. Some sort of machine sits on top of the latter, an oven-sized metal box with a video monitor decorating the front, vents opening on the back. Two levers on the right side, one red, one black. A strange silvery hat hangs off one corner. It doesn't reek of disuse like the mounds of wired equipment in the previous room. These sleek and shiny surfaces come from the competent, advanced hands of the Others.

Two new Others slouch along the far wall, looking annoyed to see us. They're younger than most of the Wardens, and much younger than the white-clad Others who brought us here. They're maybe a little older than me.

I have no idea if the lives of the Others resemble ours in any way, if they age the same way we do, or at all. All of the Others look youthful. Their skin is taut and shiny; their hair is thick; they walk ramrod straight.

The expression in their eyes isn't innocent, though.

Until now I've pegged them all as middle-aged. One of the two who brought us here, the one who drove, steps forward and speaks to the younger ones.

"These three need to be refreshed. The woman is injured but showed signs of shedding her veil beforehand. Wake her up and then make a determination."

"Should we call you if it's suspicious?" One of the annoyed boys looks up, his empty black eyes shadowed by heavy lids. Like he might fall asleep any minute, the whole situation is so dull.

"No. Do a report, then dispose of her."

Chills race along my arms and down my back, hairs standing on end as he continues.

"Refresh her Partner and the girl and erase tonight. You know what to do. Don't waste my time with your frivolous questions."

He accompanies the reprimand with a hard stare. The boy winces, gasping and clutching the sides of his head even though no one went near him.

"Yes, sir. I'm sorry, sir." A distinct tremor chokes the air with fear.

His friend pipes up. "Should we purge their doldrums while they're under?"

The white-clad Other breaks eye contact with the skinny one, who immediately lets go of his head while relief floods his face. "No, don't bother. Connecticut is on the summer purge rotation. They were just done."

The Others who brought us here exit the room. The Morgans, the Healer, and I are alone with the insolent ones against the wall. The skinny one is recovering from his fright, though he remains so pale his lips look stained against his waxy skin.

153

The stockier boy steps forward to address us. "Each of you take a cot and lie down. I will question you separately on the events of the evening."

The Healer and Mr. Morgan take the floating beds nearest the Others, leaving me the one in the center of the room. Not wanting to appear cautious, I climb on to it without hesitation. It holds my weight, doesn't sink even an inch under me.

I lie down because they told us to. The word *dispose* pulses in my head like a heartbeat. I don't want to consider what it means for Mrs. Morgan.

The Other charged with attending to her motions her cot through another doorway in the back of the room, closing the door behind him. I imagine the rooms with doors in the back go on forever.

The second boy watches him go, then turns his attention back to the three of us. "Close your eyes if you'd like; you must be tired."

The Other approaches the Healer's cot. The equipment table floats behind him, suspended just inches off the ground. Like the cots. Like the riders.

Alarm scuttles through me as the Other talks in a voice much too low to overhear. I can't eavesdrop so I turn my attention to more productive use, like trapping the heat inside of me before sweat starts dripping onto the floor.

Like figuring out what I'm going to say when it's my turn.

Thoughts of Mrs. Morgan, of what might be happening to her in the back room, try to force their way in. I push them behind a heavy door in my mind and slam it shut. If I think about that right now that'll be it. My tenuous control will snap. I'll boil the room, melt the cot, and it'll be me being disposed.

Relief battles with curiosity over learning they aren't going to purge us. Each town is on a purge schedule; once a year the Others send out a team to treat the humans to a party in town. There are massages, facials, hair colorings, rides, games. . .and purging. It's required but I've never been to one because all my families attend a summer purge.

One more thing I don't do that I'm supposed to.

The story Mr. Morgan gave at the house runs on a loop in my head. The problem will be if he changes his version. He and the Healer both relax on their cots by the time the Other gets to me. They look to be asleep. The Other's eyes bore into my body as he approaches my bed. They probe through my skin, see into my bones and brain.

Maybe it's just my imagination.

"Your name please."

"Althea Morgan." I sound calm, sleepy even. That's good.

"Tell me what happened tonight, please. Start with when you arrived home from Cell." His words are clipped and impatient. He barely looks at me, giving the distinct impression that he'd like to be doing something else. I'd be surprised if he's listening closely to my story. They probably refresh people all the time, like Leah.

"I got home the same time as always, just before five. I spent an hour or so in my bedroom doing homework, then came down for dinner."

He interrupts. "What did you eat?"

"Um, duck. And zucchini." The hesitation sends my heart tripping.

"Go on."

"We were eating dinner, and Mom started acting funny. She got up from the table. She was saying weird things—"

"Weird things like?"

A glance at his face pains me but confirms my suspicion. He's still bored. Nothing coming out of my mouth is triggering suspicion. My answer comes forth with more confidence. "Like 'where am I?' And 'who are you?' Or 'what's going on?'" He nods. "She ran to the door and I went over to see if I could help her, you

156

know? Then she fell down and we couldn't wake her up. I called for a Healer. He came. Then you guys showed up."

The simpler, the better. I can hear a slight tremble in my voice and sweat puddles underneath me, but the emotions are trapped inside where they belong. I'm doing a better job at controlling them than usual, and for that I'm thankful.

"You got up and went to her?" His eyes snap to attention and latch onto mine. "Your father didn't mention that."

14.

The panicky voice roars in my ears, making his words sound far away. They barely penetrate the fog enveloping my mind. I force my response out in a normal tone. "He didn't? Huh."

"Did she say anything to you?"

"No. She looked around like she didn't know what was going on and fell down."

My eyes flit to his face again. Looking away after a split second isn't suspicious. No one can look at the Others for long.

He sits back and his gaze returns to dull and uninterested. "That's fine."

The Other turns from my cot and pushes the floating table away. Terror clings to my body like saran wrap at what might be coming next.

He goes to the door at the back of the room, the one Mrs. Morgan disappeared through, and knocks until his coworker sticks his head out. The one who examined me doesn't bother to lower his voice. "What do you think? Got her awake yet?"

"Not really. She's been mumbling a bit. She doesn't look right."

"From what they've told me it sounds like she did shed her veil."

As my mind wrestles with the new term, the Other who had been with Mrs. Morgan grows wide-eyed. It's a minute before he gets enough of his wits back to answer.

"I never thought they could. . .you know, lose their veil."

"They can't, really. At least not on purpose. Humans can shed their veils but they lose their minds in the process. They've got so many emotions. They're trickier than most species. It's rare."

"Two in a month, Elij."

Elij shakes his head, his lips pulled into a frown. "The Term girl didn't shed her veil, it just looked like someone poked holes in it. Anyway, the Prime said to leave her that way. He wants to see if we can figure out what damaged her."

The Term girl? Were they talking about Leah? It makes sense, since they certainly didn't fix her.

"Can we refresh this one if she's shed it completely?" The skinny, nameless Other shoots worried glances behind him, as though Mrs. Morgan is going to rise from the cot and stab him in the back.

I don't know where that thought came from; the violence of it stuns me.

Elij, the refresher, shakes his head again and my heart goes still. "No. Write it up, Paj. Dispose of her."

They look excited at the prospect, not the least bit uncomfortable.

Whether they have feelings at all is a mystery. We don't interact with them, don't ask questions, not even when their movements are out of the ordinary. Like showing up at the Outing, and the Gathering.

Like kidnapping us.

Elij pats his coworker on the shoulder like a parent might to indulge an annoying child. "I'm going to refresh these three. Take care of the paperwork."

He turns and my eyelids flutter all the way shut. They've been talking loudly. If Mr. Morgan or the Healer is still awake, they've heard the entire conversation as well. Curiosity burns through my mind like wildfire, trumping fear for the moment. What do they mean by *veil*? And the scarier question, why they aren't worried about us overhearing their plan to dispose of Mrs. Morgan?

Elij crosses the room to the Healer, grabs the strange-looking hat object off the top of the machine, flips the red switch, and settles it over the Healer's head. The helmet sits there, hard and glinting. The silver is so pure it might be liquid, flowing and suspended in space.

My muscles coil, prepared to run if something goes sour.

Once the hat is in place, the Other leans down until his nose is mere inches from the Healer's. My ears strain to make out the words.

His voice is commanding, irresistible. "Open your eyes."

The Healer obeys, starting at the nearness of the Other. Pain crosses his face, likely caused by the uncomfortable, stabbing ache that accompanies the sight of the Others. He doesn't look away, but as Elij reaches back and flips the black switch on the side of the box, an odd calm seeps into his features. Maybe the hat makes the pain go away.

"Good." He shoots a quick glance at the screen on the box behind him. "Think about this evening, about everything that transpired after your summons to the Morgan house. Now imagine a blank space. Just blackness, like staring at the sky when there aren't any stars." He checks the screen again. "Very nice. Let me tell you what happened tonight, yes? Then you can try remembering again."

His voice is so pure, so enthralling that my instinct is to believe whatever he says. "Tonight the Morgans called you over because Mrs. Morgan collapsed and was rendered unconscious. The family was concerned for her well-being but had no idea what triggered the episode. You examined her and found she had suffered a brain injury. Realizing she would never recover, you declared her Broken and contacted the Wardens to come collect her. You said goodnight to the family and went home."

I stifle a gasp. His voice might urge me to believe him, but that's not what happened. The metallic hat on the Healer's head brightens and whirs, the color swirling. It *is* some sort of suspended liquid.

The Other doesn't move from his place in front of the Healer except for the brief seconds it takes to check his monitor. He waits a minute—maybe two—then asks the Healer to recount the evening again. While he does, the Other leans back and watches the screen. The Healer's voice, dreamy and detached, repeats everything exactly as the Other stated.

The new version of our evening, apparently.

Elij reaches out and picks up a syringe off the table. It's full of a silver liquid similar to the stuff sloshing around in the contraption on the Healer's head. He inserts it into the prone man's arm and the Healer's eyes close within a minute. He begins to snore, so at least he's not dead.

The Other moves on to Mr. Morgan, the table and apparatus trailing behind him. He repeats the same process, adding a few details about all the things that *didn't* happen at dinner. How Mrs. Morgan fell out of her chair right in the middle of eating her duck, flopped onto the floor for no reason.

How she never said anything at all.

Only then does it truly hit me: He's going to erase my memory. Give me a new one that doesn't include any funny business. How this is possible, or how it makes me feel, I have no idea. But that's what he's doing.

Part of me wonders if he could erase my entire existence up to this point. All of my lives. Even if he could, would I want to have never discovered that note, never traveled, never realized I'm different? I'd be robotic, unfeeling, and closed up—but not alone.

It's not like I'm free now anyway. I'm controlled by an invisible being called Ko and his ominous warnings. Is that really so much better?

Elij stands up from Mr. Morgan and turns in my direction. My eyes snap shut and I will my heart to slow down. Knowing the game doesn't make it any less frightening.

He's going to erase my memory, dig around inside my brain, and give me back a clean slate with no hint of what happened to Mrs. Morgan. A lump jams into my throat, hard as a rock and pulsing against my skin.

163

Someone should remember Mrs. Morgan. She can't just *disappear.*

Not knowing what's on the screen sends panic sizzling across my nerve endings. Elij watches it with keen interest. A transmission from the silver hat seems likely. It could show every tiny detail in my head. I have a hunch he's never seen a mind like mine before.

If they can get in there to wipe our memories and give us new ones, there's no limit to what they can control.

The Other sits next to me and positions the hat above my head. It's not touching me at all but wafting nearby. My scalp crawls as though a colony of insects march across it, snarling their little bug feet in the roots of my hair. I feel Elij lean down, can picture his face inches from mine. His breath smells oddly aromatic. A bit too sweet, like the burnt custard I threw out earlier tonight.

It takes all of my self-control not to open my eyes before he orders me to.

"Open your eyes, girl."

I answer the command. My face squinches up like when you accidentally look right at the sun. I wait for the peace to come, for my face to relax, for the pain to go away.

Nothing happens.

The stabbing ache that accompanies his face doesn't get worse, but a steady pulse remains right behind my eyes, drilling holes into my brain. Along with the ache, another presence enters my head and gusts through like a gentle breeze. The Other's gaze works its way toward confusion and all of a sudden I realize it's not working.

The pain isn't bleeding out of me like it did the men. Any minute the Other is going to turn around, check his little screen, and see my thoughts revolve around agony and not the events of tonight.

Block it out, Althea. Don't think about it. Think about nothing, the soothing voice in my mind whispers.

Waves of misery crash over me. It's impossible to think. The cot heats up under my hands, burning them, and I spend a few moments focusing on that. It helps, to think about something besides the pain.

Once that's under control, I struggle to reconstruct what happened in the Morgans' kitchen tonight. Truth and fiction blur, upset by the repeated and varied versions I've heard told tonight in this room. It's not easy to visualize with agony gnawing at my brain. Another fear, hidden until now, bursts through.

My thoughts Broke Mrs. Morgan.

That's silly. It's a coincidence. Don't think about it. Especially not right now.

The Other's eyes are so limitless that it's easy to get lost. Looking into them is like swimming in a cool, welcoming pond. The kind you can drown in if you aren't careful.

I try imagining a big rag, and use it to smear my mind blank. I have no idea if it works. Keeping my eyes trained on Elij's is the hardest thing I've ever done. At the edge of my pain-blurred vision, his lips move.

"Think about this evening, about everything that transpired after your mother called you to dinner."

I replace the blank space I cleared with a picture of what Mr. Morgan said happened at dinner.

"Good." The presence in my brain deals a gentle poke.

He gives the screen a glance, then returns his probing gaze to mine. "Now, imagine a blank space. Just blackness, like staring at the sky when there aren't any stars."

I fight off the urge to roll off the table and sprint, willing the pictures in my head to change to black and stay consistent. I use the rag again, leaving what I hope is blackness behind. The breezy presence caresses my mind again. Gentle. Lulling.

He frowns a little at the screen and my stomach flips as though it's trying to make a mad dash for the exit without me. Elij's brow knits, his confused eyes flitting to the screen before they meet mine again. My stomach gives up, falls off the cot, and splatters across the floor.

"That's fine."

He launches into the same account he gave Mr. Morgan and I let the words draw pictures in my mind. When I don't fight, the breezy evidence of his intrusion in my mind merely grazes my brain. If I get it wrong, it awards me with a rough jab. The pain sends tiny pulses trembling through me. I can't stop. It's like sitting outside in January, the wind nipping at my skin. Shiver. Tremble. Misery.

I repeat the story at his request. I wait for his verdict, my lips forcing air past them and into my lungs as he squints at his screen. The cot sags with my sweat. He didn't seem so concerned with what he saw on the men's screens. Paranoia?

Maybe. Maybe not.

Currents zap back and forth inside my head under the filmy hat. It stings but doesn't register higher than an annoyance after staring at Elij. Adrenaline pumps through me, brought on by terror, pain, and guilt, but doesn't distract my focus from that perfect image of what he wants me to believe happened tonight.

He studies my still face for what feels like forever. The wind burrows deeper inside my brain, prods harder. I keep my eyes vacant and my expression pleasant, hoping for the best as the pain inches toward agonizing. A breath before I scream, the second Other enters my field of vision and peers down over Elij's shoulder.

Double the pain. Double the trouble. He squints, too, and at a different time their mirrored expressions might strike me as comical.

"What are you staring at her like that for?"

The refresher jumps and whirls. "Why'd you sneak up on me like that? You know hearing is the one thing we can't enhance in these bodies."

I want to hug the skinny Other. He broke Elij's gaze and blessed freedom floods my head. I don't feel different; I still remember what really happened. What I did.

"Sorry. Speaking of these bodies, Deshi's on his way."

Alarms sound in my head, nerves stretching to their breaking point at the news that these Others know Deshi.

Nervousness passes over my refresher's face, too. "When?"

"Five minutes. Less, maybe. So why are you staring at her? Aren't you done yet?"

"Are you?" Elij is still sore about being startled, I can tell.

Despite the very obvious reasons for not wanting to be here right now, the emotional range of my captors fascinates me. They have feelings besides pleasure. I've witnessed anger, irritation, contrition, pain, confusion. . .almost enough to cause a sensory overload. A thought sneaks in, unbidden and unwelcome.

Deshi's coming here. He's like them.

If we're the same, that means I could be like them, too.

No. They wouldn't leave me in the hands of a human family. Being Other doesn't explain the traveling. Doubt snags my confidence with its slimy fingers and refuses to let go. I know nothing about how Others are raised, what they're capable of.

Nothing at all.

I suppress a shudder at the thought of the terrible acts the Wardens commit. Taking the Broken kids from the Outing. The way they tossed Greg around like trash. What they're doing to Mrs. Morgan. She might have creeped me out sometimes, but she's a nice lady. They're going to Break her, I know it. No more cranberry pancakes, frilly dresses, or starched white aprons. My thoughts are so soaked in terror at the prospect, it startles me when the Other who attended Mrs. Morgan answers, a hint of expectation creeping into his voice.

"I wrote the report and filed it in the system."

"Under the list of Broken?"

"Of course. Where else would I put it? Anyway, I thought you'd want to help with the disposal."

Elij grins, a sadistic shadow falling over his expression. "Yes, thanks. I've been waiting for a disposal for months."

He sounds elated, as though it's going to be fun to get rid of Mrs. Morgan. Relief mingles with guilt that his excitement distracts him from me. He stops and turns, looking back at me one more time. Nothing's inside my mind now, though.

"Seriously, why are you *looking* at her like that? Do you fancy this one? She is pretty."

Vomit shoots up and lands on my tongue. Swallowing will draw attention so it sits in the back of my throat, acidic and vile. They both watch me now.

Finally my refresher shakes his head and smiles. "It's nothing. Her mind map didn't look quite right. Like it was all just a little too perfect."

His friend claps him on the shoulder. "Just means you're good at your job. Everyone's always talking about what a great refresher Elij is going be when he's ready. And here you are, making too-perfect memories in a pretty human head."

He pauses, his gaze drifting from my face to peruse the rest of my body. My insides squirm for my outsides that want to. I feel naked and exposed.

"Too bad, the restriction against intimate contact with the humans. Some of them are so desirable. This one smells good, too." He leans over me and inhales, his eyes rolling back in his head.

I'm going to die if they don't leave.

He stands up and I release stale breath out my nose. Elij picks up a syringe of silver fluid and runs his fingertips along my arm, to my shoulder, and back down, then wraps his hand around my elbow. "I know what you mean about this one. She smells like summertime. It *is* nice. Still, she's not worth the punishment."

"Hurry up. Deshi will be here any minute and you know he'll steal the disposal if—" He breaks off and drops out of view.

Thrashing and moaning rip at my ears, the sounds of suffering twisting my heart. I swallow the puke in my throat in time for more to take its place. The noises stop and Deshi steps into view, gazing down at the Other with cold eyes. The sight of him, looking for all the world as though he belongs here, murders a piece of me.

This can't be my future. I can't be like him.

"You were saying, Paj?"

"Nothing," the skinny Other rasps from the floor. He doesn't stand.

Deshi reaches down to help him up and Elij takes advantage of the moment, plunging the needle into my vein. Deshi recognizes me, surprise contorting his odd face. He may act as if he belongs here, but he couldn't look more unlike the golden, perfectly molded boys shrinking away from him.

He glares at Elij. "What's *she* doing here?"

"Incident at her home. The mother shed her veil. We refreshed this one, her father, and the Healer who attended."

My vision blurs as whatever he injected into my arm slips into my bloodstream. My legs and arms grow heavy. Lifting them would be impossible.

Deshi steps next my cot and freezes me with his hard blue stare. "Any trouble?"

"No, sir. Refreshed. Clean mind maps. The girl's memories are the clearest I've ever created."

This doesn't please Deshi; his eyebrows knit together as he leans closer until his cheek presses against mine. My eyes slip closed and a strange buzzing noise soaks the air. The last thing I hear before I fall asleep is Deshi's voice.

It's gentle, serene. "I'm watching you."

15.

The taste of bile lingers in my mouth, my head throbs, and claustrophobia presses down on every inch of my body. My arms and legs still feel weighted, as though they've sunk into the mattress. A fleeting image of lying in the snow, how it presses in and mutes the sounds of the world, crosses my mind. That ugly orange comforter clashes with the serenity of the image. Memories crash in and tumble around me, piling up until I throw off the covers. My bare legs and arms quiver in the cold, but the cloying sense of entrapment refuses to leave. I stop wheezing as reality sinks in.

At least, what I think is reality.

I won't know for sure until I go down for breakfast.

This morning my feet don't drag, I don't linger in the shower, and I don't stop to reread the note folded inside my necklace. I throw on jeans and a sweater, brush my teeth, and hurry down to the kitchen.

The smell of strawberries and sausage wafts through the air. I summon all my courage and dart a glance at the stove. No Mrs. Morgan.

Mr. Morgan looks up from his paper and coffee. "Thea, darling, you're up rather early. Sit down and have some breakfast. They delivered something new today."

A tower of waffles topped with strawberries covers my plate. Caution paints my every move as I slide into my chair, irrational fear curling knots into my shoulders. The sense that if I make a sudden movement the entire scene will dissolve into reality. The one where Mr. Morgan remembers what happened last night and panics over the loss of his Partner, over the Others' ability to control his mind.

He seems unharmed. He peers at me over his paper again and an automatic smile slips onto my lips. Mr. Morgan returns it. Except. . .it's shaking slightly. Like the chemistry Monitor's. As though he's not sure why he's smiling, or if he wants to smile at all.

"Dad, are you okay?"

"Fine, dear. It's just, well, waffles aren't the same as cranberry pancakes."

My heart withers as he goes back to his paper and I finish eating breakfast. He's right about the waffles. The dirty dishes in the sink even strike me as sad, a visible reminder Mrs. Morgan won't be washing them. I wonder if someone will be sent to take care of it. I rinse them off and leave them there.

Breathing through the smothering secrets and grief in the house is like sucking air through a wet towel. I wouldn't normally leave for another half hour, but even braving the cold is actually more appealing than spending one more silent minute across the table from Mr. Morgan.

The dreary, barren street soaks into my bones. Fall steals away more warmth and sunlight with each passing day. Before long I stand in front of the boundary fence at the edge of the park, staring out into the Wilds. Early morning birdsong serenades me and the clean, cold scent of frost clears my head.

I've spent all my life not questioning the happiness of people, certain that something was wrong with *me* for feeling differently—for feeling at all. This morning I let myself feel everything without trying to squelch it. The crunch of individual brown blades of grass under my tennis shoes. The way the rough bark covering knots in the tree trunks scrapes across my fingertips. I gaze at an unbelievably blue sky, not worrying, not caring. Just being.

I no longer know anything about my world. Not for sure. I believed the Others when they said the boundaries exist to keep us alive, that everything they do is in the interest of our safety. Now I suspect the fences aren't to keep the animals out. They're to keep us in.

My eyes are open wide, and closing them again is impossible. What's out there, what they're keeping from us, remains hidden behind a heavy curtain, but last night laid bare a glaring truth.

The Others control *everything*. Even people's minds.

Burning rage tears into my blood, pushing it closer and closer to the surface of my skin as my palms heat up. It replaces any lingering fear in an instant, and if a Warden happened upon me I'd kick him in his pain-inflicting, lying face. An overwhelming desire to yank down the boundary with my bare hands slams into me and I make fists to keep from ripping at the electrified metal. Wild desire aches, boils through me with no outlet in sight.

I want out.

I want to hide inside that world out there, a pristine place not possessed by the Others. My foot connects with my backpack in a swift kick and it tumbles into the boundary. I close my eyes and wait for the crackle of electricity, the scent of burning material. But nothing happens.

My eyes fly open to spy my bag pressed up against the fence, perfectly whole and unharmed. I reach out a tentative hand, glancing around and behind me to check for Wardens. There are cameras on the boundary at measured intervals, but the nearest one is barely visible from here. Adrenaline speeds up my heart as I twine my fingers through the fence, half expecting to disappear into ashes, but I remain as untouched as my bag.

There may not be a way to prove the Others control minds, or that they killed Mrs. Morgan. But I could prove they're lying about the animals.

Once the idea pops into my head it won't let go, determination to prove them wrong on this one thing overshadowing everything else. Even if it's the last thing I do.

I find a foothold, take a deep breath, and brace my weight against the boundary.

Climbing is harder than I think it will be. Every time I loosen a toe or let go to grab another link my body sways back and forth on the wobbly metal. It takes longer than it should to scale the twenty feet, since I stop and press against it each time this happens, and am soaked with sweat and exhausted before I'm halfway finished.

The top of the fence lands under my grasp and I haul myself over it. A huge gust of wind pushes me against the outside of the wire. I hear a sizzle, see an explosion of sparks.

I'm frying.

No, I'm not. I open my eyes and check my body. Not fried. The breeze must have blown some debris into the barrier farther down. My brow creases at the realization that the fence is working in some places; it makes me hustle the rest of the way down. By the time I land on the soft earth my legs wobble and my breath comes in short gasps, but none of that can stop the silly grin stretching my lips.

The Monitors tell stories in Primer Cell about a time before the fences. How small children wandered away from their parents and were eaten in a single gulp by a bear, or a lion, or most often a wolf. But no beady yellow eyes peer at me from the forest. No animals rush me, or eat me, or even show themselves during my first tentative steps into the brush.

Branches sway above my head and birds continue their morning chirps, unconcerned by my alien presence in their world. Hot anger at the sheer multitude of lies recedes to make way for a wonder so complete it leaves no space for fear or rage in my heart.

A small gray animal with a bushy tail scurries up a trunk, chattering in an odd voice. I search my brain for its name, try to recall that particular science lesson. A squirrel, I think.

A rodent. According to the Others, one of the worst conduits for disease.

I remember Fils, Lucas's fish, and try to feel better.

The trees tower above me, their bare limbs forming a patchwork roof that lets the sun through in glinting patterns. I walk a little farther, far enough to miss detection by a patrol, before flopping down on my stomach. I press my face into the chilly, hard ground and breathe in deep. It should smell the same as the grass in the park, but it doesn't. Instead it smells crisp, and fresh, and promising—like freedom, whatever that really means.

I roll over onto my back and stare at the brilliant cerulean sky through the white puffs of air floating from my lips. The filtered sun dusts my cheeks, not warm but bright and comforting. Squirrels and birds dance with one another as they flit and leap between branches, greeting the new day with chatter and songs. The squirrels can hop from one tree to another as if they're flying. Some birds are huge and black, their voices coarse and raw as their songs emerge from sharp beaks. Others are tiny and yellow with impossibly fragile legs. Dazzling red and blue birds swoop in crisscross patterns, each distinct and beautiful.

The sight of a medium-sized bird with a bright orange head, a black-and-white checkerboard back, and a white breast catches the breath in my chest. My eyes follow as it flutters among its companions, finally settles on the side of a tree, and begins to peck. A hollow, rapid-fire thumping fills the forest. I don't know what kind of bird it is, and none of the others resemble it even a little bit. The freckle-backed bird goes about its business, finding another tree to pound a hole in, then yet another.

Wind meanders across me, freezing my sweaty clothes to my skin. The forest is somehow full of both blessed silence and myriad sounds; the mixture bleeds peace into an empty space inside me I'm not aware of until this instant.

Fear hovers around the corners of my consciousness, and I sense that what the Others teach is not totally false, that some form of danger likely lurks out here. A breeze sighs through the woods and whispers to the animals, as though they keep secrets from those of us without the ability to understand. They are fortunate to grasp truth without it being explained to them. Even though I can't decipher a word, this glimpse into a real world, a wild world where no being is told what to feel, who to love, or how to act, is enough. For today, just to know such a place exists spills warmth through me in grateful ripples.

The hole inside me fills the tiniest bit at the simple act of being, of *feeling* without fear. Not one animal stops and takes note, grows confused and horrified at the unhappy, redheaded girl on the forest floor.

A squirrel grabs an acorn in its tiny mouth and scurries down the tree trunk nearest me. I follow his progress, turning my neck until my left cheek presses against the ground. When he lands on the ground, his black nose and twitchy gray tail are less than two feet from my own nose.

The perfect blackness of his eye engulfs me. At first I see only my own reflection in the shiny surface, but once I look harder, dig underneath, a new understanding emerges. I see the world the way he does, from the tops of the trees, tiny feet curled around tremulous branches. I feel what it's like to leap and have the wind catch under my tail, carrying me to safety on its back. His eyes hold a special kind of knowledge, of instinct that I somehow know is part of me, too. A swish of wind sends leaves scattering his direction and he starts, dropping the acorn as he spins and disappears.

I sit up and brush the leaves and dirt from my hair, reaching out to pick up his abandoned acorn, smooth on the bottom with a rough cap. Despite my residual trepidation about disease, the idea that I could prove the Others lie about the food, also, is too intriguing to resist. I experiment after swiping the acorn clean, sliding it between my back teeth and biting down. Nothing happens. Squirrel teeth must be sharper than mine.

Determined now, I drop the acorn and stand, slamming the heel of my tennis shoe down on it. No results other than embedding it in the muddy earth. It takes a minute, but I find a good-sized, flat rock and place the acorn carefully in the center. I smash it with my foot again, this time receiving a satisfying crunch in return for my efforts. I pick apart the ruined shell and cradle what's left—a soft, orange nut—in my palm.

The animals aren't all dangerous. What about the food? The Others insist that only the food they deliver to our homes is safe for consumption. That bright red berries that grow on bushes and nuts that fall from the trees are deadly. They won't just make us sick or give us a bellyache—they'll kill us.

I lift my palm to my nose and sniff. It doesn't smell like anything really, just earthy and slightly sweet. I nibble off a tiny corner and crush it between my teeth. A bitter, sour taste coats my tongue and I spit on the ground a couple of times. I almost toss the acorn, but instead stow it away in my pocket. After several seconds, the flavor fades from my mouth and I'm not dead or even queasy.

Still, the squirrels can keep the acorns for themselves.

The Others are obviously not what they seem. The damage they could inflict is endless. Their lies—their destruction—could even spread out here, where things are pure and true.

Dread fills my veins, followed at once by white-hot rage at the thought.

If I don't leave now I'll be late for Cell, but I give myself another minute. As I lay in this bright, natural, *alive* place, I'm not even sure the Others exist at all—their world is so flat, like a drawing in a textbook.

As I scurry back over the fence with slightly more grace, I know I was wrong.

The Others aren't controlling *everything*.

They're not in control of me.

16.

The peaceful feeling of belonging bleeds out of me with each step toward Cell. The hole in my middle doesn't totally empty, and I squeeze tight around the seed of knowledge that I've been to a place where I'm not abnormal. I can prove the Others are lying to us. For the first time, my separateness from my peers makes me feel right instead of wrong.

By the time the building comes into sight, that tiny ray of light is barely visible through my thick, black dread as I remember who else will be at Cell— Deshi. In a few minutes I'll have to face him and pretend I don't know he spends his spare time torturing Others and threatening people. The words he whispered last night lingered, infiltrating my dreams and chasing the comforting shadows away. Deshi is watching me. I don't know why, or what he hopes to find out, but I can guess.

The Others are looking for something, hoping to find it by interviewing the Terminal classes in at least four cities. I'm pretty sure Deshi suspects it might be me.

I'm worried he's right.

Nothing feels different about Cell until the students start to stare at me. My whole life, even in the instances when my self-control slips, they never stare. Maybe they can tell I left the boundary. I feel so different that maybe there's a visible mark revealing my intrusion on nature.

Leah plants herself in my path. Despite her nasty attitude of late, kinship blooms with the knowledge we've both survived a refreshing with the Others. Even though, according to Elij, they left her damaged in some way, which makes her unpredictable. Which makes her dangerous.

Her hands rest on her slim hips. "Hey, you. Morgan. What's your first name?"

The question is purposefully rude, since she's heard my name called during attendance for weeks, I'm too surprised by the fact that she's speaking directly to me to be annoyed. "Uh, Althea."

"That's a funny name." Brittany walks over, her corn-silk blond hair swinging down her back in a long braid.

"Sorry." I shrug. "I didn't pick it."

My lungs constrict as Deshi moves toward us, stopping in front of me and slinging a heavy arm around Leah's shoulders. *Well, that's interesting.*

"Rumor is a Healer went to your house last night. And a couple of Wardens." Brittany toys with the frayed end of her braid, smiling up at me from under thick lashes.

There were no Wardens at our house. How many memories had the Others changed? Deshi's gaze burns holes through the side of my face, and pressure to answer the right way stifles my fading confidence.

I slide a hand into my pocket and grasp the acorn remains. "Um, yeah. That's true."

"So, what happened?" Leah's eyes shine with bright curiosity, her angelic face opposed by a cruel expression. She's delighting in this event, in the gossip.

"My mom. . .she Broke. They took her away."

Their eyes widen in concert. The stares colliding with mine are baffled, wondering. Not a sympathetic one among them. The acorn slips through my sweaty fingers. Panic rises inside me like a tide; the way they're gathered around unnerves me, traps me inside their unfeeling circle. The memory of Deshi's cheek pressed against mine, of his low, menacing voice, curls roots of dread into my abdomen. A drop of sweat puddles in the corner of my eye, burning. The ray of light from this morning's rebellion disappears and deposits me alone and cold in my reality.

Then a hand slips into mine, freezing cold and strong. Pine burns my nostrils. I cling to his sturdy presence to smother the breakdown. He looks down at me and the compassion in his eyes nearly undoes my tenuous control. I know then that whether or not I've given him permission to be my friend, Lucas *is* my friend.

The rest of the kids disperse, leaving Lucas and I alone, still holding hands. The respite allows me to dig my fingernails into my self-control. I'm not letting go. I won't give Deshi any reason to take me, Break me. Lucas's familiar scent offers comfort; nothing he could say would be more powerful right now.

I tug my hand loose and offer a small smile. Our eyes meet and that tingling, sweet sensation skims through my bloodstream. "Thanks."

His voice is soft, like a warm hand against my cheek. "Anytime."

The entire rest of the day is a blur. The girls go back to ignoring me at lunch and both Lucas and Deshi stay at a boys' table where they belong. The short twenty minutes I spent in the woods leaves me wishing for a way to re-create the feeling it gave me. Questions from last night, wondering at what it all means, distract me from hearing my lessons. Empowerment, borne of the surety that it's not me that's all wrong, but this

Other-controlled world that isn't right, resurfaces and pumps the desire to find out why I'm different through my blood like fire.

My mind takes apart the puzzle of what the Others are searching for among the Terminal classes. I need to first find out where they're holding the interviews in order to design a way to "accidentally" overhear one. It's not even totally about my survival anymore— though that's part of it; my interview is in three weeks, now—but the need to understand why these creatures with such obvious power can't simply take whatever it is they need.

I walk into chemistry and sit, vaguely noticing I beat Lucas to the back row. The lights dim once, twice, a third time.

Lucas doesn't come.

A sensation like ice water dumped on my head immobilizes me. This is more than cause for simple concern. He might as well torch the Cell, or jump off the building. Missing block accomplishes the same notoriety.

Except the emergency alarms don't sound. The Others test them once a month to make sure they work, but no whining peals assault my ears. The Monitor passes Lucas's name without comment, not even noting his attendance sheet. The kids don't turn around to look at his empty seat or gape at this unprecedented event.

Almost as though he had never been here in the first place.

A memory from my second year floats in from nowhere, of the first time I snapped at Cell. A girl whose name I don't even remember now jumped on some swings I'd been waiting for. Without thinking, I grabbed her foot—she had on these ridiculous shiny black dress shoes—and yanked her down. Her arm snapped with a loud crack when she hit the ground. It scared me for two reasons, the first being that I'd hurt her. The second was even as a kid I knew what *trust no one* meant. It meant I had a secret.

The rest of the kids on the playground stopped and stared at me. Their faces were confused but not angry, not scared. After about ten seconds of silence, someone went to the girl and helped her up. They took her inside, and I followed. We used the emergency device to contact a Healer and the girl's mother. The little girl said she fell off the swing.

She came back to Cell the next day and no one ever said a word to me.

This feels the same. As though whatever protects me from detection guards Lucas, too. Which can only mean one thing.

Wonder drowns out the Monitor. The more the events of the past few weeks run through my mind, the more certain I am that Lucas is like me. I've been waiting for definitive proof, afraid to admit it might be true, but unless he's Broken or somehow damaged like Leah, Lucas has to be a Dissident. He's not always happy, the appearance of the Wardens frightens him. Deshi's intense interest in not only me, but both of us.

A new worry quickens my breath; if he is like me, he could have traveled. We have no control over when we come and go, and as far as I know we've never been in the same city at the same time. Maybe I'll never find him again.

He could be anywhere. I have no idea where to look, but I have to try. He's come to my rescue so many times. I mean, just this morning he saved me from losing control in front of Deshi. If he's in trouble, he's earned a return favor.

Instead of listening to the Monitor, my mind races over the possibilities. Lucas had been at lunch, looking uncomfortable next to Deshi. I hadn't seen him in the halls this afternoon, but sometimes don't. Plus, it would be pretty hard to get out of the building during Cell hours with the cameras at the entrances and exits, not to mention the Warden's patrolling.

I hold my breath when one sticks his head in the door and checks the room. His eyes linger on Lucas's empty seat before he leaves.

If Lucas is still in Danbury, there's a good chance he's inside the Cell. I stare at the portrait of Water on the wall, searching his unblinking black and blue gaze for answers. I doubt he'd give them to me even if he could.

A lightbulb blinks on in my brain, causing me to sit up straight and knock my notebook onto the floor. My cheeks heat up as everyone, including the Monitor, stops while I retrieve it.

Now that I have an idea where Lucas might be, the remaining minutes drip past like honey from a spoon. When she finally dismisses us I'm out of my chair before anyone else picks up their things. Deshi intercepts me as I approach the stairs at the end of the hall.

He flashes his usual arrogant smile. "Hey, have you seen Lucas?"

"What? Nope, sure haven't."

He blocks my path. I need to get away from him before Lucas slips outside with everyone else.

"Let me walk you home, then, since your boyfriend seems to have vanished."

Warning bells clang as my mind races to find a reason to tell him no. Frustration builds, worry for Lucas boiling over, but I have no choice but to fall into step beside Deshi. The way he says the word *vanished* tugs the dread tighter around my insides. We pass through an icy blast of wind at the front door and it blows an idea into my panic-addled brain. "You know what, go ahead. I forgot my favorite pen in chemistry."

My voice doesn't waver, doesn't give away either the lie or my emotional state. I don't wait for his answer, just retrace my steps through the empty halls. My ears strain to pick up any sound that indicates students are still in the building or that Wardens lurk nearby. Nothing strikes me as out of the ordinary *except* the quiet. My sneakers make little noise on my way back to the stairwell. I head down the same flight of stairs I took the night of the Gathering.

The night I met Lucas.

My shoe squeaks a little on the hard stairs and I walk faster. My heart races, climbing into my throat. I worry the correct door won't be easy to find but it is. It looks as old, dusty, and unused as before.

I turn the knob and push it open, stepping inside with my hands in front of my face to ward off the cobwebs. There aren't any today. I swore I'd never come within ten feet of Fils again, but after this morning in the Wilds I'm more confused than anything. And worried.

The room is dim, the only light coming through the small, ground-level window sitting at the top of the wall opposite the entrance.

"Lucas?" I call his name softly.

Relief steadies my nerves when he responds from the back of the room. Where he keeps his fish. "Go away, Althea. I don't want to see you."

The tremor in his response moves my feet toward his voice anyway. The sight of his face stops me dead in my tracks. Lucas sits on a chair, shoulders sagging and appearance disheveled. His eyes are red and swollen. The realization that water attacks him, too, punches breath out through my belly.

It isn't until I consciously look around that the rest of the scene registers. Fils lies on the radiator. His bowl remains on the table above it, thick chunks of ice bobbing in the water.

He's dead. Not only can a fish not live without water, but his little body rests in an unfortunate spot. That the Others pump hot air into this abandoned room doesn't make sense. The heat, though, has left the tiny golden body dry and crispy.

"Oh." I don't know what else to say, and my heart aches as though it's trying to stretch from me to Lucas, to work for both of us.

"What are you doing down here? Aren't you supposed to be wandering around *alone*?"

His bitter, angry tone hurts my feelings and defensiveness appears without warning. "I was looking for you. What are you thinking, missing block? The Wardens noticed."

"I really don't care right now, Althea."

I approach him and rest a compassionate hand on his shoulder. He shakes it off. I don't understand how or why but he cared about that fish, and I know what it's like to lose things you care about. Longing washes through me at the memory of how it felt to have the Hammonds, then to lose them. How hard it was to leave the forest just this morning.

I want to love something and get to keep it.

"What happened to him? Did he jump out?"

"No, he didn't *jump out*. Why would he do that? Even if he did he couldn't get onto the radiator. Someone did this to him." His voice is dead, cold.

I know he's not angry with me, seeing as how I had nothing to do with the demise of his fish. He's mad and I'm the one here, so I forgive him for talking to me like I'm a moron. This time. "Who would kill your fish?"

195

Lucas shakes his head without looking at me. It had to be a Warden. Any human who found the fish would never have touched it. The sudden feeling of being watched prickles between my shoulder blades. If a Warden knows about the fish, then they've been in this room. It's not the sanctuary Lucas thinks.

"Who do you think—" The words die on my lips when Lucas stands up and kicks the chair, sending it clattering into a pile of junk stacked against the wall.

He steps toward me, stopping inches from my face. "I don't know who it was, but if I find out, they'll be sorry. They'll be so sorry, Althea, do you hear me?"

Lucas's eyes fill with water again, but he doesn't notice. I stare over his shoulder, trying to give him some privacy and swallow my own emotions. The water in the fishbowl is frozen solid because Lucas lost control of his temper. Like with me and fire.

I hadn't thought much of the ice chunks floating in the fishbowl when I first noticed them. The dead, drying fish and Lucas's swollen face had commanded my attention, but the ice is that elusive piece of proof after all. Water wells up in my own eyes and dribbles down my cheeks. I smile a real smile and don't try to hide it.

The sight of the water, along with the look of wonder on my face, sends Lucas spinning around to follow my gaze. Guilt deepens the stress lines on his face when he registers what I've seen. He stumbles backward, away from me.

"I. . .I guess maybe they killed him by freezing his water or something. . ."

He stops. It sounds ridiculous and we both know it. I reach for his hands but he shrinks away, his eyes wild and pleading. My mind lands on a possible way to show him, to convince him he doesn't have to be afraid of me. I think of the melted cup at the Gathering.

My scorched bedspread.

My handprint in the paint on the wall in the Morgans' hallway.

This whole room is chilly, now that I think about it. My own heightened feelings keep me warm, but the single windowpane is frosted over. Those recent examples aren't the only times I've melted objects with my hands. For the first time I wonder if I can do it on purpose. I've spent so many years wishing the strange accidents would stop, I've never even thought to try.

Walking to the bowl of frozen water, I wrap my fingers around it, ignoring the slippery chill it transfers to my skin. I concentrate, doubtful of succeeding. Emotions stir deep inside me—fear, loneliness, despair, guilt—and combine with the overwhelming joy soaring through me now and pulse into heat. I close my eyes, feel it surge through my palms.

My eyelids snap open in response to a gasp from Lucas. The water sloshes around in the bowl shuddering between my hands.

I can't believe I did it.

Lucas's eyes are wide, amazed. A huge grin shows off his dimple before he takes two giant steps and grabs me in a bone-crushing hug. His cold breath on my neck sends delightful shivers down my spine, and my smile bursts out so wide my cheeks nearly crack. Nothing but ecstasy filters through my body, pumping like blood. Whatever I am, I'm not alone.

"I wanted it to be true. I wondered if you might be like me, but I couldn't figure out how to know without asking. I even thought about letting the name Ko slip to gauge your reaction."

As the last words leave his lips a loud popping sound sobers us both.

The sound is deep enough to shake me to my bones. "What the. . ."

Lucas's gaze is on me, but not on my face. Instead he stares at my neck with eyes so wide they look like they might roll out of their sockets. "Althea. Your necklace."

My hand goes to the lump under my sweater, preparing to wrap around the golden metal. I pull it out, but drop it when the necklace vibrates against my bare skin. The pop sounds again. It's coming from the locket hanging below my throat. A beam of light pulses forth and we squint in the suddenly bright room as it gathers into a shape. A person stands before us. Not fully formed, shimmering instead of solid, but a person nonetheless.

It's an Other, I think. At any rate he looks more Other than human, but he's shorter than most I've seen. His features are sharp and his ears a bit larger than normal and slightly pointed on top. He's too indistinct to check for the star-shaped mark.

Lucas shifts closer to me until our bodies press against each other. The figure speaks, backing us up a few steps.

"You activated this spell by speaking my name out loud. I am Ko. You do not know me, have never seen my face, but I know you. I have watched over you from the moment of your birth." Thick emotion shines in his face, bright and warm. No one has ever looked at me that way.

"Though my features appear Other, I am not. Not entirely, and not where it matters most—in here." He stops and presses a long-fingered hand to his chest. *"I*

am a Dissident like you, Something Else entirely, and I've tried to give you the opportunity to do for your people what I could not do for mine. I cannot give you specifics in case this message is compromised, but know two things. I suspect you have found more like you, which means the time has come to fight the Others. If you do nothing, or are captured, all humanity will perish. There are those who can tell you what you need to know about your past. Be vigilant, be brave, and you will find them."

The glowing body disappears and plunges the room back into dim silence. My feet root to the floor and I sway, a little off balance. A second message from Ko has been inside my necklace this whole time. Curious, I speak his name again. Nothing happens.

"What was that?" Awe reverberates in Lucas's voice.

"I have no idea; it's never happened before." I want to talk forever, but we should leave Cell grounds. Someone knows about this room, about the fish. The Wardens infest every hallway. Where Deshi lurks is anyone's guess. "Want to get out of here?"

Lucas glances toward Fils's small, tortured body. I take his hand. "I'm sorry about Fils. It isn't fair. Bring him; we'll bury him in the park."

Lucas walks over and pries his fish off the radiator, stowing the body in a pocket. His eyes dart to mine and then away again, his cheeks splotchy and red. "Thanks. He's been my only friend for so long. I'm going to miss him, that's all."

"Well, now you have me."

His response warms my blood even more than my own internal fire.

"Now I have you."

17.

Now that it's for sure Lucas is a Dissident, too, all I want to do is sit and talk with him. Unfortunately this new, Warden-supervised world limits our ability to do that. We buried Fils in silence, bidding good-bye to Lucas's friend. He was reluctant to leave the tiny grave, and although I know it's important to him, curfew is now a short ten-minutes away. Impatience tries to quicken my steps, but I force them to slow. I haven't had a chance to tell Lucas everything about the night Mrs. Morgan Broke, about how Deshi appeared and basically threatened me.

Or how the Others can burrow inside our minds.

Lucas pushes his face into the brisk wind as it picks up, kicking leaves out of our path. It's almost like there's so much to discuss that neither of us knows where to start. But we're down to eight minutes now, and we've got to begin somewhere. Might as well go big.

"What do you think Ko meant about humanity perishing if we don't fight the Others?"

It's the most curious thing of all the curious things Ko said. I mean, the Others control the humans' minds, but they're not in danger. Right?

He shakes his head, scattering the scent of pine my direction. I resist the urge to reach out and touch him, imagine what it would feel like to run my hands through his blond curls, if the scent would intensify if I did. Now that I have permission to be myself around him, I want to let all the feelings he stirs inside me out into the open. When he glances my way I jerk my gaze free, my face surely pink.

Lucas shrugs, smiling a little. "I don't know. I've never really even felt like a part of the human race. Have you?"

The question stirs old fears, and I revisit the terrifying possibility that I—now we, along with Deshi—are Other. Because no matter what Ko said in his trick message about being a Dissident, he looks Other to me.

"No. But Ko says we're Dissident, like him, so maybe we're not part of humanity at all." Our street pops up too soon, and my watch says we've got two minutes before the front doors are to be latched behind us. "Lucas, we've got to figure out a better way to do this. We need to talk before our Warden interview."

This is week four. Three more until it's our turn.

"Actually, I've been thinking about how we might be able to discuss our. . .predicament."

My stomach jumps at the prospect. "Well?"

"I don't know if it will work." Lucas glances up and down the street, making sure no eavesdroppers lurk nearby. The little girl who lives three houses down skips toward her house, but no one else is around. "What time does Mr. Morgan go to bed?"

"Ten-thirty."

"Okay. Go out on your back porch after the Wardens' eleven o'clock patrol."

We've paused in front of Lucas's house—or the Crawfords' house, as I now think of it. It's no more his than the Morgans' is mine. We have one minute left. "Why?"

"You'll see." Lucas wraps his arms around my waist in a brief, tight hug, then runs up the walk and disappears.

An ache settles inside my chest as a fierce gust of wind whips my ponytail across my face. Eleven o'clock is a lifetime away.

Inside the Morgans', life has settled into a new routine. Mr. Morgan doesn't act unhappy, but he doesn't act the same as before either. For all the resentment of my travels, my multiple families, and the fact that none of them seem to notice my absence,

204

I miss Mrs. Morgan. The house is deflated, somehow less bright, as though she breathed life and light into it with her presence.

This evening Mr. Morgan waits for me in the living room. Completing my homework fills the time until he calls me for dinner. The kitchen table used to feel small. Now, with just him, me, and plates filled with sandwiches and raw vegetables, the kitchen engulfs us. Dinner, like all our meals, is silent without Mrs. Morgan's patter.

Even though Mr. Morgan asks about my day, tells me about his, and smiles contentedly, he doesn't seem happy. I don't usually watch television with him except on Saturdays, when family movie time is required, but tonight his bruised smile urges me to join my makeshift father on the couch.

The only programs on television are the news twice a day, and a movie at night. There are seven movies, one for each day of the week. They're all silly and lack an actual point. Sometimes they're about Partners laughing, enjoying an Outing, or they're simply funny, about people falling down or running into walls. The Others play the part of benevolent benefactors, delivering meals and graciously patching up the clumsy humans. Mr. Morgan laughs at the pictures. I don't find them particularly funny, but make sure to chuckle at the appropriate moments.

As I watch, my brain wrestles with other matters. How to broach the subject of being Other to Lucas if we are able to talk later. How to survive the interviews without being discovered.

Why Ko thinks humanity is in danger, or that Lucas and I can somehow save them if they really are.

Nine-thirty rolls around, finally. Mr. Morgan turns on the news and I escape to the welcome solitude of the bedroom. At ten the television clicks off and he walks to the bottom of the stairs, yelling up at me "Good night, Thea."

"'Night, Dad."

He shuffles into the bedroom that's now just his and closes the door with a soft *click*. I change into thick sweatpants and a sweatshirt, then flick off my bedroom light. The window seat offers a clear view of the street and I curl up among the pillows to wait. A Warden passes at ten thirty, the streetlight reflecting off his polished black shoes. He gives each house a cursory glance; all the lights are extinguished.

Lucas needs to know about the night Mrs. Morgan lost her mind. The revelation that the Others have brainwashed everyone but us strikes me as equal parts insane and obvious, now that I know. I've thought about that night in such detail so many times, but the idea will be new to Lucas.

My story organizes itself in my mind, orders the details of that night. The worst night of my life. The way Elij changed Mr. Morgan's and the Healer's memories. The breezy presence in my head as he looked into my eyes. The way Deshi seemed to cause the young Other pain by looking at him. It seems to indicate they're able to enter one another's minds as well.

My theory leaves me with two horrible questions. First, what happened to Mrs. Morgan at dinner? If the Others brainwash humans to keep them happy and content, why did it stop working on her? Second, I'm not mind controlled and neither is Lucas, but why? The obvious answer is that's what makes us Dissidents. It's why we experience bad feelings, and really good ones too. It doesn't explain the fact that I can melt stuff with a finger, but one thing at a time.

It's strange. I've grown up knowing I'm different but never truly considered I might be Other.

A different Warden passes under the lamppost. Eleven o'clock.

When he turns the corner I grab a blanket off my bed and sneak down the stairs. I hold my breath at the tiny sound the door makes when it clicks open, and step out onto the back porch. At first I see nothing, and disappointment clogs my heart.

A paper cup with a thin string trailing out the bottom catches my eye, mostly because trash is rarely lying around. There's a slip of paper trapped by the rocks filling the bottom of the cup.

You're going to think this is so nuts, unless it works. I think I used to play with one of these when I was little. Dump out the rocks, pull the string tight, and put the open end to your ear.

It's not addressed to me or signed. Lucas wouldn't be dumb enough to leave our names out for anyone to stumble across. It does sound crazy, but we've got nothing to lose, so instead of wasting time questioning him I dump out the rocks and follow his instructions. I jump as the cup vibrates in my hand and Lucas's voice comes through.

"Can you hear me, Althea?"

I take the cup from my ear and press it around my lips. "Yes."

"Wow, it works. I thought I dreamed it."

"Do you have weird dreams sometimes that feel more like memories?"

208

"Yes. I think they are memories of my real family. They call me *fils,* and it makes me happy. I named the fish because of that."

The cup is still in my hand for several seconds. Now that we're talking, a shy nervousness grips me. We only have about twenty minutes until the next patrol.

"Tell me where you spend your seasons," he asks.

It's an easy question, one with a simple answer. "In the winter I stay with the Clarks in Iowa. And the spring, Portland with the Hammonds."

"What about your summers?" He asks the question casually, but there's a reason, I know there is.

I have a theory on this, and am happy to have the chance to test it. "It's never summer."

"What do you mean it's never summer?"

"I think you know very well what I mean. I bet in your world it's never winter."

"You're right. Spring here. Summer in Georgia. Used to spend my autumns in Portland." Stunned intrigue fights with awe in his voice.

Understanding dawns like a new day, inevitable and bright. "That's why you're always cold and I'm always hot. I mean, it doesn't explain anything, but it sort of makes sense." Another question, buoyed by Ko's necklace message, niggles at me. "So what do you think brought us together here, now? What changed?"

Silence stretches between us. Something *has* changed. I felt it even before the Wardens appeared at our Outing, announced they were observing us, and began to ferry Terminal students away. It's as though someone, somewhere has kept us apart for sixteen years. The whole situation is so carefully orchestrated, the way we go to the same places but never meet. The giant hand behind the mystery of our lives, invisible until now, seems as plain as the nose on my face.

Whose hand, or what's hand, remains to be seen.

The cup startles me when it jumps with Lucas's response. "Something. The only way we're going to find out what is by hearing what they're asking in those interviews."

I nod, then remember he can't see me. "Yes. We have to know what they're looking for before we try to fool them into thinking we're not it." The cup lays flat against my ear for a while, and when I'm sure Lucas isn't going to respond, I hold it around my lips, doubt pressing against my heart. "Lucas, how are we going to fight the Others? It's ludicrous. We have nothing to fight them with."

"There must be a way, Althea. We're different. We just have to figure out what it is."

18.

Early the next week, we get the chance to spend the hour after Cell alone. In a disturbing and strange development, Deshi and Leah have begun courting. I didn't want to believe it when he put his arm around her at Cell, but Leah told us at lunch that their Parental Sanction is this evening. They'll be tied up until after dinner. Perfect.

Lucas brought me his note from Ko, which I asked to see because it's not in a necklace at all. It's written on some paper tucked in a funny plastic case, and I shove it into my backpack for later examination. The afternoon is windy and cold; strands of my hair keep sticking on my lips. Sitting outside is uncomfortable now as the weather turns colder, more bitter, every day. Autumn is on its way out, winter biting its heels like a rabid dog.

We're allowed to be in the park, but the cameras on the boundary and in the occasional tree still make me nervous. Lucas picked a good spot, hidden both from the fence and eyeball-harboring trees, but the Wardens are out there. We sit close together on our spread-out jackets and mutter in low voices.

"We have to figure out what makes us different and how to use it to fight them." Lucas waits for my reply, propped against the trunk of an elm tree.

Anger simmers at the mention of the Others, the need to expose them for what they are lighting a dormant fire. I scoot closer and pick up his hand. "It's not like the ways we're unusual are threatening. I mean, we aren't always happy, we question the authority and goodness of the Others, and no one seems truly comfortable around us."

We are also both shadows. But not to each other.

"And we smell weird, let's not forget that. Oh, and we can heat up or cool down a room like nobody's business." Lucas grins, turning my stomach inside out.

Silence stretches for several seconds while my thoughts rearrange into coherence. Taking deep breaths steadies me a bit. I make a mental note to avoid looking at his smile if I intend to utter intelligible language afterward.

The tweeting and rustling of the birds outside the boundary permeate the afternoon. The pleasant strains soak in through my ears and spread through me leaving longing in their wake. As I watch, one of the pretty blue ones flies too close to the boundary. There's a loud zap and vibrant feathers waft to the ground.

"Also, they can't control our minds," I whisper.

His head jerks up, confused eyes searching my face. "What are you talking about?"

"Lucas, I have to tell you something about the night Mrs. Morgan disappeared."

He sits up straight. "Yeah, I wanted to ask you about that. How weird was it having Wardens in the house, watching you? I don't know how you did it."

"Things were crazy. Between all of the kids disappearing, your lies about the Administrator's office, and Deshi's asking me to the mixer, my nerves were wound pretty tight."

"Deshi asked you to the mixer?" Lucas's features pinch together, and his voice sounds strange, tight.

"Yes, but that's not the point. A few days later I got home in a bad mood and Mrs. Morgan brought up the Wardens taking a baby next door. All those emotions and anger festering inside me—when they mentioned the neighbor's baby Breaking with such flippant attitudes, I lost it."

"What do you mean, you lost it? Like sweated them out?"

At first, his joking tone irritates me. How can he think of teasing at a time like this? Then again, his ability to lighten my often too-serious demeanor is one of the things I like most about him.

I *like* him.

213

The thought stalls my story for a minute, causing Lucas to think he's annoyed me with the interruption.

"Sorry. Go ahead."

"It's okay. It did get pretty hot in there. I boiled some water. And burnt the custard. Anyway, lost it as in I stood up at the table and yelled at them. About not caring about the baby, mostly, but also why they don't care when I leave. I shut up pretty fast—I realized my behavior was not Acceptable—but I couldn't switch my mind off. Mr. Morgan didn't think anything about it, just sat there chomping on his duck. Mrs. Morgan, though. . .when I looked at her eyes I could tell she saw me. Like *saw* me."

"You mean she didn't just accept that you belong there?"

"Exactly. She was scared about it, too. She shook all over, pointed at me and asked Mr. Morgan who I was and where I'd come from. She backed up and grabbed the doorknob like she was going to run away."

"What did you do?"

"I tried calming her down, so did Mr. Morgan. Nothing worked. When I went up to her, she shrank away, scared to death of me. She asked me what I am. I had to do something. I couldn't let her run all over town talking about me not being her daughter, not being like everyone else. So I pushed her and she banged her head on the door and passed out."

"You *what*?"

I shrug to hide how appalling my own actions seem to me and finish the story, including the appearance of Deshi and the talk about shedding veils.

Lucas falls silent and lies flat on his back. After a minute he pats the blanket by his side, and I stop staring and copy his pose. It's odd, relaxing like this. It's not natural for me. After a few minutes his hand finds mine again. We stay still, the breeze sifting through the bare branches and the distant sounds of the animals mingling together in muted harmony.

I wait because I want his thoughts untainted by my own suspicions. He's silent for so long I turn my head to see if he's fallen asleep. I have no idea how that would be possible given the excitement zapping between us. Maybe it's only affecting me.

He's not sleeping, but looks thoughtful. "It must be terrible to be like them. They're trapped in their own heads and they don't even know the Others have control."

To hear him say it aloud breaks down my last barriers of denial. "Yes. After what I saw that night, how they changed everyone's memories. . .something happened in our kitchen and their control stopped working on her."

"She *shed her veil*."

The words the Others used morph into a usable phrase. "They do something to the humans so they're always happy. So they don't care when their children Break or that they watch the same movies every single week."

Huh. When did I start referring to the humans as separate from us?

I whisper my worst fears through chattering teeth. "It doesn't work on us, Lucas. What if we're Other?"

Confusion sets in as Lucas laughs from his belly. The deep, warm sound wiggles its way inside me and forces a smile onto my face.

"Let's not go crazy, Althea. One thing at a time. If we are Other, I guess we'll find out in due time. There might be some perks."

"Like telling the Monitors not to give us homework."

"Going traveling when we feel like it."

"Reading each other's minds."

We laugh together now, rolling around on the blanket like a couple of children. It feels so good. Our laughter dissolves into hiccups and we lie still, gasping for breath.

"If we were Other, why would Ko bother to say we're Dissidents? We've trusted him and those notes our whole lives. I don't think we should stop now."

Sobered, I consider the facts. Ko says we're not Other where it counts, inside. He says we're Something Else. Not Other. Not human. Dissident. Reassurance pats my back like a parent's hand. "Okay. We trust Ko. But we have to do something besides just sit around waiting for the interviews with the Others, or for one of us to travel away."

There is no rhyme or reason to our travels—when it happens or where we go. I might go to winter next, but I might not. It might happen this afternoon, or at the last possible second of autumn. Often I repeat the same season over and over. Most often I spend the entire season in one place and go in order—skipping summer, of course—but not always.

That train of thought is useless. Worrying won't change anything, but I issue a quick, silent request that we stay together. Lucas and I can discuss it when our moods aren't so carefree.

He inches closer to me, his face suddenly serious. "We're going to figure out exactly what it is we can do. And we're going to do it together." Lucas's eyes flutter to my mouth and linger. His voice drops to a rough whisper. "Can you read my mind right now?"

I can't find enough air to answer, but the desire lighting his eyes tightens a similar want in my belly. The realization that he wants to kiss me pushes a wave of heat and nerves through my body. Only Partners are allowed to kiss, and kissing in public is not Acceptable.

But I don't want to stop him.

I swallow a couple of times and lick my lips, feel sweat bead up between our palms. My eyes close, as though they knew what to do all along. A sound like water roars in my ears and my heart throbs.

At the last moment an unwelcome voice pierces the air, bringing the moment to a crashing halt. "Whoa. Um. Sorry, guys. Leah and I had to reschedule the Sanction and decided to take a walk. We didn't. . ."

My eyes fly open and I spy Deshi and Leah standing a few feet away. It takes my brain a minute to catch up and for once Lucas has trouble getting back under control, too. In fact, I recover first. "It's okay. We're just getting ready to head back."

To the strange couple's credit, they don't call me out for lying. It's obvious we weren't talking or leaving, and depending on how long they lurked in the trees, they could know far more than makes me comfortable.

Lucas manages not to glare, fixing his smile as he stands and stretches his long legs. Deshi strides past and the air moves around me. My muscles tense as my eyes catch Lucas's wide-eyed gaze.

Deshi smells different.

Still earthy and wet—but spoiled. As though the dirt has gone bad or grown a fungus. The Hammonds, my spring family, are avid gardeners. We till the soil and plant vegetables and flowers. Sometimes the plants die from diseases. The most common one that kills the tomatoes is blight.

That's what Deshi smells like.

Instead of the rain-on-a-freshly-planted-garden smell, he smells like death.

I try to shake it off as the four of us walk toward the park entrance. We pause before we head in opposite directions, and Deshi gives a theatrical shiver. "Getting pretty cold, don't you think?"

The way he looks my direction when he asks the question sinks my stomach into my tennis shoes; it makes me feel like he can see through my skin and into my secrets. His threat from the other night doesn't boost my confidence.

Lucas scoots closer to me and answers, even though it's clear Deshi meant the question for me. "A little, but we don't mind. It's nice."

Deshi never looks in Lucas's direction, his penetrating gaze holding me hostage. "Nice for him. He doesn't mind the cold."

"I don't mind the cold either. It's bracing."

A belligerent tone taints my voice; more like a petulant child than a girl who almost got kissed a moment ago. Deshi holds up his hands and drops the subject. The way he looks at us, back and forth, says he let it go for now, but not for good.

19.

"I have an idea, but I don't think you're going to like it." Lucas glances sideways at me, refusing to break pace. It's almost time to be back in the houses.

"Well, try me. We have things to discuss, and a twenty-minute chat through paper cups isn't getting it done."

"Okay, well the only thing we know we can control is the cold and the heat. I think we should practice. We could use it, maybe."

"What are you, totally banana balls?" The thought strikes me as dangerous above everything else. "I could hurt you. And we could attract too much attention."

"The Wardens are going to interview us soon—do you really think they're going to miss the way we smell? Or what if they look inside your head and you don't fool them this time? We either try to find a way to fight them or we might as well give up now."

Sadness over the loss of Mrs. Morgan mingles with lingering anxiety over Greg's death. The memory of the barely restrained glee on the Others' faces at the prospect of disposing of a human trembles in my mind. They've taken a dozen of our Cellmates this autumn and they'll do the same to Lucas and me if they catch us.

The surging determination to not only live myself, but to keep Lucas alive too, surprises me with its ferocity.

We reach the Morgans' front door and stand awkwardly on the porch. It gives me flashbacks to the night of the mixer, when we were both desperate to believe the other could be a Dissident too. What Lucas says makes sense—being captured and Broken certainly isn't on my to-do list either, and the prospect of rebelling against what is Acceptable brings a thrill akin to the one offered by being outside the boundary.

"Fine. But we figure out a way to do it safely. I'd hate to set you on fire."

Lucas offers a self-satisfied grin, then pulls me into a hug. His arms are cold around me at first, but the heat from my body balances us out. Instead of pulling away quickly, like usual, he holds me until I relax against him, resting my head against his chest. When he lets go, a sense of loss shifts over me like a heavy blanket. I want to know what it's like to kiss him, to feel something other than our hands touch. The play of hot against cold, heat and chill passing between us. To know him even better.

Years of using distance as protection ensure I don't have a clue how to know anyone.

He turns to go, but I remember my idea and it pops out of my mouth. "Oh. Speaking of crazy ideas, what if we could somehow figure out what the Wardens are asking in the interviews? That way we could prepare for our own and it might tell us exactly what brought them here to begin with."

"How? No one remembers what happens during them." The previous hopeful tone in Lucas's voice turns dubious, but I don't see how his idea of igniting and freezing things is any more helpful.

"I don't know. If we could figure out where they're holding the interviews, we could eavesdrop, maybe? It's just an idea."

Lucas nods, a thoughtful look on his pale face. "We'll think about it, okay? It's a good idea, and if we could prepare that could make all the difference. I might have a way to find out where they're conducting the interrogations, at least."

He jogs home and I enter the house right on time, wondering what he meant. Mr. Morgan greets me with a quivery smile and tells me dinner will arrive within the hour. Pork chops and macaroni.

"I'll be back down for dinner. Going to do homework."

Mr. Morgan nods as I race up the stairs, change into gray lounge pants, thick socks, and a hooded sweatshirt, then sprawl out on my bed. My backpack bounces on the mattress alongside me, but it isn't the homework inside I'm after.

I dig around for Lucas's note holder.

Drawing out the small plastic square, I stare at it for a few seconds, blowing away red strands that escape from my ponytail and settle at the corners of my lips.

It's not like anything I've never seen. The front has a picture of four men and the word *Byrds*, misspelled. It takes a minute to figure out how to pry it open, but when I do I find a flat, silver circle on one side. Tiny lines run around its circumference in never ending loops, any information it might hold indiscernible. Lucas's note is inscribed on the booklet on the opposite side of the case. Ko's words are identical to mine, except for his name.

The booklet is held in by little plastic nubs but comes loose without a problem. Flipping it over, my fingers trace the faces of the men on the front. Odd groupings of words—not whole sentences but pieces of thoughts and emotions—run down the interior pages. I skim them all, then go back and read again, slower. By the time Mr. Morgan calls me to dinner, a funny trance has befallen me.

224

Back in my room with no recollection of eating, conversation, or coming back upstairs, I climb into the soft bed and read the words again. Many of the paragraphs are about love—real love—not just required Partnering. Some Partners do love each other, like I think the Morgans did, but humans rarely Partner because of love. More often the Others pair us up. What our Cellmates believe about Lucas and me, that we are going to Partner voluntarily, is uncommon.

Two sections in the booklet stick out to me, focusing on different subjects. The way the words meld into one another gives them meaning they could never have on their own. One in particular pricks my mind, settles in deep and refuses to leave.

To everything there is a season

And a time to every purpose, under Heaven

More words follow. *A time to be born, a time to die. A time to gain, a time to lose. A time to laugh, a time to weep.* But those first six repeat over and over throughout the page, as though they're the most important. *To everything there is a season.* Those words pester me, nag me, as though they have their own secrets to tell. Plenty of the words in the booklet are new to me, their definitions unknowable.

Heaven. Weep. Dance. Mourn. War.

Strange, but somehow they sound familiar when said aloud.

To everything there is a season. What is it about that line?

The overall tone haunts me, but not because I feel like I'm missing something. It's the push and pull of it.

A time to gain, a time to lose.

I gained so much these past few days. The thought of losing it is too much to bear. Lucas and I have only scratched the surface of what might be possible. Many things seem feasible now that I'm not alone.

A time to be born, a time to die. Like Mrs. Morgan. Like the baby next door, though no one knows for sure what happens to the Broken. I've never allowed myself to think about it, but after my close encounter with the Others I'm more confused than ever. They said they filed Mrs. Morgan under the list of Broken, not that she *had* Broken. Could it be that not everyone who Breaks is disposed of?

To everything there is a season.

The little thought that's been zipping outside my reach flies into my grasp. The implications speed my heart into a gallop, but without Lucas to bounce them off of, it's not easy to tell if I'm imagining the perfect way the words mirror my life, *our* lives.

*

To my surprise, I sleep sound and long, opening my eyes mere moments before Mr. Morgan hollers up the stairs for me to get a move on. The past days reinvigorated the pent-up energy I've carried around all these years. At last it has somewhere to go. My life has been spent blending in, going unnoticed, figuring out how to act normal. Now, I might be able to not only make sense of my existence, but take control of it.

At any rate, once roused, I make it out of the house in record time, waiting for Lucas on the sidewalk for a full five minutes before he ambles out.

"Morning." My grin won't stop, and I hop from foot to foot until he arrives at my side.

Lucas stops in front of me, his eyes softening as he tucks a thick piece of hair behind my ear. His fingers brush down my cheek, leaving an odd, icy-hot feeling in their wake. Then he grins. "So what are you dying to tell me?"

"I read those words inside the shiny little book, you know? Most of them were pretty, but some stuck out at me. The ones about the seasons and how they turn. The line 'to everything there is a season.' It made me think about us." My ideas bubble out as we walk to Cell. They could be way off base, but it doesn't feel like it. I've gone over it in my head a hundred times since last night and it feels true.

"You mean, because we both skip a season?"

I nod, wishing he wouldn't interrupt. "Yes. But there are two of us, and four seasons. And the note, the one from Ko, says there are more—not *another*, not *one* more. See what I'm saying?"

Understanding dawns in his eyes, excited and wondrous. "You think there are two more like us. One who misses the autumn, and one who misses the spring?" His expression amends to thoughtful. "You know, you might be on to something there."

"And the scents clinging to us, they remind people of the seasons we skip, too, right? You said yourself jasmine reminds you of summer in Georgia. The Others said the same thing the night they tried to brainwash me. That I smell like summer. Maybe you've never spent winter in Iowa but you sure smell like the groves of pine trees on the edges of the park there."

Lucas is silent for a minute, considering all the evidence carefully, which I'm coming to know reflects his thoughtful nature. We are inexplicably linked to those seasons we never experience; even our strange abilities mirror them. It makes weird sense that there are two more like us, whatever we are, out there traveling, too. One who never sees the leaves fall off the trees or feels the air turn chilly. Another who never watches flowers bloom, or endures days on end of warm rain.

The realization must hit Lucas at the same time it does me, for we both start talking, our eyes huge, matching discs. "Deshi—"

We stop. Lucas gestures for me to go.

"Deshi smells like spring. Or at least, he did when he first got here. He still does, just a rotten spring instead of a fresh one."

Lucas nods. "It makes sense, if it *is* time for us to meet, that all three of us would be thrown together. The fourth can't come here, because it's autumn."

An errant thought drags down my jubilant mood. Lucas's mention that our autumn counterpart can't come here brings back the knowledge of our ultimate separation. My heart aches at the thought of being alone again. If I go to winter, or Lucas to summer, we can't be together.

"This is crazy." My brain struggles to wrap around the reality of our lives. "Why do we travel? Why do we skip seasons we resemble? There has to be a reason."

"I'd love to be able to answer even one of those questions. Or, why aren't we pleasant, happy robots like everyone else?"

The suggestion makes me shudder. "As weird as my life is, I wouldn't trade being able to feel for anything. Would you?"

"No. Not now, anyway. A couple of weeks ago I might have considered it." The way his eyes linger on my face makes my cheeks heat up, and he chuckles. "Are you always going to turn into a furnace like that?"

"Hey, it's not like your cold hands don't make me jump!"

Lucas grabs my hand, disproving my jab when I don't jump at all but latch onto him for dear life. We stroll without speaking for several minutes until the Cell comes into view down the street. We reach the front doors, both sporting our usual smiles now, and go our separate ways. The day is uneventful, as things go. Leah spills her milk in my lap at lunch, but these episodes of hers have become common. Lucas catches me in the hall before our chemistry exam. His eyes glow as he shuts my locker for me and tugs my arm.

"There are still seven minutes before block. What's the hurry?"

"I want to show you something."

Curiosity heightens my senses as we enter the empty chemistry room and he leads me to the supply cabinets. The tops are littered with empty beakers sitting two to a tray, identical in size, along with a heating device and a thermometer.

"You want to show me beakers?"

Lucas rolls his eyes. "Just watch." He pushes the sleeves of his thin shirt up to his elbows and wraps his strong hands around the glass container. Within seconds it frosts over, emitting a series of small cracks and pops. He pulls his hands away, grinning like an idiot.

I reach out a finger and touch the glass, feeling my eyes widen. It's frozen solid. "You've been practicing."

"Yes. It took me a few tries to figure out how much power to use."

"Can you control it?"

He avoids my gaze. "I'm getting better. I accidentally froze all the clothes in my closet this morning."

I laugh, noticing now that he's wearing the same outfit as the day before. "Interesting. What are you going to do to the Others, imprison them in blocks of ice?"

"Maybe. At least I'm trying."

Lucas's response gets under my skin, but he's right. Trying to harness the heat still scares me, even though I managed to keep a tight rein on it when heating the water in Fils' bowl house. It's *fire*, though. If I lose control, or use too much, things could get ugly fast. "So what are you going to do about these frozen beakers now?"

Students will begin to trickle in any moment. He gives me a sly look that I interpret and shake my head. Now is not the time to give it a go. "No way, Lucas. People are going to be here any second. You shouldn't be fooling around with this at Cell."

He shrugs. "We have an exam today. They'll thaw before anyone notices."

Lucas and I move from the counter and take our seats as people file in. The giggling and other end-of-the-day nonsense dissipates as the lights dim and the Monitor begins block.

"Students, we've had a change of plans for today. The Wardens asked that we wait to give your first exam until everyone has completed their interview. Instead, we'll conduct an experiment. Partner with the person to your right; go pick up the trays assembled at the back."

My mouth goes dry. I shoot to my feet beside Lucas but by the time we get to the counter half the class is in front of us. Several pairs have selected trays, and the frozen beakers are gone. There's no way to find out who has them.

The Monitor projects the experiment on the screen and there's nothing to do but get started. We are to boil water over a burner, then dump it into one beaker. The other is to be filled with cold water. Afterward we'll place them in a cooler and observe which freezes first.

The hot one will. We all know it. It kind of defeats the purpose of an experiment when you complete it multiple times.

My hands shake, spilling some of the cold water onto Lucas's desk. He takes the pitcher from me in silence, nerves crackling between us like electricity. No one speaks up about having frozen beakers. Maybe they don't notice, or perhaps they think everyone else's are as well.

Lucas's hand brushes mine and turns it into ice. Not literally, thank the stars. I glare at him, lecturing with my eyes. This is what he gets for experimenting at Cell. If we're going to test the extent of our capabilities, we need to be careful. Smart.

The pot of water on the heating device reaches a boil and Lucas uses a towel to grab it by the handle and dump in into the second container. Steam begins to waft off the scalding water when a loud crack followed by the sound of water pouring onto the floor stops my heart. My body, already tense, springs forward in search of the source. A girl near the front gasps for breath, dark red blood spilling out of her clenched left hand. Her lab partner stares, open-mouthed and helpless.

The sight of the blood burns my stomach and black spots pop in front of my eyes. I stop dead in my tracks, waiting to see what will happen. The rest of our Cellmates continue their experiments, glancing up at the commotion every couple of seconds.

The injured girl makes strange whimpering noises but no water spills down her face. Her skin looks white as a sheet, colorless against her rich brown sweater and the crimson liquid puddles on her desk. She grabs her lab partner with her free hand, squeezing so hard I can see her skin redden from here. "It hurts, Emmy."

The Monitor's voice punches through my deadened hearing. "What's going on, girls? Reese, why are you bleeding?" She's calm and collected even though Reese's blood collects on the desk and floor. It's not like she's going to Break, though she does look ready to fall down.

Then again, the kids with the nosebleeds shouldn't have Broken, either.

Reese's eyes cloud over and she sways on her feet. Emmy reaches out an arm and answers for her partner. "The beaker broke, ma'am. I think it was frozen."

My heart stops and my body rocks in sympathy with Reese's. Lucas steps up beside me, close enough to touch. He sucks in a breath and holds it; my own lungs burn with unspent air.

The Monitor's eyebrows dart up in surprise. "Frozen? Why would your supplies be frozen? I'm going to have to report this. In the meantime, Emmy, take her to the Administrator's office and call a Healer."

Emmy nods, still supporting a wobbly Reese as they head out of the room. The Monitor clears her throat at the rest of us, still immobilized by the incident. "Get back to your experiments, class. Are anyone else's beakers frozen?" When she doesn't get a response she nods. "Very well. Carry on."

Lucas and I huddle over his desk, resuming our work as the Monitor puts us on mute and activates her personal communication device. She's definitely reporting what happened to the Others. What Lucas has done, in effect, is tell them there's an abnormality in this period, and with our interviews the week after next. It's one thing to sneak outside the boundary, to have secret paper cup conversations, even to try overhearing an interview, but it's another thing entirely to face the Others head-on.

A couple of Wardens enter the room five minutes later, laden with cleaning supplies and irritated dispositions. They make quick work of the blood and broken glass, then station themselves on either side of the exit. When the bell rings we put away our materials, gather our things, and get in the line waiting to leave.

The Wardens don't speak to anyone but we pass right in between them on our way out. I go first, then Lucas. They don't stop us. We separate to stop at our respective lockers. The dread burrowed inside me pulses and grows, encouraged by concern.

I don't know those girls, Emmy and Reese, at all. I've never spoken to them. Now Reese has been injured, and even though I didn't do it, part of me feels responsible. Lucas would never have frozen those beakers if we hadn't agreed to test ourselves.

I grab my coat and scarf out of my locker and slam it shut, jumping when Leah's rosy complexion appears where the door was. "Leah. You scared me."

"Sorry." Her eerie smiles sends shivers down the back of my neck. "Did you hear about Emmy and Reese?"

It's a strange question, considering we all have chemistry together and everyone saw what happened to Reese's hand. Silent warnings to tread carefully echo in my mind. "Yes, I did. Reese got cut."

Leah shakes her head, messy curls full of life. "No. After they went to the Administrator."

My fingers curl tight around my backpack. "What happened?"

Her smile stretches wider, pleased by her secret. "They had to talk to the Wardens because the Monitor reported their frozen beakers. . ." She draws out the story as though she wants me to beg, but when I refuse she continues with a quiet grunt. "They're Broken. The Wardens took them away."

20.

That could have been us.

I stomp out the front doors and pass Lucas without speaking, fighting shame at my selfishness. He jogs to catch up and keeps pace. When we're alone—as much as we ever are—I stop and face him. "I told you we shouldn't be fooling around at Cell."

The color drains from his face as he reads the mix of emotions in my eyes. "There's something besides the beakers. What's going on?"

A lump crawls into my throat, pasty like a wet piece of paper. I am angry with Lucas for being careless, but it's relief that makes me want to collapse. We weren't caught today, but the strange episode means our chemistry block could fall under even more scrutiny in the interviews. Words take a minute, first having to wiggle past the clump of thick emotions. "The Wardens took those girls away."

At least Lucas has the good sense to look guilty, too. He bends over and presses his hands into his knees, breathing deep. I want to sit in the grass and let water leak from my eyes until it dries up. Autumn has spiraled out of control, my emotions tugging me one way and then another hard enough to cause an allover ache. Lucas straightens and grabs my hands, squishing my fingers together. The pain of his grip clears my mind, exchanges guilt for self-preservation. Without a word we stumble home, our feet on some kind of autopilot. We go slow, eating up more than half of our hour in silence.

The Crawfords' house looms too soon, and I don't want Lucas to go inside. I have the ridiculous notion he can keep me safe just by walking at my side. We settle on the Morgans' front porch, my left hip pressed against his right.

"What are we going to do?" My voice shakes.

"We can't do anything for Emmy and Reese, or anyone else. Not until we can figure out how to help ourselves. And we have to do that before the interviews."

"I know."

I rest my cheek on his shoulder. There are so many things about us we can't erase or hide. We can't change what we are. We don't even *know* what we are.

Lucas remains silent for several minutes and transfers a nervous energy through his hand to mine. I raise my head, meet his eyes. A secret lurks in them, one that scares me.

"Althea, I have to tell you something."

"What is it?"

"Promise you aren't going to think I'm a bad person."

"Lucas, look at us. We're the same. I could never in a million years think you're a bad person."

He doesn't look convinced, the somber, serious expression on his face remaining in place. "It's about the day I told you I overheard in the Administrative Center that the Wardens are here looking for something."

"Oh, yeah! You never did tell me how you *really* heard that." Suspicion clouds my mind, wondering if his reasons for keeping his secret could be sinister.

"I don't know if I can explain it very well, but I'll try. That day, I tried getting information from the girls at lunch, but they didn't know a whole lot. More than I'd figured, but after that bizarre scene at the Family Outing and the realization that the Others were targeting our class, it wasn't enough." He runs a thumb over my knuckles and I forget to listen for a second. "I followed one of the Wardens. He went into the Administrator's office but I couldn't get in—you saw the cameras."

He falls silent, staring down at our linked fingers.

"Then what happened?"

"I walked away and stayed out of sight until the doors opened again." He pauses, free hand shaking as he runs it through his curls.

"So how did you know they were sent to find something if you didn't overhear the conversation?" He's taking an awful long time to tell this story, and impatience crisscrosses my words.

"It wasn't a Warden who walked out of the office. It was Leah."

"Leah? Black-haired, pissy Leah?"

Anticipation crackles along my nerves. His gaze darts to his watch and he pulls on one ear, a peculiar motion I haven't seen him make until now. It occurs to me that I've never seen him this nervous. The feeling infects me and I chew on my fingers as he finds the courage to go on.

"Yeah. She walked around the corner and I just. . .grabbed her." My mouth falls open, but he holds up a hand. "Let me get it all out. I wanted so badly to know why the Wardens were here. I thought maybe I could get her to tell me."

"You asked her? What did she say?"

His eyes glaze over, staring past me like he's seeing the whole thing over again. "Nothing, at first. She looked at me funny, then her eyes got wide and she said she was going to report me. Obviously, I couldn't

241

let her do that so I dragged her into an empty closet and shut the door."

I suck a breath in through clenched teeth. Not just because of what he's said but because it reminds me of that night in the kitchen, when Mrs. Morgan wanted to run out the door.

He pauses, meeting my eyes. "What?"

"Nothing. Go ahead."

"She looked more scared than angry. I didn't know how to convince her not to report me but my mind raced. I silently begged her to tell me what the Wardens said. I told her they aren't the good guys, that the interviews scare the living daylights out of me. It was like I'd flipped a switch. She got more and more scared and she looked crazy. I asked her to tell me what happened in the office, and she did."

"The bruises on her arms, you did that?" The shame on his face twists a knife in my heart. "What did she tell you?"

"Exactly what I told you in the park that day. That the Wardens are looking for something—she didn't hear what—and they think they'll find it by interviewing the Terms. After she spilled, her voice got soft, like a little girl's, and she asked me what was going to happen to us. She asked me what I was."

A gasp whistles through my lips. "That's almost the same thing Mrs. Morgan said."

"I was so scared. I had no idea what happened to her. And I couldn't let her go and start blabbing all over Cell about me. So I tried something. I pushed opposite thoughts at her. That she never talked to me, never even saw me. A film drew over her eyes, until she looked through me again. When I let her go, she turned and went back to block."

He stops, sitting back against the step. He pulls on his ear again, looking as though he's making a decision. Finally, he sighs. "There's more. The other day, after you suggested trying to find out about the interviews, I did it again."

"What?"

"I know, it's just that she's the only person I can think of who might know where they're conducting them, and I already screwed her up so what's the difference?" Misery deepens his voice, makes it scratchy. "She said they're conducting them in the Administrator's office, so there's no way we could listen in. And she either doesn't know or wouldn't tell me the questions."

The entire story sinks in, and the fact that my idea to somehow prepare for the interviews is a bust is the least interesting tidbit of information. Lucas's story mingles with what I learned the night Mrs. Morgan Broke, and pieces start to fall into place.

"You got around the Others' control. That night they took me outside the boundary, they talked about refreshing Leah. One Other said she'd shed her veil, but Elij said it looked like it had holes in it. You did that."

He looks up with caution, encouraged by the revelation in my voice. "After you told me what happened to Mrs. Morgan and what the Others said about her shedding her veil, it started to add up. You must have done the same thing to her."

Realization pummels my brain and water springs into my eyes. Lucas's fingers tighten around mine, his concern making everything harder.

"Lucas—" Emotions close off my throat, making it impossible to continue. After a minute I fight them off. "It's not the same. I didn't put Mrs. Morgan back together and now she's dead."

Panic, guilt, and shame wash through me with no way to escape. Instead, they bottle up until they ooze down my cheeks in fat, salty streams. Lucas scoots closer, but for the first time having him near offers little comfort.

"It's not your fault, Althea. We didn't know our thoughts could do that. When it happened, you didn't

244

even know about veils. Stop beating yourself up; I did it, too."

"Stop beating myself up? I Broke someone, Lucas! She might have acted like a robot, but she was a good person and she didn't deserve to die because I can't control myself. And don't even compare what I did to what you did. I was too stupid to realize I'd caused something I should have tried to fix. Leah's still alive, remember?"

"Althea, if you want to blame someone, blame the Others. They're the ones who put the veils up in the first place. And it's not like I did a bang-up job fixing Leah. You see how she's different. Aggressive. Angry. She's courting Deshi, to top it all off." Guilt laces his voice as it falters over the admission.

It's true Leah's different. Still, angry is better than Broken. The old, troublesome fear bends me forward over my legs for a minute. "We're not human, Lucas. We're Other. We must be."

When I look up, Lucas's beautiful, sorrow-filled eyes meet mine. He doesn't argue. How can he? We can mess with human minds like only they can. I've never known the Others to melt or freeze objects, and they don't smell odd, but humans certainly don't either. If Deshi is like us, maybe he has the answers to our questions.

"What about Deshi? He's so much like us, Lucas, but he spends time alone with the Others. I want to know what he knows. He could tell us everything about the interviews, or maybe convince the Others we don't have what they're looking for at all."

"Althea, slow down. One thing at a time. If we're Other, there's nothing we can do to change it. But Deshi. . .I agree it makes sense that he's another Dissident, and all the signs point toward that but I just don't trust him. Not the way I trusted you."

I shake my head, unwilling to totally give up on the idea. Lucas hugs me, right there in front of the Morgans' house. It's a good thing people think we're courting. His arms are strong and wrap tightly around me. The length of our bodies mold together until we feel like one person instead of two. I bury my face in his shoulder, lace my fingers together behind his back. Warmth, a mixture of our body temperatures, flows between us. In spite of everything my spirit lifts, if only a little.

I might be Other, but I'm not alone. Not anymore.

He murmurs against my hair, his cool breath chilling my sweat. "We'll figure out what to do about Deshi."

Lucas pulls away and starts toward the Crawfords'. A ragged fissure gapes inside me, tearing wider with each step he takes. The last thing in the world I want is to be alone. Mrs. Morgan, Sarah, Emmy, Reese, Greg…all gone. I can't help them, can't save them.

"Lucas?"

He turns, sadness glinting in his eyes. "Yeah?"

"Will you come over later?" It's not Acceptable, but after this afternoon, the thought of being alone until tomorrow morning makes my skin itch. If he's caught sneaking over, there's no telling what might happen. Then again, it's not the worst infraction we've committed in the past several weeks. It's not even the worst thing we've done today.

He doesn't hesitate, his dimpled smile delighting me from twenty feet away. "Sure."

The evening goes on forever, and when Mr. Morgan calls me into the living room right before the ten o'clock news I feel like it will never come to a close. He pats the couch beside him and I take a seat, shivering in soft brown pajama pants and matching camisole.

"What's up?" I ask him.

He smiles, the quivery one. "I heard from the Other Archivist today. She'll be in Danbury on Saturday morning to collect your mother's family heirlooms."

"Why? What's an Archivist?"

"The Others store family histories, compiling information and photographs. They sent some information over the Interweb Network about protocol for when someone. . .for these situations. Would you mind meeting her for me?"

"But why isn't she just coming here?" It doesn't make sense that they would ask me to meet them in the park instead of coming into town. All of Mrs. Morgan's things are here. The request plants a seed of suspicion in the back of my mind.

Mr. Morgan's eyebrows scrunch together for a moment, his quizzical smile tugging at my heart. "Would you mind meeting her for me?"

He repeats the exact same question, as though my response was wrong and he'll just keep asking until he gets the right one. I want to tell him no, but can't summon the word. First of all, he's my dad and he's not really asking. Second, his smile still doesn't reach his eyes. His shoulders slump and sadness rolls off him, and it's my fault. I'd give him anything he asked for, even though nothing can bring her back.

"Sure, Dad."

He kisses my cheek and tugs on my ponytail before sending me to bed. An hour later sudden paranoia attacks, so I pad back downstairs in sock-clad feet to recheck the back door, even though we never lock them. I smack into something hard and bounce back, stifling a shriek. Lucas's whispered voice calms me before terror takes root.

"It's me. Sheesh. I said leave the door unlocked, not tackle me when I walk in. What are you doing down here?"

"Coming to check the door."

We pass Mr. Morgan's room on our way up the stairs. I hold my breath the whole time, wishing we could actually be invisible. Despite my worry, we make it to my moonlit bedroom without any trouble and I lock it behind us. Mr. Morgan never comes into my room, but now's not the time to take chances.

Lucas smiles and looks me over. "Like your pajamas. Cute." He swipes my nose with a finger, then crosses to the window seat, climbing onto my pile of pillows.

I pull the covers back and climb into bed, sitting cross-legged and trying not to stare. Despite the cold, Lucas walked over in mesh shorts and a white T-shirt, the hard outline of his muscles showing through the thin fabric.

"Tell me your best dream." Lucas surprises me with an offhand, not-crucial-to-survival question. I know he means the ones filled with what I call shadow people, the dreams Lucas suggests are perhaps memories of

249

what our lives might have been like before Ko wrote the notes, before we traveled.

"It's weird."

"That's okay. I still want to hear it."

I take a deep breath and blow it out, bringing the images to the front of my mind. I've hidden them in the back, in a safe place, so I can still take them out and remember. "I can never see very well, and even my best one is more impressions than solid pictures. But it's warm, like the very end of spring or maybe what summer feels like. My arms and head float on top of water, hot from the sunshine. It's cool down deeper and there are people, a man and a woman, laughing and splashing nearby. I'm kicking in the water and they pass me between them, helping me get from one to the other and kissing my cheeks when I reach one of them." Warmth spills through me at the memory, as it always does, of that strange and foreign sensation of love shining around me like it never has in real life. To hide how much the dream means, I shrug. "I've never been in any water, obviously. But that's it."

A glance at Lucas's soft, enraptured expression says my shrug didn't fool him one bit. In an effort to throw the attention off me, since I feel all exposed and naked, I ask him to return the favor.

He settles back into the cushion, running a pale hand through his curls. "Well, it's snowing. I keep sinking into these huge snowdrifts all the way up to my chin, and a man pulls me out by my hands, rubbing his cold nose against mine before tossing me into another fluffy pile. Not in a mean way or anything, and I'm laughing. We both are. Then he shows me how to roll the snow into a ball, and push it and push it until it's a bigger ball and then a bigger one. We build a man made out of three huge snowballs, and give him a face made of buttons and acorns and sticks that fall from the trees. A woman comes outside with mugs of hot cocoa, making an exaggerated fuss about giving up her scarf to the snowball man, but it's red and it looks perfect around his white neck." A shy smile sneaks my direction. "That's it."

"That sounds like *almost* a good enough reason to be out in the snow."

Lucas laughs, my weak joke easing the tension borne of letting each other see into our private places. If the dreams are impressions of our memories, I cling to the possibility that the man and woman are my real parents. That at one time I did have a family, and they loved me.

But where are they now? What happened to them?

After a few moments of silence, I tell him about my unexpected outing Saturday morning, voicing my concern that it could be some kind of test or trap—like the pink drink when the Wardens first arrived. His face reflects my worry, confirming that the whole thing is suspicious at best, and Lucas suggests going along just in case.

The offer heats my cheeks. "What if we go out there to meet this Archivist and never come back?"

"We'd be together." Our eyes meet across the room, fuse as though we're connected. After another moment of silence, Lucas stands up too quickly. "I should go."

He steps toward the door, pauses at the edge of the bed, and runs a hand over the top of my head. I clutch it against my cheek, my belly full of licking fire that's so much more pleasant than the flames associated with my strange power. It spreads out until I give voice to its wants. "Will you stay until I fall asleep? I just don't want to be alone."

A quick intake of breath from Lucas hitches my heart, and for a moment I'm worried. Then I remember this is Lucas. The boy who loved his fish, who defended me after I pushed him away ten times, and whose touch makes me believe everything might really be okay now that we're facing it together. I scoot backward, peeling back the bright comforter in invitation.

Lucas's smile tightens a little, and a glinting brightness full of the same tumbling emotions doing acrobatics inside me shines in his eyes. He closes them, then takes a deep breath and slides out of his shoes. When he opens his eyes, the teasing, comfortable Lucas is back. He slides in, snuggling me against his side. As always, it takes a few minutes before our core temperatures balance out. Once they do, the bed is cozy and warm.

I think about Leah, and a sudden memory clenches my stomach. "Lucas, you can't mess with Leah anymore. That night at the refreshing, Elij said the Prime told them to leave Leah wrong in case they could figure out who did that to her veil."

"I'm not going to hurt her anymore," Lucas whispers.

"Even if we can unveil the humans, what good is it? If they can't be normal afterward, it's useless."

Lucas's disagreement is evident in his silence, and when he speaks his voice holds a hesitant tremor. "What if we could do more than one at once? Like the whole Cell, or the whole town? We might be able to get them to help us."

"No." My cheek rubs against the soft, threadbare material of his shirt. "First of all, I don't think we can. Mr. Morgan was sitting in the same room when my thoughts undid Mrs. Morgan and it didn't affect him at all. Plus, it wouldn't do any good. Everyone would go crazy all at once and run around not knowing what the heck is going on, then the Wardens would come and take them all away. We'd be responsible for Breaking a whole town. We've already got at least three lives on our heads this autumn, Lucas. That's more than enough for me."

"So you aren't even going to try and figure out how we could help? Even after what Ko said about it being the end of humanity?"

"I'm not giving up, Lucas. If it comes down to me and you against the Others, I'll do whatever it takes. Playing with the humans or their minds, though. . .if we can't really fix them, bring them back to an even keel, then we should leave them the way they are."

"You think they're better off walking around like they're happy, like everything's fine?"

My irritation spikes. He's always so sure he's right. "Yes. Unless we can keep them sane, I won't do it. What do you want to do, run experiments on them? Excuse me for being a wet blanket, but that makes you no better than the Others."

His only response is to trail his fingers up and down my arm. His touch relaxes my every muscle, making me sleepy.

"I know we're probably not human, Lucas, but I have to believe we're different from the Others, too. Ko said we can save the humans. I don't want to hurt them."

I think of the Hammonds, Val, Monica, the girls here in Danbury—even Leah. Mr. Morgan. A fierce protectiveness drops over me.

Lucas startles me with a soft response. "Okay, Althea. We'll keep working on the hot and cold, think about talking to Deshi, and keep our eyes open. Where are you meeting the Archivist Saturday?"

"In the park, where the Wardens met us by the boundary."

"I'll meet you there. Mr. Crawford wants to show me some work thing after breakfast."

The scent of him—crisp, fresh, and wintery—infuses the room. He kisses the top of my head and tucks an arm around me as he settles deeper into the blankets. "Close your eyes. I'll stay for a while longer."

Even though confusion and worry dig their fingers into my edges, my center relaxes next to this boy who knows all of my secrets but still chooses to be at my side.

21.

Saturday dawns cold and wet, the gray skies spitting rain that splatters the sidewalk with polka dots. I have breakfast with Mr. Morgan and he shows me the small box of family items the Archivist requested. Inside are a few pieces of paper that look like legal documents, some photographs of Mrs. Morgan and her parents, and identification. Nothing that looks important enough for the Others to care about.

Bracing myself for the onslaught of miserable weather, I pull on rubber boots and tug the brown-and-orange striped umbrella from the back of the closet. The wind drives bullets of water underneath my protective gear on the walk to the park.

Lucas runs up, meeting me as I pass the playground equipment. His face is flushed a healthy pink. The colder the weather, the faster autumn marches toward winter, the more robust Lucas appears. More handsome, too, if that's possible.

He kisses my cheek and crushes me in a hug, then grabs the soggy box from my arms. "I'm sorry we disagreed."

I nod, pleasure pushing back the discomfort caused by the miserable day. "Let's go. Mr. Morgan said the Archivist will be out by the boundary, where the Wardens met us."

We plod through the trees, bare and spindly without their leaves, which lie in a squishy carpet under our feet. Two figures wait outside the fence, but I look past them into the forest as an ache opens up in my core. Desire to be out there again, free from the complications born of my awkward existence in this world, burns from my toes to the top of my head.

My attention snaps back to the moment when Lucas takes my hand and squeezes lightly.

Seeing the Warden surprises me; he's one of the ten who have been constant observers of life in Danbury these past weeks. The second figure is shorter by a wide margin, and female. She stares at us, a rather pleased—albeit trembling—smile stretching her generous lips. Honey blond hair tops her tiny frame and flatters her delicate features.

She speaks at the exact same moment I realize I've been staring at her without even a flicker of pain. "Good morning, children."

I blink, sure her eyes changed from black to midnight blue and back again in the space of those three words.

"You are Althea Morgan, correct?" I nod. The Warden steps forward, making me wince as he enters my field of vision. He stares hard at Lucas. "I was not advised you were being accompanied."

"Oh, um. . ."

"I'm Lucas Crawford. We're courting."

Warmth spreads through my chest despite the uncomfortable moment. I remind myself he only said it for the Others' sake. The Warden pulls out a handheld communicator and punches some buttons. I glance at the strange, non-Other Other, starting at the expression in her eyes. It seems oddly familiar, as though I've seen it somewhere before.

"I've no indication that the two of you have taken part in a Parental Sanction. This is a requirement of voluntary Partnering."

Lucas steps closer to me, his scent calming my pounding heart. I'm glad we're downwind from the Others. The rain brings out the smells. "It's scheduled for this week."

It's not, but the Warden doesn't know that.

The Warden says nothing further, backing up and giving control to the Archivist. Something is so familiar about that woman.

"I'll just get this boundary open and take that box from you. If you'll walk this way with me, Althea, I'll ask you the necessary questions." She cocks her head to the right and begins to walk along the fence.

I hesitate, torn between gnawing curiosity about the woman and reluctance to leave Lucas. She glances back and smiles again with that look in her eyes. She seems nice. Genuine, even. The anti-Other.

I follow her along the boundary about fifty steps. Not far enough to be out of earshot or view. She digs under the leaves on her side of the fence and uncovers a small black box buried in the ground. A red button sits in the center of the top, like on the communicators. She pushes it, and back where Lucas and the Warden stand the fence opens up, exactly like where we went through in the rider the night Mrs. Morgan Broke.

The woman catches my eye and hers shift color again, filling with water. She blinks it away in a flash, smiling. "You know, I'm rather enjoying my stay nearby. The collection center is only about an hour-long walk, straight into the afternoon sun."

Before I can respond, she spins around and tromps back toward the men. I follow, glancing into the trees to catch a glimpse of the birds and squirrels. She never asks me any questions, but it's obvious she knows something.

Relief colors Lucas's face when I stand next to him again. The woman holds out her hands in a silent

259

request and he hands over the cardboard container. She passes it to the Warden without checking the contents. "Thank you for your cooperation. You've saved me some time, since my placement here expires in three days."

Without another word she and the Warden move back outside the boundary. They leave, stepping on the red button to close the fence on their way by. Lucas and I don't move as the edges of the fence slide silently toward each other, fastening into place with the faintest of clicks. The mystery surrounding the woman bothers me.

"Well, that wasn't as exciting as I thought it might be," Lucas observes.

"Hmm."

"Althea." Lucas shakes my arm, grasping my attention.

"What?"

"We'd better talk to Mr. Morgan about a Sanction since we told the Warden about it."

"Okay, sure. We can go now."

Since he broke my concentration, the freezing, soaking day reclaims my attention and I'm more than ready to get inside.

Halfway back to the Morgans', Lucas pulls me to a stop and makes me face him. "Okay, Althea. What's on your mind?"

"Did anything seem weird to you about the Archivist?"

"You mean, besides the fact she's a female Other? Like what?"

Frustration surges at my inability to pinpoint it. "Well, it didn't hurt to look at her. Her eyes changed color. And she reminded me of someone."

"Yeah, she reminds me of Others," he mutters.

It'll come to me. It's there, hiding in the recesses of my stubborn mind.

*

Mr. Morgan comes into the foyer when we enter and call out to him.

"Ah, Lucas, right? I was wondering if I might see you again." He turns to me with a stern look. "You two know the rules. We should have scheduled a Sanction before now."

His statement surprises me; I wasn't aware he'd heard the courtship rumors. Then again, Lucas did take me to the Autumn Mixer.

"I…well, I…" *Come on, words. Form a thought.*

Lucas breaks in, his voice higher than normal. "That's what we wanted to talk to you about, sir. We were hoping Tuesday evening might work for you."

Mr. Morgan chuckles. "No need to be nervous. I'll send your parents a message and check with them, but Tuesday's fine with me."

"Thank you, sir. I'll see you then."

Lucas squeezes my hand and escapes. Mr. Morgan chuckles again, then we return to our Saturday routine. We watch the movie on television for family time. It makes my skin crawl to know that up and down this street, on every street in town, in every town on Earth, everyone is doing the exact same thing. Two houses away, Lucas and the Crawfords are laughing at the same moments we are. Like mindless goons.

Afterward I burrow under the heavy covers in my bed, hoping to warm up, and thumb through Lucas's booklet of words again. I toss it aside after a while and stare up at the ceiling, willing whatever it is about the Archivist to the forefront. She's not from my memory dreams, though the caring look in her eyes mirrors the feelings they give me. Almost like she loves me.

That's it.

She reminds me of Ko when he popped out of my necklace.

The minute I think it, I know it's the truth. Her short stature, her slightly pointed ears, the nuances that make her feel Other, but not totally, just as Ko described himself. In person it's easier to see what he means. It's in their eyes more than anything. The way they seem to care for me, want to help me, maybe even love me.

Ko said there are those who know about my past. Could he mean her?

My room constricts, too small and too far from Lucas. I itch from the inside out with the need to speak with him. We didn't plan to use the cup device tonight so it'll have to wait until our free hour tomorrow morning.

Three days. She said she'll only be at the collection center three more days.

*

Lucas is waiting for me, leaning against the fence and smiling, when I fly down the front steps the next morning. For a second, I wish things were simple. That we *were* courting. That I could run out, give him a hug, and we would go meet our friends for an hour.

Instead I stop a couple of feet away. "We need to talk."

"Let's go for a walk."

263

It's the best way to talk out in the open, where Deshi or the Wardens can't sneak up on us. We head in the direction of the park. "I figured out what bothers me about that woman."

Lucas takes my gloved hand. "I knew you would."

"She's like Ko."

When the words hit his ears he stumbles a bit but keeps walking.

Lucas's eyes are as wide as the full moon, and about as bright with wonder. "You know, now that you say that, she does resemble him. I caught her eye as I handed off your box and her eyes were *nice*."

"I think she was trying to tell me something yesterday. When we walked together to open the gate she looked at me and said something about the collection center being an hour's walk into the afternoon sun."

"So?"

"Then she made it a point to tell us how long she'll be there. . ." I trail off, and wait for him to get it.

"She's told us how to find her."

"I think so, too."

"In that message, Ko said if we're brave we'll be able to find people who have answers about us. We have to go to that collection center while she's still here." Lucas's voice trembles with excitement.

264

Though I'm proud of my grudging respect for the animals living in the Wilds, traipsing through it, just the two of us, still frightens me. I'd thought there would be time to enter that space gradually, a few minutes at a time.

"I know you're worried about the animals, Althea. But this could be our one chance to find out who we are. The Others lied about Fils. They lied about what happened to Mrs. Morgan. Maybe they're lying about the animals, too."

"They are." My voice is so quiet I have to repeat myself. "They are. And I know how we can get across the boundary. I climbed it a few weeks ago, the morning after I Broke Mrs. Morgan."

A sense of loss dribbles into my heart at giving up my stolen moments, but Lucas needs to know. He does stumble this time and comes to a stop. His eyes are huge and a ridiculous, pride-filled grin lights up his handsome face. "I can't believe it. Why do you act like such a fraidycat sometimes, you little rebel?"

My face flushes, but a matching grin answers his. "I'm not a rebel, it was a bad morning and I did it without thinking. I needed to be somewhere the Others weren't."

"So, they are lying, then, about the animals? Nothing bad happened to you?"

"No, not then. I only saw birds and squirrels. I'm not sure they're lying, not totally. I mean, the animals mostly go about their business, but they have to eat, right?"

He shrugs it off. "Sure. Still, this is great news! So we're going, then?"

Though I'm not as gung ho as Lucas, not much of a life awaits me here, inside the boundary. Once the Wardens get me alone in a room it will end anyway. I have no illusions about faking my way through the interview the way I did the refreshing. Those Others weren't paying attention, and didn't have any reason to double-check anything I said or did.

The thought of my looming interview session breaks my forehead out in a sweat. I thought the ordeal with Mrs. Morgan and daring to walk alone in the forest would lessen my fear, but instead it's had the opposite effect. The sun disappears behind a cloud and a shiver zips over me, bumps standing up along my covered arms.

With a last glance at Lucas, I make up my mind. "Let's start searching for the spot I crossed right now."

Excitement joins my trepidation, widens the smile on my face. I can't wait to be back in that untouched world, the one place that makes me feel normal, at peace.

Some luck finds us, and Deshi doesn't materialize. I know the general area where I breached the boundary, but it might have been fixed, so Lucas designs a way to test the whole thing. We both gather handfuls of sticks and stroll close to the edge, tossing pieces in front of us, off to the side, and when the cameras are far away, into the fence to see if they burn. So far they all have, with a sizzle of electricity and a bright light reducing the wood to a smoldering pile of ash. Like the bird. He doesn't stop tossing sticks or look over at me as we talk.

We've been avoiding any topic that could sound suspicious if—when—we run into Deshi. It's infuriating, but the challenge of coming up with topics that sound inane but aren't is invigorating, too.

"Tell me about Intermediate Cell." Those are the three years I spent in Portland, except for the missing summers, of course. I want to know if he stayed still as well.

His cheeks color, though whether or not the question lowers his body temperature I can't say. It's too cold outside now to tell. He clears his throat and looks at me. "I spent them here. All of them."

It stuns me a little, to know he spent those three years in Danbury. Maybe that's why the kids listen to him more than me. They know him. At least, they used to.

"You?"

"In Portland. Did you make friends here?"

"Yes. A few."

The uncomfortable air around him thickens, and his rosy cheeks pluck at my curiosity. "Who?" I ask.

"Leah was my best friend." The words slide out in a whisper and regret collects in the creases around his mouth. Pieces of my heart war with one another, half of them broken for his loss of Leah, in more ways than one. The rest relieved she's no longer close to Lucas. If he had never traveled again, perhaps the two of them would be courting. I hate that idea.

We keep walking, tossing sticks in between our muted footsteps. The leaves smothering the ground are a dirty, mushy blanket atop the dying grass. *Squish. Squish. Squish. Zap!*

While trying to decide on another seemingly innocuous topic, I remember I've still never told Lucas how my necklace looks like the Wardens' scars. I'm scared he'll see what I see—another link between us and the Others. Then again, we're never going to learn anything if we're too scared to see the truth. *Squish. Squish. Squish. Zap!*

"Lucas, have you ever noticed the raised red marks on the Others' necks, below their left ears?"

He gives me an odd look. "No. I've never looked at them for more than a second."

Squish. Squish. Squish. Zap! "Oh. Yeah, I hadn't either until the Gathering. Then, while they were trying to refresh me I got a pretty good look."

"And?"

I chew on the tip of my index finger. "And the scar is shaped like my necklace. A star with only four points."

"What do you think it means?"

Squish. Squish. Squish. Tink!

We stop short at the new sound, conversation forgotten as we stare like idiots at the intact stick lying beneath the fence.

Lucas throws another. *Tink!*

This time we're watching and nothing happens. The small, brittle piece of wood hits the metal and bounces off, landing on a bed of leaves near the first stick. I run my eyes along the area, searching for cameras while pretending to peer at the clouds. The nearest one on the fence is about thirty yards from where we stand, and pointed straight inward. We're not in its line of sight.

Hesitant but growing bolder with each step, Lucas approaches the boundary. He puts out a hand, ready to touch it where the sticks did. I suck in a breath, loud enough to be heard, but he doesn't pay any attention. Part of me wants to stop him, but we have to get out. Even though I touched the fence a couple of weeks ago, my short fingernails dig into my palms as Lucas's fingers creep closer and closer to the entwined metal, finally wrapping around the section in front of him.

He doesn't disintegrate. My breath blows out in a huge gush of relief. Lucas backs up a little and stares at the boundary, surprised.

"The Ko woman said it takes an hour to get to the collection center. We'll have to go soon."

"Tonight, Althea. We only have two more days. I'll meet you on the back porch at eleven."

"Let's go back. It's cold."

Lucas grins, snatching my hand and rubbing it between his. As though that will warm me up. "You could start a fire. Have you been practicing?"

"No, I haven't had the chance." I change the subject. "We should both bring a flashlight tonight."

We stumble on Deshi as we pass the playground equipment near the front of the park. The look on his face irritates me more than usual; he's smirking as though he's pleased with himself. It reminds me of the night he hurt the young Other, and I'm frightened to know what's brought it on this morning. The way he shows up unexpectedly has always put me on edge, worries me he's eavesdropping. Whether he's like us, or like the Others, Lucas is right—he's not trustworthy.

"Hey, guys, what's going on?"

Lucas answers in a cool, collected voice, slipping an arm around my back. "Nothing, really. Taking a walk, that's all."

Deshi snorts, glancing pointedly at my fingers tucked inside my sleeves. His sideways remarks about my comfort level in the cold make me think he knows something. Perhaps he's trying to figure out if *we're* like *him.*

"Can I walk a little ways with you?"

It's not as though we have a choice, so the three of us step out onto the sidewalk. The silence isn't comfortable with Deshi on my left; in fact, it presses down from all directions and deadens my limbs more than the cold.

We make it a few blocks before Deshi smiles wider. "So, you guys have interviews next week, huh? Are you nervous?"

I smile back, and slip into my best blank gaze and lifeless tone of voice even though sweat heats my body under my clothes. "No, why would we be?"

Deshi stops walking; we've reached our street. "No reason. It's exciting is all. It's going to be a day you'll never forget."

22.

The Warden passes under the streetlight and I swear he looks right at me in my window seat before he keeps walking.

Lucas waits out back like he promised. I step out onto the porch, tugging my coat tight around me as the bitter wind whips down the block and blows my hair around my face. Pulling it up into a ponytail would've taken less than a minute. Now it's going to drive me banana balls all night.

Leaving it down is almost worth it when Lucas lights up, grabbing my hand. "You look pretty. I can smell the jasmine better when your hair is down. The breeze blows it around, and. . ." He trails off, embarrassed or out of words, it's hard to tell which.

I rescue him. "Breeze? Feels more like a gale."

"Really?" He lifts his face into the bracing wind. "I think it feels nice."

Patrolling Wardens and bright lights make using the streets hazardous, so we stick to backyards until we dart through the park entrance. Once we leave the playground there are no lights, and stifling darkness presses in. I want to turn on my flashlight, but Lucas stays my hand.

"Not yet. Not until we get out."

My eyes adjust within a few minutes. We make our way to the dead section of the fence in good time. Lucas marked it earlier with a small strip of fabric torn from the inside of my coat. He tests the spot again and we get the same nonreaction.

Lucas turns, lifting an eyebrow. His eyes sparkle, teasing me. My heart skips a couple of beats and I think I manage a smile back, but who knows? His lips move and I try to focus on his words.

"You want to go first?"

"You go ahead. I've done it."

"Show-off."

Lucas tosses his flashlight and backpack over, looking suspiciously like he might be enjoying this little adventure. His strong hands grip the metal and nothing happens. Wedging a toe in between the wires, he hoists his full weight onto the fence and starts to climb. I chew on a finger, frightened the Wardens or Deshi are going to stumble upon us at any moment. Lucas's tree-climbing experience comes in handy as he ascends the twenty feet or so with graceful speed.

Climbing is as unnatural for me now as it was the first time, and violent shakes attack my limbs by the time I sling a leg over the top and start making my way down. When I get within a reasonable distance of the ground, I release my grip and drop the remaining few feet onto the muddy earth. Lucas's arms steady me, hold me up when my knees go weak. My face is inches from his, our breath mixing in frosty white clouds.

The heat inside me starts at unbearable and climbs upward. I'm breathing too hard, as much from this moment as from the chore of scaling the boundary.

He stares into my eyes and his brow furrows. "Althea, can I kiss you?"

My head refuses to take the order to nod, frozen in shock and fear. Not the kind of fear that pounds inside me at the thought of the Others, but an exhilarating sort. Never mind that we're standing out in the open, that we just crossed a forbidden boundary. I lick my lips and answer in a throaty whisper. "Yes."

I can't believe I said it. I can't believe this is happening, or how badly I want it. He better do it soon, because I'm about to break into pieces from sheer expectation. His arms tighten as they pull me against his chest, and he bends his beautiful face to mine. When our lips touch the intensity rockets out of my body and spins around in a mad swirl. The dizziness makes me clutch him tighter.

His lips are cool, refreshing against my red-hot ones. The kiss deepens, my lips parting just a bit as my head shifts to one side and my arms snake around his neck. It seems to have lasted for hours, but at the same time it's over so fast. Our foreheads press together as we gasp for breath. When my eyes open, they meet Lucas's. After a second of bemused staring, he smiles and my muscles relax.

"We should go."

My entire body has the shakes, and just supporting my own weight makes black spots dance in front of my eyes. My mind slogs through dark, cloudy pools and my voice sounds far away. "I don't know if I can walk three steps, never mind an hour."

The words slip out, and it isn't until afterward that I realize honesty might be overrated in this particular situation.

He raises an eyebrow. "That good, huh?"

I whack his arm and stalk past him, then stop at the sight of the endless blackness. My trepidation at being outside the boundary crashes back into my consciousness. We flick on our flashlights once we enter the trees.

Lucas snorts as I shrink closer to him. "Baby."

In spite of his teasing tone, he slides his hand into mine and holds tight.

We set off in the direction the sun sets, like the woman said. The peace of the Wilds is harder to find in the pitch black. There are too many shadows, too many places where animals bigger than a squirrel could hide.

We've been walking a long time when a rustling stops us in our tracks. My entire body freezes as a pair of soft, fearful eyes emerge from the blackness. My fingernails dig into Lucas's arm. He grunts at the pain and follows my gaze.

"Oh. It's a deer, Althea."

He whispers, as though he doesn't want to frighten her away, voice full of awed wonder.

It's a girl, I think, because it doesn't have antlers. Her breath escapes in nervous puffs, and her ears twitch. Finding us out here is probably not part of her evening plans. Though she stands still, muscles ripple under her velvety-looking skin. She looks ready to run. A sudden surge of envy that she *can* run stutters through me. She's not trapped. Only her fear and uncertainty hold her in place.

I wish that were true of me. Then again, maybe it is.

"I know what it is, Lucas." I try to capture his annoying tone. "The question is, what are we going to do about it?"

In answer, he reaches a hand around his back and unzips the front pocket of his backpack; he brought water, snacks, and extra blankets for me.

The soft noise of the zipper startles the deer and for a second I think she's going to bolt, but all four hooves stay rooted to the spot and her nose twitches. Lucas draws a small, clear plastic box out of his bag; vegetables roll around inside it. He grins, puts a finger to his lips, and takes a small step forward.

Urgency creeps into my answering whisper. "What are you doing?"

He steps closer to the deer without responding, fingers working a carrot out of the container. The air in my lungs starts to burn. I force it out in a silent exhale.

The deer behaves the opposite of how we've been led to believe. She's timid and unsure, her initial instinct clearly flight. Nothing about her posture suggests violence or disease. She's beautiful, in fact, from the tip of her nose to her fringed white tail.

Lucas extends a hand with the carrot on his palm and the beam of light projected from my flashlight jumps up and down. Against her better judgment, the deer reaches her nose out and sniffs the air. Her lips start forward, then back off. Forward and back. Lucas trembles with the effort of holding still. He gasps when she snatches the carrot from him, pulling out another and holding on to it this time as she nibbles. His grin is infectious.

"Come here, Althea. Don't be scared of her."

Wonder blooms in my belly, and the joy on his face brings me closer to the animal. I go slowly, sensing her hesitance, until I stand next to Lucas. He hands me a carrot and I cup it, stretching my arm out until my open palm sneaks under her face. She could bite my hands off, but I don't think she will.

Breath fills up my lungs and I hold it there, standing like a statue as her kind face dips down. The air whooshes out as her lips whisk the carrot out of my hands. She's so perfect, so utterly pure. My heart feels ripped open; the stitches I used to close it up when I left Portland and the only semblance of an actual family I ever knew are busted and gone. This animal, with no effort at all, makes me care again. Makes me feel alive and a solid part of the world, instead of like a stranger shimmering on its edges.

In this instant, I think I understand the real reason the Others separate us from the animals.

Lucas shatters the moment when he extends a hand to touch her side. At the first feel of his fingertips on her flank she pulls back, carrot forgotten as it falls to the earth. Her eyes flick in fear and she bounds away, tail disappearing into the trees before either of us utters

278

a sound. Lucas turns back, his eyes moist. "She was so soft. Scared of us, though. Wonder why."

"You shouldn't have done that."

"Why not? Did she look violent to you? Or like a million germs crawled over her?" His defensive tone raises my hackles.

"No. I meant scare her. You shouldn't have tried to touch her without. . ."

"What? Without her permission?" He quirks a smile my direction.

"No. I was going to say until she was comfortable."

"So, what do you think now, about the animals?"

I consider as we continue deeper into the trees, offering a smile of reconciliation. The answer is nothing the Others have ever told us. "I love her, and I love it out here." A sad sort of loss sweeps through me. I'll never see her again. "But deer eat plants, you know, not people."

He laughs; the sound relaxes me even more. I check my watch after a few more minutes and am startled to see we've been moving for well over an hour. We emerge from the thick trees and stare not at the collection center, but at the park boundary. We went in a circle.

"Well, that didn't work." Lucas's wry tone makes me laugh.

"We're going to have to try again tomorrow."

A huge oak tree to our left has a triangular cutout near its base, almost like a little cave. Lucas kneels and unloads the contents of his backpack, shoving them into the hole.

"What're you doing that for?"

"Easier than sneaking them back out tomorrow, right?"

The walk home is slow; for once we have plenty of time. Neither of us talks, and my mind wanders back over the horrors of our recent lives, irritation at missing a chance to talk to the woman depressing me. We hide in the trees as a Warden passes by in front of our houses on his 2 a.m. patrol.

When the coast is clear Lucas catches my lips with his, surprising me, then turns and sprints inside. I follow his lead and drag myself up to bed.

*

The next morning a funny feeling captures me and holds me tight in its clutches. The past several days contain both infuriating and wonderful memories. They jumble inside me, resulting in nausea more than anything. The odd mood persists through breakfast and follows me out the front door. Lucas waits on the sidewalk in front of the house in between ours, his smile a little awkward. It hasn't dawned on me to feel weird about kissing last night. He sort of looks like he feels weird though.

"Hey." Lucas pecks my cheek, sounding normal.

We make small talk on the way to Cell, avoiding a rehash of our failed attempt last night. A heaviness settles over me as we part ways for our morning blocks.

Deshi, looking and smelling like a corpse, accosts Lucas at lunch so they sit alone instead of with us girls. I can't say this upsets me, but it makes me nervous for Lucas. He acts pleasant and chatters away to Deshi during the period. The performance looks good from here.

In chemistry, the Monitor appears on the screen and calls our attention to her lesson. It might be possible for my Cellmates to focus, but for me it's out of the question. All I can think about is how little time we have left to figure out what we're going to do alone in a room with a Warden.

After block, Lucas leans over to whisper in my ear, his cool breath tickling my neck. Tingles work their way up and down my body, delicious and long lasting.

"I have to use the wasteroom. Meet you out front."

I imagine turning my head toward him, our mouths touching. My eyes close, and I lick my lips, nodding my understanding. He lingers a moment, breath skimming loose strands of my hair against my skin. We're frozen. Like we're stuck together, each unable to move. Lucas finally straightens up, but when our eyes meet his tell me moving wasn't easy for him either. His lips tip up, making my heart go even faster. He has to get out of here before I die. This day has been hard enough on my heart and my nerves without him smiling at me like that.

My way out of the Cell is unobstructed with no Deshi to intercept me. Come to think of it, except for at lunch today, I've barely seen him around lately. I bounce from one foot to the other, having trouble standing still while there's so much to figure out. A few minutes later Lucas strides toward me, his face ashen. Terror melts out of him and puddles in my queasy stomach. "What happened to you?"

He doesn't answer. "Just walk."

It takes an eternity to walk beyond Cell grounds. My knees tremble hard by the time we leave everyone behind. Lucas stops walking and bends over, putting his hands on his knees and gasping.

"Lucas. Lucas! You're scaring me. Tell me what happened."

"I saw something." He stops, swallowing hard before he continues. "I was using the wasteroom like I told you, and Deshi came in while I was in the stall. I knew it was him because of his death cologne. It's

282

nauseating, worse than the last time we smelled it. Much worse."

"And?"

"I stood on the disposal so he couldn't see my feet. I don't know why. So he did his business and went out to disinfect his hands and I peered out through the crack in the door. His face—" Lucas stops, paling further at the memory.

Patience isn't easy right now, but he rewards mine by picking up the story again when he's ready.

"The reflection in the mirror wasn't his face. It was an Other. Deshi's an Other."

23.

"No, he isn't. He can't be an Other, Lucas. We've spent time with him, talked with him. He's a human Barbarus." My voice climbs to a higher and higher pitch. Defeat washes through me even though part of me has known it since the night I Broke Mrs. Morgan.

"I'm telling you what I saw, Althea. He's an Other hiding in human skin."

A dark, unbidden realization slithers into my conscious mind. It makes me gasp out loud and grab Lucas's arm for support.

"What is it?"

"What do you think it means that an Other chose to make his body smell like springtime? That his eyes are blue like ours but all wrong in his face? That he sought us out to latch onto, kids who are different, too?"

If possible, even more color drains out of his face, until he resembles a snowy winter day. My thoughts become his and my fears register.

His voice echoes the one screaming inside my head. "They know about us: how we smell, how old we are, that we're Terms. The Others are here looking for us."

"Why?"

It's the biggest question of all and neither of us has the answer. We separate in front of the Crawfords' house, parting ways with more ease than usual because we have another attempt at reaching the collection center scheduled. This time I have a plan to keep us from going in circles.

Back outside the boundary later that night, I point up at the sky. "How good are you at astronomy?"

"As good as anyone else who's been taught that crap for two hours a day for ten years."

"Me, too. So, the sun goes east to west, and the Archivist said walk into the afternoon sun. West. We just need to get our star bearings and make sure we walk in the right direction."

Lucas nods, studying the winking lights smeared across the midnight sky. Finally he lets out a relived chirp. "I've got it. If we keep Regulus in front of us, we should go the right way, and straight, too.

"You're a genius. Let's grab some waters and get moving."

We find the huge tree without any trouble and I squat down to retrieve the items Lucas stowed in the trunk last night. A squeak emits from inside and I pull my hand back, but not fast enough. A furry black-and-white animal runs through a wet, cloudy stench and escapes into the blackness.

My eyes sting and water as a racking cough rattles my lungs. Fire licks its way down my throat, burning pain searing the tender tissue.

This is it. I'm going to die.

Lucas runs to my side and kneels on the wet earth, holding a hand over his nose and mouth as he inspects me. The coughing subsides and he hands me a water bottle out of the now unoccupied tree trunk. I pour the clear liquid over my face, and use a blanket to gently rub it around my burning eyes. After several minutes my eyes and throat have recovered, but the stink clinging to me isn't fading, not a single bit.

I've never, ever smelled anything like what that thing sprayed on me. I've never heard of such an animal, don't know what it's called, but I wish it would come back so I could kick it. It gives me none of the warm fuzzies offered by last night's deer encounter.

Lucas watches my self-cleansing from a few feet away, his eyes sparkling and merry. "Are you okay?"

"Oh, what, you think this is funny? What if it kills me!?"

Lucas dissolves into laughter, working hard to stay on his feet. I get up, snatch another water bottle, and crash through the brush.

He catches up but keeps his distance. "I'm sorry, Althea. It's not funny." He has to wait until his stupid grin is under control before continuing. "I'm sure you won't die, but if you're worried let's go back."

"We can't go back. The woman is only going to be there one more day. If I'm going to die from animal poisoning, I'd rather do it out here, anyway."

Lucas speeds up and leads the way, staying a step or two ahead of me. "Sorry. Gotta stay upwind."

He settles down after about a half an hour and I forgive him for laughing. Now that it appears I'm not going to keel over dead, I suppose there is humor in the situation. It would be a lot funnier if it had happened to him, though.

This makes two animals we've encountered, and neither one tried to kill us. In fact, they both exhibited fear—the deer running and the little furball tonight spraying me with his foul odor in order to escape. My opinion continues to change, little by little, experience by experience. These animals, so free and wild and uncontained, seem to be doing nothing more than living their lives. I even forgive Stinky. I must look pretty scary to him.

If we opened the boundary, they'd probably choose not to come in.

The Others' determination to separate the uncontrollable speaks volumes about what they might do to Lucas and me, two creatures also outside their influence in so many ways.

"Althea, what else do you think we can control?"

"What?"

He sighs, exasperated at my lack of attention. "You know, we can control hot and cold. We can get around the veils or whatever controls human minds. I was just thinking. . .what if we could stop traveling? Or only do it when we want to?"

The idea swishes into the recesses of my mind, forcing me to look at my life in a different way, a way in which I'm in control of what happens to me. Not traveling at all would be my first choice, but if we could do it ourselves we could get out of autumn, escape Deshi and the Wardens and our interviews. My shoulders sag at a memory. "The day after the Gathering, Sarah's father said Wardens were at the Upper Cells in all of the places we travel. We can't get away. Besides, traveling has hidden us before because they've never been aware of us. But Deshi's an Other and he certainly isn't going to forget about us if we disappear. If anything it will prove beyond all doubt that we're worth looking for."

"But as a last resort, maybe. We can't avoid them forever, but jumping seasons could buy us some time."

"You think we could do it the same way we use the hot and cold—by focusing our emotions and pushing?"

"The big problem is figuring out how to stay together when we try it. I mean, we could pool our emotions together maybe, if we were touching."

The suggestion immediately makes me wary. "We might hurt each other."

"Especially you, with those fire hands."

"Funny."

We walk on, checking the sky every ten minutes or so to maintain our direction. My watch says twelve-thirty when Lucas stops, stretching out an arm to block my path. Up ahead, lights filter through the forest.

We creep forward, taking care to make as little noise as possible, and stop at the edge of the clearing. A small clapboard building rests in the center, spotlights directed outward on all four sides. No sound or movement suggests anyone is around and no lights glow in the windows.

Lucas pulls me back into the trees, pushing a finger against his lips as he gags at my nearness. Worry tinges my excitement and adrenaline pumps through my blood. His breathing and the pounding of my heart fill the silence, but nothing else. Then I hear what Lucas does. Squishing noises like the ones our footsteps make in the leaves.

Coal black eyes poke around a thick tree and the terror abates. It's not some version of threatening wildlife, but her. The Other we trekked out here to find.

"Hi." Pleasure fills her eyes, now the color of midnight. "It is so nice to see you two together, I. . .*what* is that smell?"

She leans toward me and takes a delicate sniff before retreating several steps and laughing, a tinkling sound more pleasant than anything I've ever heard. She reaches out to Lucas but he pulls back, closer to me.

The not-Other sighs. "I'm happy you decided to come. It's good you don't trust me; Ko did an excellent job with those notes. If you'll come inside we can talk."

A squeak slips through my lips and Lucas's breath slides out of his lungs in a gurgle. She *is* connected to Ko.

"Who are you?" Lucas demands.

"A friend to Ko. And a friend to you, whether you know it or not. I'm Cadi."

Enticing us out here could be a trick, but in all honesty, that doesn't make much sense. The Others have incredible technology and mental capabilities at their fingertips. If they did know for sure Lucas and I are the ones they're looking for, they'd just come and take us. They can change everyone's memory back to normal afterward and it will be as if we never existed at all.

Jitters bounce through my insides, half excited, half nervous. The woman, Cadi, starts toward the little building, and I meet Lucas's eye.

He shrugs. "This is why we walked all the way out here. You ready?"

"We don't have to trust her all the way yet, right?"

Lucas's face tightens before he gives a curt shake of the head. "No way. Let's just see how we feel after we talk to her."

He takes my hand and we step into the clearing.

Cadi glances back and a small smile tugs at the corners of her pink lips. "I must say, I'm impressed the two of you have the nerve to leave the city boundary."

Pride fills her voice and my curiosity grows. Anticipation speeds my heart at the prospect of learning more about my life. A million questions infuse my thoughts and fight to get out of my mouth first, but caution still holds me back.

She stops at the front door and faces us. "Why don't we go inside and get you cleaned up, Althea. That smell is impossible. Lucas, if you don't mind, please turn around and close your eyes while she gets out of those clothes. I'll come back and get you once she's soaking."

Lucas hesitates and I know he's worried about losing sight of me. Normally I'd agree with him, but cleaning this stench off is worth a small risk, an opinion I communicate to him with a look.

Cadi notices our silent conversation and smiles. Lucas walks ten paces away and turns his back. I strip off all four layers of clothes, my limbs trembling more and more violently each piece I remove. Bumps decorate my pale skin and my teeth chatter. When nothing but my bra and underwear remain, Cadi tosses the rest in a pile, takes my hand, and leads me inside. My thoughts are frozen into a complete blank.

We pass a small living area and an even smaller kitchen before entering a mint green tiled cleansing room. A huge, white basin with clawed feet takes up more than a quarter of the room. Candles flicker on the edge of the tub and sink, casting shimmying shadows on the walls.

Cadi leans over and turns on the water, plugging the bottom when the liquid starts to steam. "This part is going to be unpleasant, I'm afraid, but that smell isn't easy to get rid of."

"Do you know what did this to me?"

"It's called a skunk. Scared little things, really. Nearly sightless but they have a good defense mechanism, wouldn't you agree?" She raises an eyebrow at me, humor lighting her face.

"Sure," I respond dryly. "Am I going to die?"

"No. Goodness, how I hate what the Others have done to this planet. Let's go out back."

"Out back? Why?" The thought of going outside, into the freezing wind, hurts my head.

"I need to hose you off and scrub you down with a solution that will break down the scent."

I have no idea what she's talking about and honestly don't care. If it will get rid of the smell, fine. I follow her out of the cleansing room, casting a longing look at the steaming water, and try to prepare myself.

Ten minutes later icy water droplets cling to every inch of me as Cadi leads me back inside. A glimpse in the mirror reveals blue lips and frozen strands of hair. I strip the rest of the way and sink into the tub. Steaming water stings my frosty skin at first, but feels better than just about anything, ever.

"Let me get Lucas settled and I'll be back." She leaves with my soaking undergarments pinched between two fingers.

My eyes slip closed in the darkness. It's so quiet, so peaceful, and for the first time since I lay on the forest floor I don't feel as though someone is watching me. My chin rests atop the bubbles and my mind shuts off, thankful to have a break. Glowing yellow patterns flicker on the tiles. I just breathe in the solitude. In. Out. In.

The door opens again and Cadi slips in. She kneels at the end of the basin by my head. She's changed into lounge clothes, a pale green pair of pants and a matching top. She grabs a couple of bottles from under the sink and squirts shampoo into her palm. "You have questions, Althea?"

Only about a million.

Cadi rubs the fragrant suds into my hair and kneads my scalp. She works on me in silence for several seconds. There are an infinite number of questions but few that Lucas won't want to hear, too. My brow scrunches and I nibble on the tips of my fingers as she finishes with my hair and moves on to my back. No one has ever taken the time to pay attention to me, to take care of me. I don't know Cadi at all, but I let her do it. A feeling of protection fills the room, as though this little cabin offers safe harbor.

It's silly to feel that way. It's an Other facility in the middle of nowhere.

It's Cadi that's making me feel like this, not the building. She and Ko are strange that way.

"What are you if you're not an Other?"

"What am I? All this time in the dark about you and your question is about me?"

The words choke off at the end and I twist to look at her face. Water floods her midnight eyes and she looks at me like the people in my dreams do. Whatever she and Ko are, they do care about us. She couldn't fake the raw, jagged emotion written all over her. But why?

"What's the water in your eyes called? I get it, too, and Lucas has had it before, but no one else does."

"The humans call them tears. And they all have them, but tears are brought on by emotion. When they come it's called crying, or weeping. It's how everyone would purge feelings naturally, if they could."

"Tears." I try out the word, happy to have a name for the water and also, a definition for one of the words in Lucas's strange, haunting booklet. I examine my fingertips, wrinkled and pink from the water, and take the washcloth from Cadi. Even though my clothes absorbed much of the smell, I'm not ready to get out of the water just yet. "So, what are you?"

She seems to think about it for a minute. "The gulf between our languages is vast. Your vocabulary is quite limiting."

"Hey!"

She shrugs. "It is not your fault, Althea. The Others have nothing to gain and much to lose from teaching language or history." She searches her mind for another few minutes while I practice using my patience. "I am an Augur. It is the closest definition. I am not wholly Other, nor am I human. My forebearers were from a planet called Sprita. We had one primary emotion— love. Our planet is. . .*was* peaceful, full of respect and happiness. When the Others arrived, no one stood against them; fighting is not in our nature. We welcomed them, offered them sanctuary. The Others spent many years on Sprita before moving on. No one survived their habitation except those they took with them when they left."

"They took you with them," I squeak out. Greg asking what happens to the Others' hosts hops out of my memory. This is almost worse than no one surviving.

"Some of us, yes. My people have specific abilities the Others wished to copy. They took a dozen of our women when they left and extracted genetic material. Experimented with controlling the genes they wished for themselves. It worked, to an extent. I am an example. So is Ko." A ghostly smile haunts her face. "We are not the first to be taken. Or the last. Many species do not survive the aggressive gene manipulation. Or do not behave as intended."

A shudder of what looks like revulsion wracks her tiny frame. I'm unwilling to push her on what is obviously a distressing point. The hot water turns lukewarm and I want to get out anyway, to return to Lucas. "Cadi, why are you and Ko helping us?"

She watches me through sad, resigned eyes. "You remember what I told you about Sprita? We wish a different outcome for Earth. You could be the answer."

I get out of the water and rub myself dry as Cadi leaves the room, then returns with my clothes. They smell clean and fresh, like they dried in warm air. "How?"

She winks. "Magic, Althea. Come. I'll tell you more."

Whatever magic is.

I dress and enter the kitchen to find Cadi and Lucas staring at each other over steaming mugs of hot chocolate. A third cup waits for me in front of the seat beside Lucas. My stiff fingers warm as they wrap around it.

He leans over and sniffs, then gives me a nod of approval. "Much better." He steals one of my hands, then turns a suspicious gaze on Cadi. "I have a question. Why are you here now, after sixteen years of leaving us to fend for ourselves? Something's happened, hasn't it."

It's a statement, not a question. We know something has.

"Yes, things have changed as far as the two of you are concerned. First of all, you must know we did not leave you to fend for yourselves. Ko is the reason you have survived until now." Her eyes darken further and grief pulls at her perfect, sharp features. "He wrote you those notes and helps you travel between seasons. His abilities kept you safe after your parents could no longer hide your existence on their own."

Lucas clears his throat, opens his mouth, and then closes it again. He finds his voice before I do. "What abilities?"

"The hologram stored in Althea's necklace is a good example. Spritans have advanced capacities for altering perceptions. We can't change reality, just the way it is perceived."

"I've never heard of such a thing," Lucas scoffs.

"There are a great many things in this universe you've never heard of, young man. I promise we are more than capable of producing results. Ko is a powerful Augur. I possess an adequate amount of knowledge in this area as well."

Her words attempt to penetrate the barrier between what is known and what is possible. My brain pounds and stretches, clearing space for the new ideas.

"Why did he help us?" Lucas is harsh with Cadi. He's obviously frustrated and having a hard time trusting her.

Cadi stares back at Lucas, and he avoids her emotion-soaked gaze. "Althea can fill you in on my past, but Ko and I have our reasons for keeping you alive. In the course of protecting you as you've grown, we have come to care for you very much. Almost as if you belong to us."

I've been stuck on her original statement this entire time, when she mentioned our parents. My heart climbs into my throat and tries to beat, tightening my airway with a painful pinch.

"You said Ko took over because our parents could no longer protect us. We have parents?"

She sees our earnest, hopeful faces and shakes her head. "Yes, of course you have parents. The Prime Other wants you *because* of your parents. After all, you're the only children born to an Other and a human."

My jaw drops open. We *are* Other. At least, part of us is. Lucas's eyes find mine and dismay flows out of them into my heart. Cadi places a hand over our linked ones. Comfort drips from underneath it and into my blood, but it can't thwart my shiver.

"I thought relationships between Others and humans are forbidden," I say.

Her eyebrows shoot up in surprise, giving her a comical appearance. "How do you know that, Althea?"

"Long story. I heard some Others talking about me once, and saying it was too bad intimacy is forbidden."

Lucas grunts and I remember he didn't know that part.

Cadi continues, keeping her hand on ours. "The kind of love humans experience between a man and a woman is peculiar to this planet. The Others had never encountered it before. Your Other parents were sent to the four corners of Earth to help subdue the planet. In the process, they fell in love. The emotion caught them off guard with its distinct power and the desperate ferocity with which they protected it. Their Partnering with humans resulted in your births."

She stops, taking a deep breath and staring off into space, as though gathering her thoughts. "Any Other beside your parents would have been killed for breaking the first rule of habitation—no intimacy."

"Why not our parents?" Lucas's mouth pulls down into a frown.

My heart beats wildly, wanting to know, not wanting to know.

"The two of you doubtlessly realize you possess strange qualities." She waits for our assent. "The Others have not been able to locate a planet that can sustain their existence indefinitely. When they arrive in a new atmosphere, their presence changes its makeup. The air becomes cold, so bitter that every living thing withers and dies within seconds. They need the cold, feed off it. They also need the indigenous population and environment to support them as long as they want to stay. This is where your Other parents come in."

Cadi pauses, taking her hands off ours and using them to support her weight as she leans back in the chair. She sucks in a deep breath before going on.

"Your parents are the Elements."

24.

The world stops. If Lucas hadn't put an arm around me, my face would have smacked the table. "Our parents are the Elements? But how—" I stop. So much about me makes sense. At last.

"They control the climate on the host planets—the seasons here on Earth—and maintain a livable environment. Without them, the Others would not be able to stay long."

"But there are four of them." Even in his shell-shocked state, Lucas tosses a lure into his statement, trying to confirm our suspicions.

"And there are four of *you*, which you've likely figured out. Smart kids."

"What do they want from us?" The thought of spending two seconds in a room with any of the Elements simmers panic in my blood.

"The Others don't want anything from the four of you. They just want you. They'll dispose of you, in all likelihood, unless they discover some way you can be useful to them." Cadi pauses again while she prods at the mini marshmallows in her cup.

"If all this is true, how come they've never found us? I mean, we're just walking around like everyone else. They aren't stupid." Suspicious Lucas is back, poking at Cadi's story for holes.

"No, the Others are not stupid, Lucas. The furthest thing from it. They've never found you because they haven't been looking. Your existence has been kept secret until recently, when. . .I will just show you what happened when the Others learned of your parents' love affairs, and what has happened to Ko this autumn. It will be easier."

Before we can react she reaches out to touch us, snapping the thumb and forefinger of her free hand together. The kitchen dissolves and we're in a different place. I assume it's a house, though it's unlike any I've ever lived in. It's much bigger, for one. The floor underneath our feet is a cherry-colored wood with thick rugs covering it at regular intervals. Straight ahead, an impressive staircase spirals up toward the vaulted ceiling. It twists out of sight above our heads.

To the left is a sitting room, a fire roaring in a cutout in the wall. I take a few steps back but it remains confined as it crackles and pops. Couches, chairs, and end tables surround a glossy black piece of wood with part of the top propped into the air. The piece is backed by a huge wall of windows; frost decorates the glass in lacy patterns. Warmth and familiarity hug the room, creating an inviting atmosphere very different from the cold, hard spaces in which I spend my days.

To the right is a hallway, perhaps leading to the kitchen considering the metallic clinks and smell of garlic and onion coming from that direction. At my side, Lucas's face shines with surprise, his eyes wide as he takes in our surroundings. Cadi watches us, her own features reserved and closed off. The despondent, ravaged expression in her eyes starts a shiver down my spine. Whatever it is we are about to see, she's not looking forward to it.

As we enter the sitting room another cluster of chairs and couches come into view opposite the fire. Four Others perch on the edges of the furniture, silent and surrounded by nervous energy. I recognize them in an instant and my sweaty hand slips into Lucas's.

The Elements.

I glance at Cadi. "Can they see us?"

"No." She shakes her head, shiny hair bobbing up and down. "This is only a memory."

A voice snaps our attention back to the seated foursome.

"I can't believe this is happening." Fire's voice flows like water over rocks in a stream, bubbly and fresh. The quality doesn't mask the defeated tone.

The voice in my head, the one that sounds like mine but not really, because it's smarter, prettier—it doesn't quite sound like mine because it's *hers*.

I suck in a breath and lean into Lucas. My hands clutch his arm, leaving indentations in his shirt. I jerk away when the blue fabric starts to smolder. Lucas and Cadi both look at me, concern reaching out from their gazes and colliding with my heart. I shake my head, unwilling to share.

The man sitting next to her, Water, puts his hand over Fire's. "We knew what would happen if the Prime found out about our affairs, Flacara. We all hoped he wouldn't, but he has." His voice is low, pleasant like hers, and just as forlorn.

"We should have been more careful, Apa. Sent our Partners away with the children five years ago." She jerks her hand out from underneath his as the fire crackles and climbs higher in its confined space. It writhes, gaining force as though she commands it, brandishing the undeniable truth.

She's my mother. She talks in my mind. I say it to myself so I can try to actually believe it.

One of the men speaks. I recognize him from the portraits, of course. Earth. "You were the least willing of all of us to give up your daughter, Flacara. Now we must deal with the consequences."

Even though Cadi assures us they're unaware of our eavesdropping, fear tumbles around in my gut. Parents or not, I'm uncomfortable in the room with them. At the same time, their countenances are different than I expected, somehow. In their pictures they appear evil, cold, even merciless. Here, now. . .they are more human than they should be. Far more so than the Wardens.

Water speaks up from the couch again, desperation breaking his previously calm demeanor. "Ko will help us."

Fire—no, *Flacara*—won't be placated. "Why would Ko do anything for us? After what we've done to him and his people? We destroyed his home, enslaved and then murdered his own mother. He must hate us."

Despite the anger she's projecting, her sorrow is clear. The men aren't afraid of her. Earth answers with words infused with kindness. "The Spritans don't know how to hate, Flacara. You know that. Ko and Cadi see our children as this planet's hope. Perhaps they are right. We've witnessed the small talents they've inherited from us. Perhaps they could save this planet when we exhaust its resources and move on."

"You know I agree with Pamant." Air, who has been quiet until now, adds his two cents. "Ko and Cadi aren't offering aid because they want to help us. They

306

want to help the children—and the humans. And so I trust them. We all agreed to trust them. Where is Ko, anyway?"

As though on cue, the heavy front door bangs open behind us and a small man bustles into the room. It's hard to tell, since we've only seen an insubstantial version, but it looks like Ko.

He brushes past us without breaking stride and goes to stand in the empty space in front of the fire. The Elements sit up straighter as the tension thickens.

Flacara speaks first, terror lacing her words. "Well? Are they safe?"

Ko takes a moment to catch his breath, unwinding a long, magenta scarf from around his neck and shaking snowflakes out of his dark blond hair. It, as well as his other features, matches Cadi's almost exactly, right down to his impossibly dark blue eyes and short stature. "The children are protected. They will travel between seasons without detection, and I've put other mechanisms in place to help ensure their safety. None of it's foolproof, of course, but. . ." He shrugs and trails off.

Water, the one they call Apa, stands. A chill descends from him that frosts over the windowpanes. Puffs of white breath emerge from our lips in a room that felt warm ten seconds before. Lucas's fingers

307

tighten on mine. His eyes are full of wonder, fear, and disgust—the same mix of emotions running through me. I turn back to the standing man, beautiful perfection in flesh.

That's Lucas's father.

He walks toward Ko, who stands his ground. The shimmering firelight provides a clear view of the star-shaped scar on Apa's neck, the sight rolling fresh shock through me. It's black, and instead of a simple red outline of a star, it's filled in as though someone colored it. Instead of *resembling* my necklace, it *is* my necklace.

The necklace must always have been meant as a clue to the truth—that I'm connected to these aliens, these Elements.

Apa speaks, frosty breath accompanying the words as they leave his lips. "*Not foolproof* isn't good enough. How will you harbor them until they are old enough to care for themselves?"

"Cadi and I have the power to move them at will, in case they unintentionally attract attention. They will each be surrounded by a. . .what is a good word? Curse this limiting language! Ah, let's say an invisible bubble that prevents humans from seeing them clearly. Their hosts, the children at Cell—no one will notice when they are gone. They will hardly notice when they are there. Your children will not stay in one place too long, and they will never visit their natural seasons." He pauses as Flacara gasps and starts to weep quietly. "It's better that way. If the Others become aware of their existence, they will search for them where they would be most comfortable. I've provided each of your children a note, encased in a clue. As they get older they will understand what it means."

"Will they be together?" Earth speaks, his black-and-blue eyes pinning Ko with an intense stare.

Ko shakes his head. "No, Pamant. They will not meet. I thought it best to keep them apart. That way, if something happens to one, well, they won't all be compromised before we can come up with a solution."

"What about Ben?" Flacara poses the question, voice devoid of hope. She twists her long red curls between her fingers the way I sometimes do when I'm upset. Her eyes are downcast, tears winding over her cheeks. In spite of everything, her sorrow tugs at my heart.

"Ben is dead. So are Na, Gisela, and Sophie. I'm so sorry. The Others executed your Partners this morning. I hoped they would only banish them with the Broken, but the Prime is angry." Ko's own voice is full of remorse; tears well up and leak out of his eyes. His voice lowers to a whisper. "The Prime is enraged."

The words hit my ears and though I understand what they mean it takes a minute for them to soak in. The truth. The Broken might not all be disposed.

Ben must be my father, and he's dead.

Lucas's mother is gone. Two additional human lives, parents of our kindred we have never met, were snuffed out because they fell in love with the strange, beautiful people sitting in this room. Heaviness settles in my chest and my heart beats sideways under the weight. My father is dead. I'll never know him, never see him smile at me or kiss my head the way Mr. Morgan does sometimes. The scene in front of us interrupts my spiraling train of thought as it continues to play out.

"They're dead because we loved them." Air, who has been silent for some time and whose real name we don't know, stands and stalks toward the front window.

Lucas's father follows him to the front of the room and sits on the small bench behind the strange black piece of wood. Without warning, a haunting and beautiful sound emerges from inside the bulky wood.

My breath eases out of my chest and my ears soak up the sound until it fades several minutes later. "What was that?"

"The humans call it music. The instrument is a piano."

"It's beautiful." The echoing strains ache in my heart. In some strange way the sound reflects the thick air of mourning hanging over the room. Shared grief settles in my blood and drags like sediment at the bottom of a stream.

Apa stands from behind the piano and puts his hand on Air's shoulder. "Come, Vant. There is nothing we can do to bring them back. We loved them. They loved us. We did not lie to them, and we all knew the risk. Let us mourn. Then let us prepare for our own punishment." He grinds out the words, and the choking quality in his voice tells me he's holding back tears.

Horror numbed my thoughts upon first learning these people are my family. Still, the fact that they loved their Partners and are scared for us—their children—is obvious. Watching them grieve, comfort one another, and strive to ensure our safety confuses the terror their faces have triggered my entire life.

Without warning, Cadi snaps her fingers and the warm, stately house disappears. We're in a cold, impersonal building and a new scene. It looks and feels like a Cell, more institutional than anything else. The ceiling stretches out of sight, exactly like the giant

311

black building the Others took me to in the Wilds to be refreshed.

Cadi walks forward with her head bowed. "This happened seven weeks ago."

She reaches the end of the hall and pushes open a metal door. It protests as it swings inward, hinges squeaking loud enough to make me glance around even though Cadi has promised no one can see us. The room is full of Others, and the urge to turn and run pumps adrenaline into my muscles.

My fears quiet when our approach goes unnoticed. The Others sit in silence on raised platforms, like bleachers, and surround us on three walls. There are six Others on a bench at the front of the room, on the fourth wall, and they've restrained Ko in a chair facing them. He doesn't struggle, but watches them with careful eyes.

The Other in the front and center looks down at him with an unforgiving, infinite black gaze. Three thick obsidian bands ring his neck. I've never seen him before, though his position of authority rings loud and clear, not only because of his seat or slightly altered appearance but simply by his countenance. I lean over to Cadi, barely daring to open my lips. "Who's that?"

"The Prime Other. Their leader."

The Prime Other.

He leans forward, fixing his prisoner in place with a glittering black glare. "Do you know why you are here, Ko?"

"Yes, sir. You drugged me and probed my memories while I slept last night. You know I helped the Elements almost twelve years ago." He states this matter-of-factly, no trace of disrespect in his tone.

Cadi's gaze never leaves the scene, but she addresses us. "The Others' minds are connected in a series of tunnels and caverns. They speak to one another, give orders, display pictures. They can cause pain. Unimaginable pain."

Her voice cracks and falls silent as the Other stands, looming over the heavy table. "Your sympathy to the plight of the humans concerns us more than your allegiance to the Elements. They have been dealt with."

Ko shrugs. "Separating them was wise."

Cadi whispers again, her head angled toward us but her anguished eyes glued to the scene. "Together, the Elements are more powerful than the remaining Others combined. After the Prime learned of their treason, he separated them physically."

The Other settles back into his chair with a disgruntled snort. "I am not interested in your opinion on the Elements. I am now aware offspring resulted from these abominable Partnerships. I want them."

"You cannot have them. Their exact whereabouts are not known to me or anyone else, and it shall remain that way. Pardon me for saying so, but your probes are no match for my mental abilities in this area. You are powerful, but the secrets surrounding those children are too well protected for you to—" He breaks off with a gasp, writhing in agony as his head snaps back and pounds against the chair over and over again.

An eerie wail slips from his lips, the sound stabbing me in the heart until I can't stand it for another moment. My hands cover my ears but the piercing noise only softens. The screams of the Other boy Deshi knocked to the floor with a simple glance ring in my memory, mingling with Ko's as they grow louder.

Cadi turns her back on the scene, shoulders shaking as it goes on for several minutes. Finally Ko goes limp, liquid trickling from his bottom lip where he bit it. It should be blood, but it's a golden color instead of red. Dark amber circles that weren't there a moment ago ring his eyes and the midnight blue of them is shot through with deep yellow veins. Another rivulet of golden blood trickles from his nose. His head lolls off to one side and he makes no effort to right himself. Lucas's hand finds mine and we both squeeze.

We figured they could enter one another's minds, but seeing the torture confirmed firsthand shakes me. The thought of the presence that prodded my mind the night Mrs. Morgan Broke swirls dizzying nausea in my gut.

I hear Fire's voice so often, proffering comfort and urging me forward. If she can get inside my mind, all the Others can.

"Now, Ko. Are you going to tell us where to find the children, or are we going to have to pick their location out of your dying brain? In case you've forgotten, all we need from you Spritans is your genes. Your bodies are disposable." The Prime Other's voice is soft and laden with menace. The subtle hint of glee sickens me. Lucas's hand rubs the small of my back but offers no comfort.

The Prime's voice leaves no room for doubt. If Ko keeps our secret, it won't be without great personal cost. I doubt it's possible to withstand the kind of abuse the Others are capable of dishing out. Not for long.

Not forever.

Cadi snaps her fingers. I blink several times, adjusting to the candlelit kitchen in the building in the Wilds. I put my arms around myself, trying to hold it together. A short while ago it felt safe here. Now, no place will ever feel safe again. Lucas's eyes meet mine, full of all the distress, confusion, and guilt fighting for prominence in my own heart.

Cadi tries speaking but her voice breaks and she pauses, blinking rapidly. After a deep breath she finds the strength to continue. "I'm not sure how much he's revealed about your enchantments—protections—or your possible talents. Their means of torture are. . .convincing. He is strong, but no one can hold out indefinitely. They might know everything. At the very least, they are searching for you. Quietly, at the moment."

Responsibility for Ko's predicament has the substance and weight of a giant lead ball tied to my heart, pulling against each beat. My entire life his name, his note, has anchored me. His name was my promise that someday life will make sense. To see him imprisoned, suffering over the knowledge of my existence, makes a lump settle in my throat and my eyes burn.

"They know how we smell." Lucas's voice sounds hard, dead.

Cadi's head snaps up. "Are you sure?"

Lucas tells her about Deshi and dismay streaks her features.

"They will stop at nothing to find you. Nothing."

"But why? Why do they care about us at all?" The obnoxious, high-pitched whining of my own voice makes me want to slap myself, so I focus on calming down.

"The Others are seekers of knowledge, for one thing, and are scholars in the area of gene manipulation. They want to answer the simple question of what you might be capable of, given your parentage. Also because they can't run the risk that you possess a hidden ability that could undermine them. Your planet is apparently rich in the resource they need to survive. They aren't ready to go. Last, the Elements humiliated the Prime by deliberately disobeying him. He'll make an example of them by killing you."

Our odd talents will be the death of us. The heat, the cold, the undoing of the human veils. Lucas's hand squeezes my knee, hard. It feels like a warning. I keep my mouth shut about our abilities.

Lucas keeps his hand on me, chilling through my jeans. "What's the resource they need? How do they choose their host planets?"

Cadi keeps her eyes on her cold cocoa and bites her lower lip. She passes a hand absentmindedly over the top and it steams again. "I can't answer that. It's a secret the Others guard with single-minded tenacity. Only they know the source of their survival. From the moment of birth each Other mind is constrained, to a certain extent. The part of their brains harboring the secrets of their people is cut off from their ability to communicate." She shakes her head, looking frustrated. "I'm sorry. It's not easy to explain. But this restricted area in their brain is impenetrable, as far as we know."

"So, they're good at the mind-control thing and erecting these veils that make people believe they're happy with the way things are. How did they do it, though? Take over Earth? There are so many more humans than Others." My teeth clack together as late autumn wind rattles the windows.

"You're cold. Let me help."

Cadi snaps her fingers again and the kitchen goes black.

Nothingness surrounds me, and in the moments before my vision returns, the smell of jasmine, fresh and in bloom, wafts beneath my nose. Honeysuckle. Roses. Next, a warm, satisfying breeze tickles my cheek. Water laps gently, rhythmically. Tension unwinds from my neck and back as comfort and calm envelops me.

A small hand presses down on my arm. "You can open your eyes."

The scene that greets me nearly knocks me out of my chair.

Wait.

I'm no longer sitting in a chair, but a boat. The floor is greenish blue water, and in front of me the sun sinks toward the horizon. The foliage is in bloom; the yellows, reds, pinks, purples, and blues dazzle me. The trees are green and lush like the grass covering the ground underneath them. Small pricks of light blink in the dusk.

Lucas gasps in amazement beside me, looking around in every direction. Cadi reclines in the bow of the boat with us, wearing shorts and a tank top. Her tiny feet are bare. She's adjusted other small details as well. Instead of long pants, Lucas wears tan shorts and a short-sleeved polo shirt the same color of blue as the one he had on before. Instead of sneakers, he has on flip-flops.

Looking down at my own clothes, I feel a bit naked. The modest jeans and sweater have been replaced with a light pink dress. Small embroidered white flowers adorn the flowing skirt, which lands a bit shorter than Mrs. Morgan would have approved of. The top of the dress exposes a fair amount of my chest, and is supported by skinny straps. I've heard of these—sundresses. Never had an occasion to wear one, though. My feet are still stuck in my dirty white sneakers, but she's stolen my socks.

I'm not cold, despite the generous amount of exposed skin. The hot breeze moves through the trees, floating the intoxicating aroma of the flowers out to the boat. A force—powerful, foreign, yet somehow recognizable—blossoms in my center. It flows through my organs, spills out my pores. I feel like I can do anything.

This is so strange. And awesome. Definitely awesome.

Lucas regains his powers of speech but doesn't stop staring at me. "What is this place?"

"It's not an actual place. It's summer. I thought Althea might like to see it."

She was right. "How did we get here?"

"Just a trick of the imagination. A rather simple one, honestly. We aren't physically here, we are still sitting in the kitchen."

"I belong here," I breathe out.

Cadi studies me with a sorrowful stare. "Yes, you do."

Lucas grimaces and wipes his forehead, already beading with sweat. "Little warm, don't you think?"

Cadi laughs, the sound lilting and dreamlike. "For you, Lucas. If we get another chance, I would be happy to show you winter, though I much prefer summer myself. No offense." She leans back on her elbows and dangles her bare feet over the edge of the boat. Her toes make little circles in the water. "I'll answer your question now that you're comfortable. First of all, the Others don't control minds but emotions. Their veil separates beings from powerful feeling, anything that might inspire one to act out. Love. Anger. Affection. Jealousy. Protectiveness. Your species has more than most, a factor they did not expect and that gave them trouble at the beginning. They Broke many thousands before figuring out they have to purge the pent-up emotions."

The word catches my attention. "Purge?"

"Yes, the yearly purging. The Others set it up as a tradition, but the point is to give them access to large groups at a time. They drain the bad feelings: the passionate urges, the trapped resentment, and anything else that won't work in their favor from behind the veils. If veiled humans aren't purged, they Break."

After years of wondering what is wrong with everyone, this makes so much sense.

Most of it, anyway.

Lucas interrupts the silence. "So, even though we don't get purged, we aren't Broken because the Others never put up veils in our minds."

"Because they didn't know about us until this autumn." I never thought I could feel so thankful for being different.

"Yes. Your minds are your own. Mostly."

"You said the Others communicate through some kind of tunnels. We're part Other. Can they get inside our heads, too?" It's a concern that's been plaguing me since the first time I heard Fire's voice tonight.

Worry lines crease Cadi's smooth forehead. "I have never sought you out in the tunnels, but it's possible. They can enter mine—and Ko's, as you saw." She studies my face with great concentration for a moment. "The Others, the way their minds are connected, it's like a huge cavern. A hive. They exist on many levels, in countless tunnels, down twisting paths. Each Other has their own alcove. They could find you, if they suspected you had one."

It's always when my guard falls that Fire's voice spreads through my mind. I resolve to try harder to keep her out. If she can find me in there, what's to stop the Prime Other, or Deshi, from doing the same thing? They're both staring at me, so I change the subject. "The Elements are different than I expected."

Lucas nods. "Me, too—warmer somehow. They seemed more human than Other to me."

Cadi's eyes soften as she hears the longing we're trying to hide. "They are Other, children. Before experiencing love and parenthood, the Elements were as callous and merciless as the rest of their race. I will not tell you lies about the things they have done, the worlds they have helped destroy. Still, they are changed. Loving their Partners instilled humanity inside their alien bodies. I am not surprised you sensed it when you saw them for yourselves." Her eyes hold no judgment. "We need to go soon. The Others monitor my whereabouts."

Lucas gives me a sideways glance full of suspicion. "Why does she look like that?"

Cadi laughs, the infectious tinkling putting a grin on my own face. "The two of you have most likely not even grazed the potential of your abilities. Your natural season brings them closer to the surface."

"Wait, what do I look like?"

He screws up his face. "It sounds stupid."

"Oh, come on. I want to know!"

"Like you're glowing, okay?" His cheeks deepen to a scarlet red.

Cadi and I both laugh, and after a minute Lucas chuckles as well. I grab his hand and hold it in my lap.

"One last thing. You told us how they control humans, but how do so few Others conquer whole planets?"

It's a good thing Lucas is here, I'm too infused with glee over being in the warmth to think up proper questions. Cadi leans over to pick at her big toenail. I notice for the first time that her toes are fused together.

"They do it by not making a show, not presenting a threat. The Others land on a new planet without detection, and the first thing they do is determine the most significant rulers in each quadrant. Then they send the Elements in, one to each."

I pipe up. "I thought it hurt them to be separated."

"It does, but it's not for long and they can communicate in their way. Voluntary separation is easier." She sits back, scratching her cheek. "On Earth, the Others sent Pamant to a place called China, Apa to France, Vant to Brazil, and Flacara, your mother, to America. Each had a small contingent of Others with them. They began slowly, but within six months the leaders of those countries were veiled and under the control of the Others. They began peaceful negotiations with more humble countries to join them. The ones who resisted were taken by force. Many people died, more were Broken and disposed of. For a few years, the four original countries remained.

324

Eventually Earth's population dwindled until now everyone resides in what used to be America."

My mind reels. More places exist on our planet than just the Other cities. Until a few weeks ago, I never guessed something more than animals and death lay outside the boundaries. I want to see a map, a picture of this America, these places the Elements fell in love.

The three of us lapse into silence and float, gently rocked into a daze by the rippling water. It's so lovely. As the sun slips toward the horizon a new whirring noise greets my ears. "What's that?"

Lucas answers. "Cicadas. They're bugs. Huh. Guess you wouldn't have heard them before."

The sound is wonderful. I kick off my shoes and copy Cadi, dragging my toes in water as warm as a bath.

Lucas sits up so fast the boat nearly tips over. "What time is it?"

As the sun slips away, Cadi snaps her fingers one last time. An overwhelming sense of sadness conquers me as we find ourselves back in the collection center. Cold air worms its way under the door and around the windowsill, chilling me.

A clock chimes five times.

"Althea, we've got to go. It'll take us more than an hour to get home and wake up is at seven." Lucas pulls me to my feet and we yank on our coats and boots. Cadi follows us out the front door and to the edge of the clearing, stopping abruptly.

I look back at her. It's not fair that she knows everything about me when *I* don't know the first thing about me. The urge to break the rules, to stay out here talking all day and night, claws at me. Cadi catches me off guard and hugs me tight. She stares at Lucas for a moment, a fond expression tilting her mouth. "It's odd, Lucas not wanting to trust me. He's always been more trusting than you. It's rather sweet."

I wonder what she means by Lucas's distrust being sweet. "Can't you come with us, or stay longer? What are we going to do about the interviews?"

Her eyes darken and look deep into mine. "I am not free to come and go as I please, Althea. I can't even step outside this clearing unaccompanied. Come back tomorrow night, if you can manage it. I can help you escape, if it comes to that. I still have hope Ko's work will hold."

I nod, hugging her back and breathing in her woodsy scent. Lucas and I adjust our sky bearings to take us east, and use the stars to navigate our way back to town. The night is cold and dark, but the blackness eases to a silky blue over the next forty minutes. We don't speak. The revelations of this night crack and sizzle along my synapses, warm my heart and chill my bones.

Who—no, *what*—we are is so unthinkable.

A loud growl knocks me out of my thoughts and back into the real world. Lucas stops, looking as dazed as I feel. We slip through a couple of bushes, stopping short when we see some animals in a standoff.

Small and grey with black stripes ringing their tales and eyes, the creatures don't notice they have an audience. Two bigger ones have a smaller one cornered against a tree. The little one vacillates between whimpering and growling as the larger ones advance, loud snarls ominous and menacing.

One attacks the little guy and he squeals. Lucas runs forward with two sticks in his hands, banging them together. When he gets closer he uses one to fling the assailant off its victim and into the bushes. It scurries away, and the second bully follows suit. My heart races and all four layers of my clothes soak through with sweat in seconds as Lucas bends down to check on the littlest creature.

I scream for him to stop and run straight at him, but it's too late.

25

The animal launches from its huddled, protective stance into Lucas's legs, knocking him backward onto his butt. It snarls and bites and claws; Lucas struggles and grunts with the effort to get free. I race over to kick it, but it lets go and runs the opposite direction of its attackers, disappearing into the forest.

I shoot a panicked glance around the area, but we're alone again, at least for now. Lucas's face is white and slick with sweat. He takes several deep breaths as I drop to my knees and wrap my hands around his face. His left pant leg is ripped open and dark red blood colors the frayed edges.

"Are you okay?"

Pain flickers as he tries to smile. "Fine. I guess you were right about the animals, after all."

My hands drop to my sides. "You shouldn't have gotten so close. He was frightened to death already. You look like some sort of giant to him."

Lucas reaches out a shaking hand to tug his ruined pant leg over the injury. "Well, well, what's this? Althea defending the animals?"

"I'm not defending them, exactly. I'm saying *you* were stupid. This isn't our world, out here. It's theirs."

He flinches as his fingers graze a gaping slash along his calf. My stomach turns at the metallic scent of blood but I push it away and lean in to inspect the wound. Flaps of jagged skin open to reveal red tissue and bubbles of something white.

"It's deep, Lucas. We need to get home. Can you walk?"

He nods and struggles to his feet. I pretend not to see him wince, and set a slower pace as we walk the last twenty minutes to the boundary. Lucas doesn't have as difficult a time with the climb over the fence as I expect. But the incident with the animals makes us later—it's nearly six forty-five before we get back to our street. No time to fix Lucas. "Get that thing cleaned and bandaged."

"Remember dinner tonight, with Mr. Morgan."

It's Tuesday, time for our Parent Sanction. If Mr. Morgan approves of our courtship, then we'll have to schedule one with Lucas's fake parents, too. If we live that long. "Right. See you in a bit."

I race home, shutting off my alarm about five minutes before Mr. Morgan shouts a good morning up the stairs. My heart thumps as I take a shower and stuff breakfast in my face.

Mr. Morgan is even keeled this morning. "I spoke with the Crawfords. Lucas will definitely be coming here this evening for dinner. I've ordered something special."

I nod and take our dishes to the sink, kissing him goodbye and hurrying out the front door for Cell. The sight of Lucas waiting for me, looking clean and healthy, eases my tension a bit. "How are you? How's your leg?"

"It hurts, but I'll live. I cleaned it in the shower and made a bandage out of a shirt."

"Is it still bleeding?"

"Yeah, but it's slowing down." He tries to hide a limp.

I choose to ignore the development, instead punching him lightly on the arm. "So are you ready for our Sanction dinner with Mr. Morgan tonight?"

"As ready as I'll ever be."

We fall silent when students litter the sidewalk in front of us. We pass through the front doors of the Cell and go about our day. My legs jiggle all the way through, fingers tapping tables and desks. A super annoying twitch finds my right eye after lunch and refuses to vacate the premises. A reminder to calm down, issued to myself every few minutes, keeps the sweat to a minimum. Lucas joins us girls at lunch, but his presence isn't as soothing as usual. Since my brain resists focusing in block or paying any type of attention to the Monitors, I let it linger on all the reasons fueling this crazy, trapped feeling.

Cadi.

Learning the Others are looking for me.

Hearing that the Others murdered my human parent, that Fire is a prisoner.

It's everything. Most of all, it's not being able to ask Cadi all the questions we need answered. It's driving me completely crazy.

By the end of chemistry, my heart races with anticipation. In a few hours we'll be back with her, maybe figuring out how to get out of here.

Lucas and I plow through the front doors when Cell ends, but not fast enough to avoid Deshi. Tearing my hair out—or his—doesn't seem wise, so instead we agree to join him on a trip to the pizza parlor.

Our Cellmates must have decided on bowling, because the restaurant is all but empty when we grab a table. We're alone. With an Other. One who seems very interested in the two of us. After last night I second-guess every move, wonder if I'm giving us away.

The video screen on the table takes our order, and five minutes later three hot slices of pepperoni pie slide

331

off the conveyor belt and onto our table. It should look and smell wonderful.

Should. But doesn't.

Eating wouldn't be easy even without Deshi's rotting mushroom smell permeating the air, but I've got to try. Lucas blanches as he takes a bite but Deshi is too intent on his own meal to notice. He looks up after a minute, still chewing. It doesn't stop him from talking, and keeping a smile on my face while I watch strings of mashed-up cheese hang from his teeth is excruciating.

"So, why do you guys think the Wardens are *really* in town?" He watches us both with measured intensity.

I don't know what period Deshi has chemistry, but I suppose it doesn't actually matter.

Lucas swallows his bite of pizza with some effort before he answers. "I'm sure it's no big deal. Maybe they're looking for some of us to work for them or something. That would be cool."

"Work for them?" Deshi sounds surprised, and to be honest, so am I.

"Yeah, you know. Like assistants, or rider pilots, or something."

This just keeps getting better and better. Lucas is totally winging it.

Deshi keeps eating and watching Lucas with thinly disguised irritation, then turns his gaze my direction. When he first arrived in Danbury he acted too open to seem all the way human, but friendly. Now, he seems impatient all the time. It ramps up my fear, the notion that he's anxious for something to happen, that we're running out of time.

"What about you?" Deshi lobs the question at me this time.

"Me? No, thanks. I want to work in Travel like my dad."

His tight smile lances open my bravado. "No, I mean what do you think of the interviews?"

"Oh." My palms feel slick, pizza grease mixing with sweat. "Not much, I suppose. Maybe what Lucas said. Maybe something else. Who cares?"

"Just wondering what you'd say. You two are so interesting." Deshi bites into his slice with more force than necessary. The smell of decomposition makes me think the skin he's wearing is nearing its expiration date. Maybe that looming deadline is what's making him so irritable.

Does he only suspect us or does he know? He can't be sure or he'd alert the Prime Other.

Wouldn't he?

We finish up our snack and tell Deshi we've got to go get ready for our Sanction. I hop in the shower at home, more to be alone than anything else. The revelations from Cadi's memories are too much to handle all at once. I mean, I've met my mother—in a sense—and learned that the Others executed my father. I've watched the only person I've trusted my entire life—until Lucas—tortured for information about me.

The Wardens are here searching for us.

My mother talks in my mind.

It's still unbelievable that Fire is my mother—the most powerful of the Elements. The woman whose reflection I've stared at as it hung on Cell walls and felt nothing but fear. Even in the room with her, watching her cry over the death of my father and worry about my safety, indecision dominated.

There's a spark of something good in her, and knowing she loved me pushes my fear into a slide toward uncertainty. I think about how my father must have loved her. Enough to risk death to be together. They gave up everything for each other, and then for me. Their child.

Until now, love has been an abstract emotion. It's a word people use, like *I love roasted potatoes*. When people Partner they promise to love each other, but it means nothing. Or at least it didn't before. When

Lucas's father's face tightened, voice scraping out the words *"we loved them. . .they loved us,"* I felt it for the first time. Love. What it must be.

Out of nowhere the memory of Lucas's kiss bubbles up. Those feelings he sets off in me don't have a name. It's not love. Not yet.

But maybe something like it.

Okay, Althea. Focus. Thinking about normal teenage things such as Lucas coming over for the Parental Sanction helps take my mind off everything else. My growing feelings for him should be insignificant in the grand scheme of my life. Still, the idea of this dinner sends squirrels chasing one another around in my stomach.

Hot water runs over me, washing in rivulets down the drain. A hard stream pulses from the showerhead, kneading the strain out of my neck and shoulders. I wonder what Lucas thinks about tonight, if he's sorry he kissed me, if—in a different world—he'd want to court me for real.

It may be selfish and trivial, but having Lucas at my side is the most important thing right now. Even the thought of being captured and killed by the Others can't win out over thoughts of the boy with blue eyes like my own. No one else understands what I'm going through, what it means to find out I'm not human.

He's the only person on Earth who gives me hope. My past and future are tied up in this one boy. To break the connection would cause unimaginable pain. Ko and Cadi both mentioned that separation caused the Elements discomfort. Could it be the same with us?

I turn the shower off and towel myself dry. Perusing my closet for something that doesn't look like I'm trying too hard, I settle on a knee-length brown skirt and a soft, light pink sweater.

Makeup is hard to do, but looks okay after some work. My hair is thick and I'm unused to wrestling it into something other than a ponytail. Tears fill my eyes as I remember how Mrs. Morgan would curl my hair. The mixer was probably the last time it will ever look so pretty. Curling it myself would turn into a disaster, so instead I dry it and brush it out straight until it shines. I search my reflection for traces of my parents. Maybe my father's ears, or freckles, but the red hair is surely a gift from Fire.

I still can't think of my mother by her real name. I try it out. *Flacara.*

Nope.

The door rings and my stomach flutters. The mirror confirms the red tinge creeping into my cheeks. So much for makeup.

"Thea! Your young man is here. Come on down!"

He called Lucas my "young man." And right in front of him. Balls.

Calm down. Lucas isn't going to think anything of it.

The voice in my head—*her* voice—makes sense, but I tell it to shut up.

Even though he kissed me, it's not like we've had any talks about anything serious, never mind Partnering for real. The only reason we're even having the Sanction is because that Other questioned us in the park.

The fluttering increases at the sight of Lucas, setting me on edge and causing my hands to shake. He looks handsome in tan pants and a light blue button-down instead of his typical jeans and T-shirt. The shirt matches his eyes, which seem to reach out and hold me from across the room. He smiles. The fluttering turns to flapping. Like a flock of birds have joined the wrestling squirrels.

"Hey, Althea."

"Hi." Oh, no, that croaked out. I clear my throat.

"Well, dinner won't be here for a few minutes, so why don't we all sit down and watch the news?" Mr. Morgan beams at us, waving one arm in an inviting arc toward the living room.

Lucas and I follow him through the arched doorway and settle onto the empty love seat. Mr. Morgan takes the couch, choosing to focus on the television instead of us. He seems nervous, too, and it's nice not to be the only one, because Lucas is as cool as a cucumber. He nudges me with an elbow when Mr. Morgan's not looking, his eyes smiling in amusement at the jumping anxiety fluttering about the room. I don't know how he takes things in stride like that. I try to copy his playfulness, crossing my eyes at him until the voice on the television captures my attention.

A human reporter stands outside a home, loitering next to an irritated Warden. "Sir, can you tell us what happened here today?"

"A tragedy. A couple lived in this house and the man Broke. His Partner either didn't realize the nature of his issue, or refused to report it. He killed her, then took his own life. Their young boy has also been removed." Worry trickles into the Warden's unemotional tone.

The reporter goes on, the same pleasant and unconcerned air about him. "This is interesting news. Have you ever heard of anything like this happening before? I know I've never witnessed it in Portland."

Portland? Without thinking about Mr. Morgan being in the same room, my hand finds its way into Lucas's. Everyone's eyes are riveted to the television.

"No, nothing of this magnitude. We all know people Break, and we remove them from the general public. Violence is unheard of, until now."

The Warden turns and walks away without waiting to see if the reporter has any additional questions. A small child sits forgotten on the front steps, his elbows balanced on his knees and his head resting on his hands. His eyes are dry and empty as he watches two floating cots meander out the front door on the screen, controlled by a white-clad Other like the ones who collected Mrs. Morgan. The outlines of bodies are visible under the sheets, and bright red splotches stain the white fabric. My stomach churns at the sight, which reminds me of Greg's head smashed open on that rock. Reese's hand sliced open in chemistry. The blood dripping from my Cellmates' faces at the Family Outing.

I resist the urge to bury my face in Lucas's shoulder.

Mr. Morgan looks unbothered; he just grunts and sits back. Then the door rings again, making both Lucas and me jump up from the love seat.

Mr. Morgan shoots us an amused smile. "Hungry, kids? Don't worry. I'll get the food. You two go on in and set the table."

Hungry is the last thing I am after seeing the news report.

As we step through the kitchen door into the cold, brightly lit space, Lucas turns to me. "What do you make of that?"

"I don't know. But if they put this veil up, erase our memories, feelings, and who we were before, but then it's suddenly gone. . ."

"It must be like waking up and having no idea where you are, who you are, what year it is, anything. Terrifying," Lucas finishes for me.

The unbidden thought of the white, blood-soaked sheets rises in my mind's eye. It dawns on me I have no idea what humans would act like without a veil. "If the humans *are* violent, maybe it's better this way. If they have no emotions, they can't get angry."

"You don't mean that."

Lucas walks over to the cabinets and opens the doors one by one until he finds the plates. I take the stack from him and place them around the table, then point him to the glasses while I get silverware out of the drawer.

"I don't know. I guess just because they have the capacity for violence doesn't mean they all act on it. I like my emotions, most of the time."

We pass each other in the center of the room and he gives me a gentle bump on the hip. "Except for when my kisses make you swoon, right? Then emotions can be a bear."

He's grinning, and I can't help but return it. "I did not *swoon*, Lucas. And don't go acting like you didn't enjoy it."

Lucas pecks my cheek, cooling the flush crawling across it, and pulls away just as Mr. Morgan enters the kitchen. He arranges the food on the table, and the meal is indeed one of my favorites: lasagna, salad, and garlic bread. It smells wonderful, but my stomach remains queasy as I fill the glasses up with ice and water.

Dinner is quiet and uneventful. Lucas holds my hand under the table, intertwines our fingers as Mr. Morgan asks him about the Crawfords and what they do for a living. He marches out the typical parental questions, wanting to know what Lucas would like as a Career, his favorite subject in Cell, and more random information that means nothing to the two of us. The surreal nature of the dinner scene twists longing through me.

If only those things *were* important to us, too.

*

Lucas is waiting for me on the back porch several hours later, anxious to get going. A sickly pallor glistens on his face and fatigue engraves lines around his eyes.

"Are you okay?"

"I'm fine." His words slur; he sounds exhausted.

"Lucas, if something's wrong—"

"I said I'm fine. Let's go."

We cross the boundary and use the sky to get our bearings. No animals impede our path tonight, and though I'm no longer afraid of them on principle, I'm happy to be left alone.

Halfway to the collection center, Lucas's breath turns ragged and shallow. I debate asking how he's doing again but doubt he'll give me an honest answer. The dread in my gut returns and warns me to keep an eye on him. It's probably the animal scratch from last night. He wouldn't let me see it after dinner; he insisted he took care of it. His hand is damp and clammy when I slip mine inside it, and my worry deepens.

We near the clearing and I come to an abrupt stop, pulling a stumbling Lucas with me back into the brush. A rider idles in front of the collection center, the back hatch open. Four Wardens swarm away from it and across the grass in the front and the back of the building, then hold their positions.

Cadi.

The Wardens talk among themselves, their voices carrying in the still, quiet night. "Why are we wasting time on this half-breed?"

"Chief said the Prime's office lost contact with her for a period last night."

Not all of them are visible from our position, but one issues a foreign, teeth-chattering sound. Its high pitch stabs my head, leaving an ache and twitchy fingers. I barely stop my hands from covering my ears.

Not thirty seconds after it begins, Cadi's voice shatters the quiet. "What are you doing here, Wardens?"

Her voice holds no fear. I have enough for both of us. My mind races, skipping over ways to help her, to get all of us out of here. It lands on nothing.

Cadi strolls off the porch and all four Wardens wait to trap her, fanning out in an arc to prevent her escape. Even in the dark I detect the hitch in Cadi's step.

One of them snorts, an ugly noise. "You know why we're here, Spritan. Let's go. Come quietly, if you know what's good for you."

"You can't hurt me. My knowledge is too valuable and we both know it. Imprison me, yes. Kill me, no."

A pleading undertone marks her words. The Wardens sense it and laugh. Two of them circle behind her as a fifth figure emerges from the rider and strides toward Cadi with purpose.

"We can't kill you, Cadi, not yet. Hurting you, though, is a different story."

The voice, familiar and sickening all at once, immobilizes me.

Deshi. He's here.

26.

Without warning, Cadi pitches forward onto the grass, landing hard on her knees and keening with an agony that curls my toes. She thrashes around, the scream gurgling into breathless gasps as she twists onto her back and pounds her head into the ground. The urge to shout, to run to her, thumps inside me, but there's nothing to do. All that would result in is confirming Deshi's suspicion about us, and then he'll know Cadi's helping us, too.

Cadi goes still, limp as a rag doll, and he walks to her side, pressing a black-booted foot into her face. Her voice is almost too soft to hear, broken and laced with defeat. "Let's just get this over with."

Deshi kicks her in the ribs, hard enough that the cracking *thunk* carries to the trees. His voice, low and thick with hatred, attacks her. "Don't play with me. My father and I know you're helping their abominable children."

Tears spring to my eyes and my fists clench hard, fingernails biting into my skin. Lucas's rattling breath snags. Cadi rolls onto her back, chest heaving. She remains silent, probably unwilling to risk another kick.

345

Deshi continues, still murmuring in his grating tone. "What did you think, Cadi? That after my father discovered what Ko did, he would trust you? You should have known he only sent you here, so close to town, as a test. Not only have you confirmed their identities, you've verified where your loyalty lies."

Terror lashes through me, my knees weak and my stomach spasming to the cadence of his voice.

Cadi peers up at him from the ground. "You're lying, Chief. You don't know who they are. Their enchantments are exceptional."

He laughs and the evil sound rends my shreds of confidence. Lucas slips his fingers in between mine, our hands shaking.

"Maybe your Spritan abilities did obscure them, but no longer. You can't protect Lucas and Althea any more than you can protect Deshi. We haven't found the fourth yet, but we know he's in Portland after the incident today."

I swallow a gasp—he knows our names. Not only that, but what does he mean, she can't protect Deshi? Isn't *he* Deshi? He doesn't seem to need protection to me.

We have to run, hide, anything but stand still, but the heavy weight of duty makes me stay, and witness what will become of Cadi. Once again our existence

346

threatens a life. I can't comprehend the fact that there are people, more than one even, willing to die to keep me alive.

"If you know who they are, what are you doing out here?"

"I've known about Lucas and Althea for weeks. Found a fish in the Cell basement and killed it, then installed cameras in the stairwells. My father asked me to watch them, to make sure they didn't escape, but to wait until the interviews to bring them in. He wanted to find out which side you're on."

"Now you know." Cadi stands and stares him down.

He returns her gaze, not backing down but taking a step forward. "You accomplished nothing in the end. I'm going to bring them in as soon as we're finished with you."

As he stops talking the Wardens converge, too fast for Cadi to make a move. She doesn't even try. They pick her up and haul her to the rider. She begins to struggle when they toss her in the back. From our position at the corner of the house, we have a direct line of sight into the open hatch. The light above their heads illuminates the scene and it's like watching a movie in slow motion. Tears trickle down my burning cheeks, every inch of me on fire.

The Wardens in the rider hold Cadi down by her shoulders as her legs continue to flail. Her foot connects with one of them and he grunts before backhanding her across the face. She goes still for a moment, and when she returns to struggling her movements are more subdued.

Deshi's gruff voice shouts orders at the two in the rider. "Get the vial and make her drink it. I refuse to deal with this conspirator any longer."

One of the Wardens digs in a bag and produces a vial. He pinches Cadi's nose closed until she can't hold her breath anymore and opens her mouth. The liquid pours in, and the Warden clamps his free hand over her lips so she can't spit it out. It takes her a while to give up and swallow, but she finally does.

Sweat soaks through my clothes and drips into my eyes. I picture running across the lawn, jumping Deshi from behind. Pulling his hair, biting him, scratching his eyes out. I know I can't, though. Getting thrown in that rider with Cadi won't help anyone.

My eyes are glued to the tiny, beautiful, caring woman who tried to help us, to warn us. The last thing I see before the harsh trunk light blinks off is Cadi's midnight gaze. As the door slams shut she goes still, and her eyes go dark.

Lucas tugs my arm, pulling me into the trees. He releases me once we're well hidden and I drop to my knees, clapping both hands over my mouth to keep the cries from spilling out. My eyes, wide and filled with tears, refuse to focus.

"Althea, look at me."

I shake my head.

"Look at me!"

He kneels and takes me by the arms, wrenching my hands away from my face. He's shaking as his hands latch onto my biceps with a death grip. His fingertips squeeze painfully, pressing through my jacket and sweater and into my skin.

The shattering of my control surges, explodes, and the blast of heat sends Lucas backing away. The tears roll unchecked and sobs wrench from my chest. Trying to stay quiet only makes them harder to contain.

Lucas stares at me with a lost expression. The anger and sadness abate after a while and I want nothing more than to curl up into a ball and disappear. Instead, I throw myself at Lucas and he catches me in his arms. His emotions run high, too, as evidenced by the immediate chill that transfers to me upon touching him. I don't care, and burrow closer until we are both a more natural, warm temperature. His fingertips trail up and down my neck, providing comfort with each pass. I want to stay here forever, but I can't. We can't.

I have to be strong. For Lucas. For Cadi. For us all.

I pull back, a little embarrassed by my outburst. He reaches over and rubs the tears off my cheeks.

His voice trembles and the thick sheen of sweat on his pale face glows. "I'm so sorry, Althea, that you had to see that. I know you liked her."

"I can't believe we didn't help her—" My words choke off in a sob.

"We couldn't. Cadi came here hoping to give us a chance. She wouldn't want us to give it up."

An awed tone creeps into his voice and for the first time, I think *he* likes Cadi.

"Is she. . .is she dead, Lucas? Or Broken?" The possible answer scares me, but the need to know outweighs the onslaught of pain.

"I don't know. You heard how they talked to her, and we saw how different she was. Cadi wasn't one of them, not really."

He keeps using the word *was* instead of *is* and it's enough to signal his belief. He thinks she's gone.

"This is our fault."

He wants to say it's not, I can read it in his face. He can't though, because it *is* our fault. Maybe didn't hurt Cadi, but our existence hurt Cadi. After

350

spending all my life feeling so unimportant to everyone, it's hard to imagine the opposite might be true.

Now Cadi's gone, leaving an ocean of unanswered questions in her wake. Deshi knows about us, is planning on taking us away during our interview—or perhaps before. Maybe now, tonight. Either way, there's no way I can face him again.

"Althea, we have to go."

Lucas slides an arm over my shoulders and pulls me close, making walking difficult. We keep kicking each other's feet as we slog over the wet, smushy ground. The way he leans his weight on me is bothersome, and this morning's limp is more pronounced. After several minutes my thoughts are too much to bear in silence.

"What do you think they'll do to us?" The words, whispered and laced with fear, signal my surrender.

Lucas stops walking. "We're not giving up, Althea. I'm not going to let them do anything to you. We're going to run. As long as we're together, we can make it."

"Make it?" I shake my head, unmoved by his empty promises. "Make it where? The Others won't stop. We've both seen firsthand what they're capable of. We'll be Broken by this time tomorrow, if that's what they want."

My whole body sags, limp with defeat and begging to crumple. It was my idea first, that we could somehow run and find a way to fight, but seeing their power on display with Cadi sapped my belief. Sure we can run, but they'll find us. Even if there were a way to travel away together, our world is a very small place. They know the cities where we travel.

Lucas's arms go around me as he whispers indistinguishable words into my hair, cool breath sending shivers down my neck. A renewing strength flows into me, sparking a desperate fire in my belly. Maybe running can only prolong our lives, but maybe it will buy us enough time to find a way to change the game.

It's small, but it's hope just the same, and it bolsters my spirit. "We'll need to take some food with us, to tide us over until we figure out what to do."

"Yes. We'll go home, grab a bag, and go. If we both fill up and take care with how much we eat, hopefully we'll be okay until we travel again."

Having a plan makes me feel better. Stronger. And in a blind rush to get out of Danbury. "We should hurry and get back. Deshi could be anywhere."

We walk the rest of the way in silence. My thoughts are a jumbled mess. I want to wish I were human, but the idea of not feeling confuses me. The

352

intensely good but sickening emotions Lucas causes in me aren't worth giving up. Not for anything. What I want is a chance at the life we might have had if the Others had never arrived on our planet.

Of course, that doesn't work either. Without them neither of us would exist.

At least I have Lucas; at least we are in this together.

"You know, I have to admit the two of you surprised me tonight."

Lucas and I stop, turn slowly. We haven't quite reached the fence, haven't made it out of the Wilds, and Deshi's already caught us. How he got here so fast is beyond me, but he's here all the same, stinking of rotting flesh, smirking, pulsing revulsion and fear.

Lucas stands up straight, supporting his own weight in a show of strength. His sickly pallor and sweat-drenched clothes contradict the movement and I tense, ready to grab him if he topples. Deshi strolls from tree to tree, eventually choosing a position between us and the boundary, a three-foot-wide stream at his back.

"How did the two of you get past the boundary?"

We remain silent. I'm not telling him anything.

His gaze focuses on Lucas, a sick smile twisting his thin lips. Words, spoken softly, shout a warning. "You want to play games? Fine by me."

Lucas stiffens and drops to the ground at my side with a groan, grabbing his bad leg as he hits the earth and writhes. White, foamy bubbles gather at the corners of his mouth; his eyes squeeze shut as he groans and tears slip down his cheeks. Pain smudges purple circles under his eyes and something inside me snaps.

I step in front of Lucas and meet Deshi's gaze, holding my hands out in front of me. He thinks I'm asking for mercy.

I'm not.

Fury, white-hot and brimming with hatred, surges through my blood, bubbles out of my veins, and pools in my palms. Without thinking, I push it at Deshi where it belongs. His clothing and hair burst into flames.

He screams, and my stomach twists. Lucas struggles to his knees and gasps, his hands seeking mine. I help him up and together we watch Deshi flail, beating helplessly at the blaze devouring his clothes and licking his blistering skin.

In spite of everything we've learned about what happened to our parents, what the Others plan to do to us, my heart seizes. I told Lucas if he experiments on humans he's no better than the Others. If I let Deshi die, I'm a murderer.

I rush at him, vaguely aware Lucas's voice calling me back. Ignoring the glowing inferno, I push my hands into Deshi's chest and shove him backward. He falls on the bank of the stream, still squirming, beyond the ability to help himself. I plant a foot between his shoulder blades and roll him into the water. The flames extinguish almost immediately and Deshi lies still, burbling water caressing his ruined body.

Adrenaline bleeds out of me, leaving horror and exhaustion in its wake. I sink down onto the muddy riverbank, riveted by the destruction wreaked by my so-called talent. His skin is bright red and swollen with white blisters, charred in places. His hair is mostly gone; only a few chunks remain.

Soft, hesitant footsteps approach and then Lucas sits at my side. "We've got to go, Althea. He's an Other, and by the sound of the conversation back at the collection center, one with a powerful father."

Deshi's chest inflates, deflates, inflates, deflates. He's not dead. I wonder if even Cadi knows how to kill an Other. "What are we going to do with him?"

Lucas's animated response opposes my dull, lifeless tone. "I don't care what we do with him. Leave him. He hurt Cadi. He meant to hurt us."

The wheels of my mind turn, creaking and protesting the process of thought. Cadi said the Others

355

can talk to one another, that they can draw mental pictures and share them through their minds. If Deshi has a cavern in those tunnels or whatever, then I suspect even if he's unconscious the rest of their infuriatingly competent race can locate him. "He's not going to die, and they'll know how to find him."

"They can find his mind in the Other hive."

I nod. "The best we can hope for is to keep him out here, stall them so we have enough time to grab our things and go."

Without a word, Lucas reaches out his hands and places them on the surface of the stream. The water freezes, first around his hands but stretching all the way to the other bank in a matter of seconds. Only Deshi's eyes, nose, and mouth remain above the solid surface, his body sealed beneath the ice.

"Let's go." Lucas struggles to his feet, grimacing with each tiny movement.

"Lucas, you've got to tell me if something's wrong with you."

"It's nothing. I'll be fine."

I don't believe him, but have no choice other than to follow as we cover the rest of the way to the boundary and climb it. For the first time it takes Lucas longer than me. He's hobbling and gasping for breath by the time we reach the Crawfords'. His hands are on fire, hot even to my touch.

He jerks out of my grasp and starts toward the house. "I'll meet you out back in five minutes. Five minutes, Althea. No longer."

Light snores waft from under Mr. Morgan's door and make me question what's real, if the events that transpired in the Wilds these past two nights are a dream. My filthy hands and jeans, along with the stunned horror gurgling inside me, convince me they actually happened.

I run to the bedroom to grab a duffel bag. In goes a pile of warm clothes, along with a couple of blankets, Lucas's note holder, and a toothbrush. As an afterthought I toss in a couple of textbooks, unsure of what information we might need in the weeks to come. Down in the kitchen I sneak bread, crackers, and bottles of water in with the clothes.

In four minutes I'm on the back porch, breath expelling frosty clouds into the air. The first snowflakes of the year drift down, dusting the early morning grass. Lucas is still inside. In the silence, another line from Lucas's booklet rings in my mind, a group about children being beyond the control of their parents and how times are always changing.

Your sons and your daughters

Are beyond your command…
For the times they are a-changin'.

After the massive, life-altering revelations of the past two days the words seem written especially for me.

Lucas and I are, without a doubt, beyond the command of our parents. All of them. The times are changing. I've felt it all autumn; change thick in the air, choking me. It started when the Others found out I existed, and it's not going to stop until they capture me. Or until Lucas and I figure out a way to stop them from ruining this planet.

For the times they are a-changin'.

I've hardly slept in three days and my eyes feel as though someone poured sand inside them and then stomped around on it. The five-minute mark comes and goes. Anxiety blooms, Lucas's face flashing through my mind in a pattern until an aching need pulses through me. He said not to be late.

Grabbing my bag off the deck beside me, my feet take off running. I stop in the Crawfords' backyard, intending to peer through the kitchen window and survey the situation. I need to see him, to make sure he's okay.

On my tiptoes in the new snow, I poke my head up and peek through the blinds into the kitchen. It's empty. Nerves wrestle in my stomach, tangling like my hair in the wind; I can't wait another moment. The back door opens easily with a push. My wet sneakers drip snow across the clean tiles on my way to the stairs.

It's not quite four a.m. on Wednesday morning, so there's no reason to think the Crawfords aren't slumbering away, dreaming mindless dreams about whatever the Others approve. The house is identical to my own, so I take a guess that Lucas's room will be in the same spot as mine.

The comforter is dark gray with cream-colored sheets peeking out from underneath. Lucas's familiar wintery scent lingers on his things. At first it seems deserted, this place where he should be, but as I turn to make sure I haven't missed him somehow, I see a bare foot sticking out of the closet.

Inside, a dark bloodstain seeps into the carpet underneath Lucas's body.

27.

O n my knees at his side, I reach out a tentative hand, nearly collapsing from relief at the sight of his chest moving up and down. It seems too shallow, but I am not a Healer. His skin, though, I know is wrong—it's too hot. Cold beads of water sprinkle his forehead and upper lip, making his neck and arms slippery. He must have been changing his clothes, as he's in his undershorts, the wound on his leg burning bright red. Streaks reach from the festering center up and down, toward his ankle on one end and disappearing under his shorts in the opposite direction.

Distress over his health and our dwindling chances of disappearing from Danbury before Deshi returns presses against me like a malevolent shadow, stealing my breath and shunting hope away.

"Lucas," I whisper as loud as I dare. When he doesn't respond, I touch my hands to his cheeks, shaking him.

His eyes flutter, trying to open, but only the whites show and he mumbles something unintelligible. Tears gather in my throat, but I swallow them and bite my bottom lip before smacking Lucas's face. When that gets me no response, I sit back on my heels to think. The taste of blood coats my tongue from where I chewed through the skin on my lip. We're supposed to be running away right now, escaping this place and our troubles.

But Lucas can't run. I can't carry him like this. And I'm not leaving without him.

My thoughts race, searching for impossible, hidden answers to the question of what on Earth I'm supposed to do now. A set of violent shudders wrack Lucas's strong shoulders and slide down his body, eliciting a sharp, unconscious cry as his leg scrapes the carpet. The only real option squeezes my heart in a vise.

I'm going to have to get Lucas a Healer.

He's hurt far beyond my ability to help him alone. Something about that animal scratch has infected him from the inside, perhaps even spread to his blood. I want to get away, but Lucas needs medicine. His life trumps my escape, and I cling to the hope that Deshi will remain out of commission long enough for a Healer to fix Lucas and for the two of us to get out after all.

It's hard to talk around the throbbing mess in my throat, so I lean down and press my lips to Lucas's cheek. He calms, at least it seems that way to me, and the shudders lessen to shivers. "I'm sorry. You need help, and I'm not leaving you alone. I'm not."

I get up from the carpet and take two steps to Lucas's nightstand. I can't call for help, can't be caught here with him, but the Crawfords can. My arm swings in a calculated arc, swiping the table lamp into the wall. It smashes into pieces, the shattering ceramic loud enough to wake Lucas's fake parents. I hope they're not deep sleepers.

The inside of the shower is dry and dark, and I wipe silent tears with the back of my hand while I hide and wait. The Crawfords don't disappoint me, creeping down the hallway moments after the noise interrupted the early morning stillness.

"I'm telling you, Robert. I heard something." A woman's voice, tired and scratchy, winds its way through the cleansing room doors.

"We'll just make sure Lucas is asleep and then—" The man's whispered reassurance breaks off with a gasp.

"What happened to him? That's a lot of blood."

"I don't know, Janet," he answers.

Shuffling sounds tell me they're checking out Lucas's condition, and I bite my lip to keep from shouting for them to contact a Healer. After what feels like hours, Mr. Crawford leaves the room to place the call. I wait another lifetime—but probably it's less than five minutes—before feet trample up the stairs.

"Can you tell me what happened?" asks a voice that is not Other at all.

It might be a trick of the imagination, but it sounds like the same portly, mustached Healer who came to our house the night Mrs. Morgan was taken away.

Mrs. Crawford's response comes quickly, steady and strong. "We heard a crash and it woke us. When we came upstairs to check on Lucas, we found him in the closet with the blood on the floor."

"How did he get this cut on his leg?"

"We don't know."

"I think your son will be fine, although he does have a nasty infection and requires immediate treatment. He'll need to be observed, so I'll need to report this incident. Where is the communicator?"

The Healer and Mr. Crawford leave the room again, and the similarities to my own experience slick my palms and neck with sweat. I had hoped the Healer would simply give Lucas a pill to make him better. If he reports this to the same Other who required Mrs. Morgan to be taken to a Regional Healer, Deshi will be informed of the development once he's rescued.

Springs squeak, and the image of Mrs. Crawford sitting on the edge of the bed heats my blood further. I would give anything to be out there holding Lucas's hand, trying to soothe him, but she's not even touching him. My heart breaks in half at the thought that he might feel scared and alone.

This time when the stairs creak, more than one pair of feet pound the thin carpet. The cold slam of their Other-like gait shrinks me into the cold tile, both to get as far away as possible and to use it to cool the fire slinking under my skin.

The voices in the room now are clearly Other, and the harmonic tones make my hands clench into fists. I remind myself that this is what Lucas needs. I have to let the Others take him right now, if that's the way to fix the infection raging through him because of that stupid animal.

"We will accompany your son. Healer, would you please take Mr. and Mrs. Crawford downstairs and complete their statement? We'll get Lucas settled on his transport and get out of your hair." An Other, indistinguishable from all the rest, dismisses Lucas's parents.

Three pairs of feet shuffle from the room. The Others—are they Wardens? The white-clad Others? I have no way to know. And even though my worry for

Lucas dominates every breath, I also hope they stay out of the cleansing room.

"What on Earth happened to this kid?"

Noises accompany their conversation. I think of how they treated Greg, and push it from my mind. The Healer can help Lucas. They'll be careful with him.

"I personally don't give a shit."

"Really, Hanaj? You're going to curse like a human now?"

When the first voice doesn't respond, the second continues. "You know he's the male that Deshi told us to watch. Lucas Crawford. We can let the Healer treat him, but we can't let him go to the Observatory Pod until Deshi talks to him."

Oxygen stales in my lungs. I'm afraid to breathe, scared they'll say something important and I'll miss it. I press scalding hot hands into the shower wall, trying to maintain some kind of composure. They know about us, and they're going to take Lucas somewhere to wait for Deshi.

"We haven't heard from Chief since last night."

That's what Cadi called Deshi, I realize.

"So, we'll take the kid and the Healer to the Cell and keep him in the Administrative Center until Deshi shows up and tells us what to do. Orders are not to dispose of him." The Other who spoke like a human earlier sounds impatient, his words clipped.

They don't say anything else, apparently agreeing on their course of action. Despair fills me. Instead of sending Lucas with a Healer to get help, I've shipped him off with a bunch of Others who'll turn him over to Deshi. The notion that I could still stop what's been put in motion, that using my heated body to overpower two Others and get Lucas away would be much more feasible than taking on Deshi, flutters around but I slap it away.

Lucas still needs help, and I can't give it to him. Being with the Others, even Deshi, is better than being dead. Isn't it?

Helplessness tightens my chest, making it hard to breathe. I bite my knuckles to keep from crying out as they exit the room, leaving a looming silence that says I'm alone up here. After a moment or two I creep out of the cleansing room and back into Lucas's private space, the lingering smell of him making me want to collapse.

Through the window I see the Crawfords' front door bang open and the Others and the Healer exit, and Lucas following on a floating cot. One gestures the bed toward the rider at the curb, then they get inside and slam the doors shut.

The rider, taking away the only person who means anything to me in this world, disappears. My knees give out, dropping me on the floor with my back against Lucas's window seat. I remind myself that all is not lost. I know they're taking Lucas to the Cell, and he'll be there at least the rest of the day. Even if Deshi manages to get help extricating himself from that stream this morning, they have interviews and no one is talking to Lucas until the Healer fixes his leg enough to wake him up.

The earliest they'll be able to move him is this evening. I have the day to figure out how to get into the Cell and get Lucas back.

Before I can find the energy to pick myself up off the floor, footsteps patter down the hall. The Crawfords enter the room, staring at me with comical, surprised expressions a moment later. He's wearing blue-striped pajama pants and a white T-shirt, his ebony skin visible through the worn threads. Glasses perch on his thick nose, magnifying his dark brown eyes. Her legs are pale and bare beneath a nightgown the color of sapphires.

They stop inside the doorway, seemingly unsure of what the protocol is for finding strange girls sitting on the floor of your son's bedroom.

Mr. Crawford clears his throat and attempts a smile. "Hello. What are you doing here?"

I'm careful to keep my frustrated thoughts to myself so I don't Break them, too. "I was, um, looking for Lucas?"

Mrs. Crawford's smile wobbles a little. "He had an accident and had to go away with the Healer. But he'll be back." Confusion thickens in her grass green gaze. "I don't think you should be here."

"Yes, you're not supposed to be here."

Their puzzlement over my intrusion on their already bizarre morning worries me. In the past, no one has commented on my outbursts or pointed out instances where I am somewhere Unacceptable. But now that I know how strong a hold the Others have over the humans, I worry it's too engrained, that Mr. Crawford will report my appearance to the Others. There's only a small chance I'll be able to save Lucas, and getting caught turns that into no chance at all.

Weariness settles in, joining a bone-deep resistance to using my powers to deal with the Crawfords. But time is precious. Deshi could already be awake but still trapped, using his brain tunnels to contact help. The longer I stay hidden the better. I drag myself off the carpet and frown. "Get in the closet."

Their faces morph into masks of stunned bewilderment, almost making me laugh. Mr. Crawford recovers first, putting out a hand to stop his Partner as she steps forward to obey. "No. I think it's time for you to leave."

I step toward the bed, pulling a pillow from under the comforter, and stop beside Mrs. Crawford. Nausea bubbles up as I press the cotton between my hands and push the heat. Acrid smoke rises up, filling my nostrils. I thrust the smoldering pillow toward Mrs. Crawford's chest as flames sprout and flicker from under my palms. It's so hard to say the words around the vomit in my throat. A picture of Lucas at Deshi's mercy flashes in my mind and makes it easier.

"If you don't want me to light her on fire, get in the closet."

It's the weirdest thing, watching them try to process fear without any knowledge of how to be afraid. Their empty eyes flash with emotion, but it quickly disappears. Then Mr. Crawford grabs his Partner's hand and drags her with him into Lucas's closet. They huddle together along the back wall, clothes falling around them like the snowflakes outside.

Tears burn my eyes. "I'm sorry. I'm so sorry."

Before the sight of their blank faces changes my mind I slam the door shut. I press my hand to the brass doorknob, heating it until it melts and spreads from the door to the jamb, effectively trapping them inside. I tell myself they'll be fine; when they don't report for work in a couple hours, someone will look for them. It was good practice at trying to use only the right amount of heat, I suppose, though thinking of scaring them—even if they didn't realize they were scared—as practice makes me sick.

The morning is cloudy and cold. Small lacy flakes continue to waft down from the iron gray sky. My watch says it's just past five, still two hours before the rest of the world will wake up and greet the day.

I grab my bag where I dropped it in the backyard and run for the park. I can't go to Cell right now. I can't go to the Morgans'. Deshi, screaming and on fire, skitters through my overwrought brain. There's only one place I can go to wait out the hours until I can try to save Lucas, and although I want to go get him now, at least I'll have time to strengthen my plan.

And time to come to grips with what I'm going to have to do.

The houses drop from sight and my feet break into a sprint. They don't stop until I've reached the dead section of the boundary, thrown my duffel bag into the Wilds, and scrambled over the top. I pick my way through the underbrush, stopping at a tree with a funny-shaped trunk. Instead of being a perfect circle it has an indentation in one side, about three feet across and two feet deep. I curl into the tree's roots and close my eyes against this impossible situation as hopelessness tightens my chest.

My tension starts to unwind as a plan begins to form. It's not very good; in fact, it's reckless and will most likely get me locked up right along with Lucas, but it's all I've got. It'll probably end up with me captured right along with him, but that's better than being alone again.

I spend some time scanning my chemistry and physics books, researching the melting point of glass and similar materials. Practice would be beneficial, but my emotions flounder around so violently it frightens me that the animals in the Wilds could suffer if the fire gets out of hand. Out here, with nothing but flammable trees and brush as far as the eye can see, flames would be disastrous. Not to mention they would give me away. I'll have to hope that my fire hands, as Lucas termed them, don't let me down when I actually need them.

Exhausted, I unzip my bag, pull out one of the blankets, and wrap it around me. Snuggled inside, aching and raw from both the cold and grief, worry tramples my tenuous hope. My blood carries it from my head to my heart and down to my stomach until my entire body trembles from holding it all in.

Thoughts of Lucas, of what the Others might already have done to him, make me feel ill. I hope the Healer fixed his leg, but if I ever see Lucas again, I am going to punch him right in the face for not telling me how bad it had gotten.

*

Night falls on the forest. Deshi is free of our makeshift imprisonment. Three Wardens opened the gate and rescued him several hours ago. They passed within twenty yards of me, never guessing, never looking.

It's too late to turn back. Alarms have been raised. I didn't go home or to Cell, and the Wardens return and sweep the park. It's after curfew now and they call my name, loud enough for me to hear from this side of the boundary. The fence rattles and I stop breathing.

A laughing, melodious Other voice shatters the still night. "What are you doing, idiot? He said not to bother checking out there."

"I know, but she's not human. How do Chief and the Prime know what she'll do?"

The first one snorts. "She was raised human, though, right? If Chief says she'll walk right into our hands, then she will."

Heavy feet thud into the earth. The second voice, deeper but no less pleasant, sounds sheepish. "I'm not questioning the Prime or the Chief. Just wanted an excuse to get out of this town."

They walk away and my lungs release a shaky breath.

Weeks ago, back when only my life depended on me, I would have given up. Now Lucas's life is in my hands. He's made life tolerable, been my friend and confidant. I can't let him go. Besides, he would do the same for me. There's not a doubt in my mind.

The moon rises as the sun scoots into tomorrow, casting a haunting, silvery glow over the trees and underbrush. The peculiar silence full of sounds that only exists in the Wilds drapes the night. Stars twinkle all around and for a moment I ponder Cadi's stories. I wish I could see Sprita from here; Deasupra was light years away, when it still existed.

Sounds materialize, hoots and scratches that bring back the memories of our mishaps with the animals. A howl echoes in the distance, haunting and free. It sends shivers along my spine and up my neck. The serenity this freedom offers is a lifeline; I clutch it and hang on. I'm free now, like the animals. If I get Lucas out, I'm never going back in there again.

A rustling comes closer and a scraping sounds above me. My muscles don't even twitch, trusting the natural world to behave as it should. Lucas might laugh at my calmness after what happened to his leg. My smile fades as I wonder if I'll ever hear his playful voice again.

I keep waiting, knowing that the longer I hold out, the fewer possibilities there will be for disaster to strike. The humans need to be tucked safe in their homes before I march into town and stir up trouble. I sense someone—something—watching me. It could be an animal, or perhaps Deshi is out here searching for me after all. Like a small child afraid of the dark spaces under my bed, I draw the blanket up around me and bury my face. If I can't see them, they can't see me.

When it's time to go, the moon is high in the sky. Dark, wispy clouds pass in front of it, not dense enough to staunch the light. I tear my eyes away from the void and make my way cautiously back to the fence.

Shadows hide me on the way into town. My heart whispers one last wish for help. If Cadi is listening, maybe she'll throw a bit of luck our way. I'd feel better just knowing she lives.

Four Wardens loiter on the sidewalk, talking. I jerk farther back into the shadows and slip behind a tree trunk large enough to obscure me. I'm afraid they'll hear my gasping breath from where they stand, even though their conversation is far away, barely audible over the sound of my heart pounding in my ears.

"This is dumb. Why didn't we bring them in weeks ago, when Chief found the fish?"

"The Prime wanted to find out who was helping them. Plus, you know how they like to play with the humans."

"He better be right about her taking the bait at the Cell. The Prime isn't going to be happy if he loses the girl."

The Wardens split up and wander down the block, voices fading as they head toward the park. Disgust heats my face and hands. The reminder that Deshi and the Prime Other have known about us for weeks feels cold and slimy inside my mind, an unwelcome invasion. A hot flash of anger follows, spurring me forward with new determination. I know now the idea to keep Lucas at Cell is a trap set for me, but if Deshi thinks they're getting Lucas or me without a fight, he's got another think coming.

I'd worried before about the front doors of the Cell being locked, but now that I know Deshi is counting on my stupidity—or loyalty, depending on how you look at it—I feel sure they'll be open. He wouldn't want to lock me out of his baited snare.

The door pulls open easily in my left hand, confirming the trap. My right palm stretches toward the camera watching my every move. Wild, thrashing emotion travels down my arm into my hand. When my palm feels as though it will explode from the heat bubbling under the skin, I push the heat out of me. It hits the camera, melting it in an instant. An acrid smell hangs in the air as the charred, gooey lump falls off its mount.

Maybe that was a bit much.

Ignoring the dead camera, I head into the building and straight to the Administrator's office. No point in trying to be sneaky. Deshi is expecting me; I don't want to keep him waiting. Chances are, as soon as that camera melted someone alerted him and the Wardens to my presence. Dread pulses and burrows, but the prolonged adrenaline rush deadens the sensation.

The hallways are dark and strangely eerie with the lack of voices and banging lockers. The cameras I pass along the way melt with a flick of my wrist now. A sense of strong, heady power buzzes in my fingertips. Along the way I experiment with pressure, and by the time I pass through the last doorway just the lens melts, the rest of the camera staying mounted on the wall.

When a Warden steps around the corner we both startle.

I avoid his gaze, having no desire to experience the pain of their brain invasion, and scramble backward. My own feet trip me and I land in a heap.

Panic tingles through my limbs and mixes with adrenaline. Massive knots of tension wind tight inside my every muscle. Instinct I didn't even know existed until this moment takes over when he bends and grabs me. Before he gets a good grip I plant both feet into his chest and push with all my might.

He flies backward into a row of lockers, taking strands of my hair with him. He hits hard but stays conscious. I shoot to my feet and take three steps over to where he lies.

His arm lashes out at me. I grab his wrist and the world goes black. I see Lucas. His face is bloody and lumpy. His eyes are purple and closed. I can't tell if he's breathing. Someone laughs. It sounds like Deshi.

The Warden jerks his arm out of my grasp and the world comes back.

There's no time to think about what just happened. Surprise colors the Warden's face; he must have noticed my little foray into his mind. Or into all the Others' minds, their tunnels. Before he recovers I pick up one foot and smash it into his face.

His head snaps back, cracks against the white linoleum. The crunch of bone and flesh tear through my stomach as he goes still. I should tie him up so he doesn't come after me, but there's nothing to bind him with or to.

A kind of trance befalls me, and staring at the flecks of blood and mucus on my dirty tennis shoe fascinates me for several seconds. I shake it off and move again toward the center of the Cell.

No Wardens hang around the outside of the office. They must at least be watching. After all, there's only one way into that office and it's through the front door.

This must be the part where I get caught.

28.

I run the back of my sleeve across my forehead and it comes away soaked through with sweat. Outward calm masks nothing but foreboding. Pure and powerful, it courses through me but doesn't slow me down as I draw up to the doors.

The cameras on either side of the entrance melt in tandem and I confront the problem of the locks. The door won't open unless someone inside hits a button. My chemistry book confirmed that glass melts, but only at an extremely hot temperature. I'm afraid to try and push that much heat out through my hands, so I press my entire body against the crack between the doors. With every emotion simmering so close to my surface, it's never been easier to summon the blinding heat. Fiery warmth oozes out from under my clothes. At first nothing happens.

Then the glass starts to give.

I pull my face away from the superheated doors, afraid they'll burn me. They don't. The fact that the heat is generated within me somehow protects my skin and keeps it from melting.

The glass in front of me bends and begins to liquefy. It gives the rest of the way under a firm kick delivered by my bloody shoe. No one appears to stop me when I step through the hole I made, and Lucas is nowhere to be seen. The clear path should relieve me, but instead it has the opposite effect, turning the entire office into an elaborate ambush. Once I go into the back office, there's only one way out.

The knob on the Administrator's door is cool underneath my trembling palm and doesn't resist. Inside, Lucas lies faceup on the purple carpet—the sight of him nearly breaks all my resolve. Blood cakes his forehead and left cheek; his eyes sit closed. They are purple and swollen, exactly the way he looked when I touched the Warden. Lucas is still wearing shorts, and the wound in his leg has been dressed. The white wrap smells like decay, and bile rises into my mouth as I fling myself to the floor, gathering his head into my lap.

I run my fingertips over the gash on his forehead, resisting the urge to yell when he flinches away from my touch. I bend and press my lips to his, sobbing when his eyes fly open in surprise. They fill with confusion and pain before they focus on me.

"What are you crying about, you big baby? Does this mean you care?"

I can't stop gasping long enough to conjure a smart remark. It doesn't look like he can see much out of his left eye.

Suspicion rolls over me, trumping relief. "Why are you alone?"

He shakes his head and winces. "Some Wardens and Deshi smacked me around a while ago but they left to take care of something. A Healer's supposed to come work on my leg some more. Apparently Deshi thought the pain would make me talk, but he doesn't want me to die. Yet."

His words set off alarms in my head. "So no one's guarding you?"

As though I invite intrusion with my words, the door to the Administrator's office flies open. I shoot to my feet, ready to fight, but stop at the sight of the Healer.

And Leah.

The Healer stares at us, openmouthed, and works at producing a sentence. The false smile drops from Leah's mouth when she sees Lucas's damaged body. The blood drains out of her face as a disconcerting array of emotions march across it. Confusion. Anger. Sorrow. Fear. Her eyes flick from Lucas, to me, to the Healer and don't stop. I rip my eyes away from her when the Healer gets words out.

"Who are you? Why are you here? Excuse me, I'll have to report this."

"Wait." I cross the room before he can leave. My heart begs me to reconsider. Every cell in my body screams against what I'm planning to do.

Lucas is barely able to sit up. He can't do this; I have to.

The Healer's eyes are wary and slightly panicked at my approach. His gaze flutters to Lucas and indecision registers. Healers don't deal much—or deal at all—with people getting the sense beat out of them. His gaze pulls back to mine and I push away the self-loathing threatening to interrupt, shoving thoughts toward the Healer instead.

You don't want to tell the Others anything. Look at us. We're just kids, nothing suspicious. Help us.

A fascinating change takes place on his lumpy, old-man features. His eyes, emerald and hard, start to focus on my face instead of looking through me. Fear slides in and mixes with confusion. "What am I doing here? Who are you?" He glances around, his fear growing. "Where are we?"

"Calm down. You came because you're a Healer and Lucas needs help." My words don't sink in and his agitation grows. His eyes widen and flash back and forth, reminding me of the night I Broke Mrs. Morgan.

382

Lucas's urgent voice rasps through my growing dread. "Use your mind to calm him down, Althea. I don't think it works when you talk."

I try it and the Healer calms down. He crosses the room to Lucas, opens his medical bag, and pulls out gauze, a bottle of liquid, and a syringe of fluid. He cleans and bandages the cuts on Lucas's face, then studies the gaping wound on his leg. "The pills I gave you earlier broke the fever, but the infection is bad. You need a shot directly into the wound."

Lucas's face contorts as the Healer cleans the gash, then injects the syringe into his leg.

"Will he be able to walk?" I need to know he'll get some strength back soon. We're going to have to run.

The Healer nods, his back still to me as he tends his patient. "Yes. This antibiotic is potent. He should improve in less than ten minutes."

I want to go to Lucas's side but leaving Leah alone seems like a bad idea, given everything she's been through. She's a loose cannon, an unknown entity. Lucas busted her sanity, and the deranged look in her eyes declares she's capable of anything.

The Healer straightens up, handing Lucas a cold pack for his eye. It's been a little less than five minutes, and we can't wait any longer. Five minutes is five minutes too many.

Lucas lurches to his feet, wincing and clutching his midsection. He puts minimal weight on his left leg.

"Can you walk?"

"Don't worry about me. Let's go." He jerks his thumb at the Healer and Leah. "They can't come with us."

"We can't leave him here like this. The Others will Break them." Guilt twists in my stomach. This is why our powers are worthless. They hurt people.

"Well, try to put the veil back up then. Just hurry."

The situation calls for decisive action and fast choices, and I wish Lucas would do it. He's at least tried fixing a veil before.

There's no time to argue, so I turn to the Healer and look into his eyes. I force the voice in my head to sound soothing and calm. *You never saw us. You came to heal Lucas, like they ordered, but he was gone. Everything is fine.*

His eyes glaze back over, staring through me.

Lucas grabs my hand and gives me a tight smile. "You did it. Let's go."

"Wait."

Leah's trembling voice stops us dead. We both turn to look at her, and the desperate tears in her eyes slice me open. Her pleading expression stops me, even though we don't have time to deal with her. "What are you even doing here?"

Her gaze slides toward Lucas, then to the floor. "I saw him earlier, while I was working in the office. I made up an excuse about forgetting my backpack and came to check on him, but the Healer was already here." She takes my free hand. "Please. Please don't leave me like this, half in, half out."

It sounds like she's talking nonsense, but she's not. Not really. Lucas puts a hand on her shoulder, flinching when he puts weight on his bad leg. "Which way do you want to go?"

"Take it out. Them. Take them out."

His eyes meet mine, begging permission. Conflicting voices battle in my mind. "Lucas, I think it would be better to put the veil back up, if we can."

A visible shudder rolls through Leah. "No. No, please. I can't go back. I'll pretend." She drops my hand and steps into Lucas, wrapping her arms around his waist. "Like you. I'll pretend."

Our eyes meet over her jet-black curls, silent conversation ending in a decision.

I nod. "Leah, look at me."

She obeys, turning away from Lucas.

You're Leah Olsen. The Others keep humans in line by controlling their minds. You're different than

385

everyone else now, but you must act the same. You must.

The crazed, cloudy anxiety in her gray eyes evaporates like fog on a warm spring morning. Her gaze is clear and determined. Scared, but a healthy amount. She gasps. "You have to go. Deshi and the Prime mean to take you away."

Lucas squeezes her hand once before letting go.

She wraps me in a fierce, quick hug on our way out of the inner office. "Thank you, Althea."

Our feet trade the silent thick carpet for hard, tiled floor. Lucas stops at the hole in the door, reaching out to touch the edges of the melted glass. He turns to me, eyes wide. "You did this?"

"Yes. Who else do you think did it?"

The amazement in his eyes irks me, like my stupid talent is something to be proud of, when all it's good for is destruction. His eyes grow serious and I get the feeling he knows what I'm thinking.

"Just where do the two of you think you're going, exactly?"

Lucas and I lock eyes, afraid to turn and confront the smooth, honeyed speaker. The clipped tone tells me it's a Warden.

The question is, how many of them are here?

29

"Very interesting, what happened in this Cell tonight. Don't you think, Rahaj?"

Lucas and I whirl together, joined at the hand. Mine is slick with sweat, and turn clammy upon contact with his icy one. Two Wardens stand outside the ruined door, smirking at us. One is tall, taller than anyone I've ever seen.

He speaks again. "Guess the stories are true. Chief is going to be upset he missed this."

The shorter one steps through the hole, pulling his arms tight across his front to avoid touching the melted edges. "Which one of you is the fire-breathing dragon, anyway?"

I have no idea what a dragon is, but with the fire reference, he must mean me. The tall one laughs, planting himself in front of the opening.

We have nowhere to go.

"Are you kidding, Rahaj? The girl is Flacara's daughter. Look at her hair."

For someone else to acknowledge Fire as my mother solidifies the fact in my mind. My stomach feels funny, amazement and loathing fighting for a spot.

The second one squints at me as though he's trying to see someone else in my face. He comes closer and my heart races at the thought of him touching me. The memory of the younger Others talking about liking me—wanting to do things to me—returns with enough force to make me gag. Lucas steps between us at the last moment and the short one's leering face disappears from my vision.

"Get out of the way, boy. Or did you enjoy the beating you took earlier?"

"Don't touch her. If you're going to take us, just get it over with."

"You hear that, Lanej?" I can't see his face as he addresses his cohort. "Sweet, isn't it? Young love?"

The tall one barks a laugh. "Adorable. These humans and their love. Maybe we should tell them what it did to their parents. How the Prime tore their minds apart until they begged to die."

"Move aside, hero," Rahaj leers. "I want a good look at your girlfriend."

Lucas grabs the short Warden's hand and he howls. The sound is unlike anything I've ever heard, deep and guttural. Agonized.

He pulls away from Lucas with some effort, a tearing sound accompanying the split. Lanej runs through the doors to help his cohort.

The two of them are still between us and the exit. Stepping up next to Lucas, my mouth falls open and my stomach heaves at the sight of Rahaj's arm.

It's missing skin. A *huge chunk* of it.

"Lucas." The word rips from my throat. What has he done?

Lucas doesn't answer. He's in some kind of daze. He turns to me and his eyes focus a bit. "Althea. I saw something when I touched him. The room they tortured Ko in. The Prime ordered the Wardens out after us. How did that happen?"

"I don't know. I saw something when I touched one earlier, too. Their minds are connected, like Cadi said."

Lucas snaps out of the dream state faster than I managed to in the hallway, frantically wiping his palm on his shorts. He tugs me closer to the door as Lanej straightens up and sidles back to his position blocking our escape. He looks scared but still unwilling to let us go.

He turns glaring eyes on Lucas. "What did you do? Fix him."

"I can't. I don't know how."

"He froze my skin to his hand and when I pulled away it ripped. . .off. . ." Rahaj attempts to explain but the pain lacing his voice makes his words hard to hear.

My hands itch to cover my ears, to block it out.

Leah's pretty face contorts and she does cover her ears, then drops to her knees in one corner of the back office. The Healer squats beside her, patting her head and looking more confused than ever. They're not going to be any help to Lucas and me, but at least they're safe.

Lanej obscures our path but no longer looks sure he wants to be there. The need to get out overtakes every other emotion stewing inside me. The fear, the pain, the loathing over hurting people. Or even hurting Others.

Pushing it all deep down, I screw up my courage until it sticks. "If you don't want to get hurt like your friend, I suggest you get out of our way. We're leaving."

"No. What are you going to do? You're just a couple of kids." He sounds like he's trying to convince himself. It's probably what Deshi said when he asked them to detain us.

"Really? Why don't you ask your skinless friend over there? I'm guessing you showed up here because of the melted security cameras. How about I do that to your face?"

"You wouldn't dare."

He's no more sure than I am. "Do you want to take your chances or just get out of the way?"

"You can't hide. There isn't anywhere you can go where we can't find you. Don't you want to come with us, find out more about who you are? Meet your parents?" He's baiting me, desperation tingeing his voice.

Those boys who disposed of Mrs. Morgan were so frightened of Deshi. The Prime tortured Ko without remorse, the sick pleasure on his face giving away his enjoyment. The big question at the moment is whether this Warden's fear of punishment from his own kind is enough to trump his fear of us.

He glances at Rahaj, and I follow his gaze. The Warden Lucas hurt has fallen unconscious. His eyes are closed and he slumps up against the wall. In front of my eyes, the flaps of remaining skin grow back toward each other.

He's healing. We have to hurry.

Lanej's features harden as we step toward him. He's going to stand and fight. To be honest, I'd be more scared of the Others than me, too.

My loathing of what I'm about to do intensifies. Lucas lets go of my hand, granting silent permission to take care of the Warden standing in our path.

"Don't go crazy, Althea."

I think of the melted cameras and know what he means. The intensity of heat that melted the door would turn the Warden into a puddle of flesh and bone. A question about what they look like underneath their humanesque costumes tugs my curiosity.

Lanej shrinks back against what's left of the door. His face slackens as he realizes there's nowhere else to go. My fingertips trace along his forearm, the pads heating up one by one.

He screams and jerks, even though the only evidence of my touch is angry red streaks. He's more frightened than anything; he realizes it and lunges for me. Scare tactics alone aren't going to do it.

Lucas strides forward but I beat him to the punch. Wrapping both hands firmly around the Warden's right arm, I let the heat go.

I'm inside his mind. Alarms shriek. I see Ko's torture chamber, like Lucas did. An Other skids in, stops in front of the Prime. *"They've breached the hive."*

The Prime's face twists into a horrid mask of a human face. *"Go get them. Use everyone. Do not underestimate them again."*

Tentacles reach into my brain and probe, cautious but soon dealing a painful jab. I gasp at the explosion of pain, then feel a slap on my cheek.

The Administrative Center reappears. The Warden jerks out of my loosened grip, dropping to the ground in pain. The skin that sat under my palms oozes and drips from the bones of his arm. He joins his friend in some sort of sleep state. I wonder if that's what Deshi did last night, if they heal faster that way.

Lucas holds my face. He's talking. For a second I can't hear, then sounds comes back.

"Althea. I'm sorry I smacked you. You looked. . .you wouldn't come back."

"They know we're here. The Prime is coming. They're all coming. Right now."

The wounds on Lucas's victim have nearly healed. Knowing the damage isn't permanent makes me feel better.

Also worse.

Lucas waits outside the door. His voice is sharp. "Althea. Move."

My body responds to the command in his voice. I step through the melted glass and we move back to the

Cell entrance with swift steps. My last glimpse of the Danbury Administrative Center is an image Leah's clear gray eyes watching me go.

Running isn't an option for Lucas, who still hugs his bruised side and limps. His steps are surer though, and hopefully the antibiotic has begun to work.

Gathered shadows conceal us against the outside of the building. Sirens explode, wailing through the frosty black night. I've heard them before, when they're being tested, but never in use. Tonight they're calling together a search for us.

Three months ago I would never have dreamed of causing physical damage, inflicting mental trauma, or running from the Wardens. Never would have believed that being Something Else meant I'm half Other.

Never would have guessed that animals aren't the most frightening part of this world.

The idea of finding someone like me was still a fantasy, too. I glance sideways at Lucas, taking in his concerned profile. He's worth it.

Lucas turns, meeting my eyes. "We should go. Who knows how long it will take them to get here. We need to get outside the boundary where there's more places to hide. They'll probably look for us in the park first."

Cold sweat soaks my body. "We'll go as fast as you can manage."

I lead the way, stepping onto the sidewalk but staying close to the brick exterior of the building. Lucas keeps up as we race across the street and melt into the trees on the opposite side.

That's when we see them.

Two riders pull up in front of the Cell and ten— no, twenty—Wardens get out. Half go inside the Cell. The rest head toward us. Toward the park.

They know the best place to search for us. At least Deshi never learned exactly where we crawled over the boundary. They'll have to waste some time searching.

Without a word, we hurry ahead of them. My breath explodes in gasps that I work hard to keep quiet. The sound of Lucas's wild inhales pounds in my ears, keeping time with my heart.

The Wardens' footsteps slap the pavement behind us, gaining with each forward motion. Lucas grabs my hand and yanks. I stumble and fall, bringing him down with me. He grunts softly as we hit the dirt, but gathers me in his arms. We roll behind a large clump of holly bushes near the park entrance.

There's no time to voice my irritation as the Wardens jog past less than a minute later. If we'd kept running, they would've caught us. Now they're in the park, roaming around between us and our escape route. Once the sound of their boots slogging through the piles of wet leaves disappears, I turn and whisper to Lucas. "Now what are we going to do?"

He shrugs, then flinches. His face has paled again and shines with sweat. "I don't know. Getting out of sight was the extent of my plan. Wait?"

"Yeah, for how long? It could take hours to search the park, and what if they don't leave? They could just set up along the boundary and wait." I look around, appraising our hiding place. The front of me is already sodden from the damp ground. "These bushes are thick, but they'll find us eventually."

"Have you got a better idea?" He hisses the words, heavy with exasperation.

"Well, excuse me for not wanting to get caught. You know, since we've just seriously injured a bunch of Others and proven beyond all shadow of a doubt that we have powers they'll want to kill us for. And you're welcome for not leaving you behind, by the way."

"Thank you for coming to get me. And for doing what you had to do to get us this far."

The thought of what I've done makes my temples throb.

I change the subject, keeping my voice at a murmur and my ears open for approaching death. "What happened this morning?"

"I don't know. I got dizzy and fell while I was packing. The next thing I knew I woke up at Cell."

"I asked you a million times if you were okay. Why didn't you say something?"

He continues as though he didn't hear me. "I guess the Wardens threw me in the office and let the Healer fix me enough to wake up." Lucas's face screws up like he wants to punch someone. "Deshi showed up and changed into an Other right in front of me. Two Wardens held me down, wouldn't let me fight back while he hit me."

In another time, a different place, the defensiveness in his voice might make me smile.

Anger at the Others bubbles up as I take a closer look at his marred features. I bury it as best as I can. "He's been playing with us for a long time. Are you okay now?"

"I feel better. I'm not going to pass out again, at any rate." Lucas gingerly fingers the cut on his forehead, then pokes the edge of his swollen eye.

"Can you see out of your eye?"

"Quit worrying about me. I haven't felt any pain since I woke up to you kissing me."

My cheeks heat up even though I know he's lying. "Shut up. What do you think, you're charming or something?"

He grins, mouth sitting lopsided because of the swelling. "Tell you what. We get out of this thing alive and I might let you kiss me again."

The statement, meant as a tease, sobers me instead. "Getting out of this thing alive is a big, fat question mark at the moment."

Only the sounds of the icy wind howling through the trees and our even breathing interrupts the silence for several minutes. My watch says it's ten thirty. Light from the streetlamps pools in puddles on the road as my ears strain. I hope the Wardens leave the park soon. As though they hear my silent urging, eleven come into view at that moment. They talk in low voices, words indiscernible until they are almost on top of us.

"They'll turn up. Where could they go?"

"Did you hear what came over the line? What they did to the guys at the Cell? The Prime will not forgive anyone for losing them."

I hold my breath as they pass within four feet of us, arguing about the best course of action. My lungs burn in protest, but I don't let the stale air escape until the Wardens are well out of sight.

Lucas hauls me to my feet. "Let's get out of here."

My legs are stiff and cramping. I limp beside Lucas until the numbness wears off, then trot to keep pace. He seems better, no longer holding his side or grimacing with every step.

Even though the Wardens who entered the park walked back by us, my unease grows as we pass the playground equipment. The trees provide some shelter, as they always have, but not enough with their leaves strewn about the ground. They cast long, spindly shadows in the moonlight.

We make it to the boundary and wind our way around to the spot we can crawl over. I know it like the back of my hand by now, couldn't miss it if I suddenly went blind. Lucas reaches out to grab the fence.

He turns to say something at the last minute, which is why the explosion of pain on his face is so clear when the angry outburst of sparks illuminates the night.

30.

The fence is working.

The truth stumbles through my mind, which is as sluggish and in shock as my body. Lucas flies back from the boundary in slow motion, crumpling to the ground. The light and sparks fade before his twitching body hits with a *thud*. The sound brings me to my senses and I throw myself down beside him for the third time today.

"Lucas! Lucas, answer me!"

He doesn't move, doesn't even a groan this time. In the silence, the sound of footsteps whips my head around. Deshi walks out of the trees and ambles toward us as though he hasn't a care in the world. The marks from last night's burns have faded to pink puckers in less than twenty-four hours.

"Too bad about that. Not sure if he'll wake up this time. Kind of surprised he did after I planted my fist in his face before."

My back leans into Lucas's side; I know there's no way to protect him. "How did you know?"

"What, about where the two of you snuck out?" He shrugs and leans against the nearest tree trunk, crossing his feet at the ankle.

The relaxed pose is odd, false. In a series of seconds, he becomes indistinct, shimmering like the Ko in my necklace, then solidifies into an Other. Tall. Blond hair. Limitless black eyes. Cold cruelty encased in perfection. His star-shaped scar is bigger and an angrier red than I've ever seen, and he has a thick black band around his neck—just like the Prime's, except it's only one line instead of three.

"I didn't, not really. I searched the boundary after I got out of that stream earlier. Cool trick, by the way. Apa would have been proud of his boy. Anyway, I should have figured it out sooner."

"Yeah, well, I guess dealing with your rotting skin suit took up too much of your time."

"Maybe." He slinks toward us.

I swallow my terror to keep it from showing. The sick, twisted smile crawling across his beautiful face tells me I failed. I press my lips together, unwilling to risk revealing any information.

He stops a few feet away and sighs. "It's adorable that the two of you thought you could get away. Interesting though your powers are, you can't kill us. But, oh, how I've enjoyed playing this game with you."

His voice dips deep, dripping hatred. "The storied half-breed children of the Elements. The products of sickening unions. You all deserve to die."

"Why don't you kill us then?"

"My father, the Prime Other, wants you alive." His eyes ferret out the shock on my face. "Oh, you didn't know who you attacked earlier? He wants to know more about your talents in case, you know, it's something we can use. He'll enjoy hurting you for what you did to me. For your parents' betrayals."

He takes another step forward and my hand goes involuntarily to Lucas's shoulder.

"Well, take us then. Or are you too scared?"

He laughs, an eerie, frightening noise. "Of you? Hardly. I saw what you did back at the Cell, and haven't forgotten the temporary setback you dealt me in the Wilds this morning, but I'm a fast learner."

Lucas stirs, and despite the fact that we're dead meat, tears spring to my eyes. "Lucas."

His eyes flutter and then open. He puts a hand to his head and groans, revealing burn marks on his palms. "What happened?"

I don't answer, cutting my eyes at Other Deshi, who keeps coming closer. Lucas's eyes follow and widen in shock and fear. He regains control in a flash and shoots to his knees beside me.

Without warning Deshi's hand snakes out and twists around Lucas's upper arm. He yanks, pulling Lucas toward him on the ground, and then drags him to a standing position by his hair. Deshi holds Lucas like a shield. There's no way I can shoot heat at Deshi and be sure some of it won't graze Lucas. There's a slippery-looking scarf wrapped around Deshi's hands, a barrier between him and Lucas's skin.

Protection from the cold.

At my step forward, Deshi grins and shakes his head. "I wouldn't do that. I believe the Prime would forgive me for killing one of you, as long as the second makes it into custody. I'm not sure I care which one of you it is."

Lucas struggles to get hold of Deshi or escape. This time I wouldn't feel bad about burning someone but there's no clear shot. Lucas's stare holds mine, full of emotion and strength. One last, desperate idea comes to me in an instant. If it doesn't work, we're toast.

We're toast either way, eventually.

I stare at my friend, my kindred, and beg him with my eyes to understand. He struggles to comprehend before realization arrives and he gives a small nod.

My mind performs a frantic search of its contents, trying to find anything that could make it work. We have to use the cold, the heat. . .or the place it comes from.

After tonight, finding the place inside me that generates the heat is easier than I ever expected. Now it swells, and every bad feeling, every happy emotion provided by the past few weeks mixes together in my core. I feel it surge, and try to focus the energy on traveling. If we don't succeed, our lives are over. If we do, we may not be together when we wake up.

You have to touch him.

Stay away from me, Fire, I growl in response.

Ice crystals bead on Lucas's forehead as sweat pours down my face. At the last second I trust my mother and lunge forward, crashing into him. Deshi has his hands, so I press as much of me against him as I can in that split second.

I hear Lucas's voice, already far away. "I'll find you."

The next instant, the world goes dark.

EPILOGUE

My eyes crack, adjusting to the dark room. I'm inside, that much is obvious. That feeling of disappearing, the one that scares me more than anything, presses down, suffocating me. A scream gathers at the back of my throat as I struggle to convince myself I exist.

It works in the nick of time, like always.

I'm in bed. Alone.

The comforter is thick and deep blue. It reminds me of Cadi's eyes when she'd get upset. Without moving, my ears pick up the howling wind rattling the window in its frame.

Sliding my feet into the slippers waiting beside the bed, I make my way over to the window. I collapse onto the cushioned seat and press my forehead to the frosty glass. My breath blows white patterns as the snow swirls outside. It clings to the spindly tree branches and sticks to the ground, deep drifts piling up against the curb. Tears slide down my cheeks.

It's winter. I'm in Iowa. It means, among other things, that Lucas is gone.

He can't come here. I don't even know if he's gotten out of autumn alive. The loneliness, kept at bay by his presence the past several weeks, nips at me like a hungry beast. It will eat me alive before long. There is nothing left to combat it.

I've gone against what I believe and used violence to save us. The Others know who we are, what we look like. They may not know where I am this instant, but it won't take them long to find out.

My locket vibrates against my chest, not as violently as the day Ko popped out but hard enough to make me jump. Nothing appears this time, so with a trembling hand I pull it over my head and open it up. My note is lodged inside, as I expect. I pull it out like always, unfold it with care. The sight of the altered words catches my breath in my throat:

Althea—

Lucas is safe. We will help in any way we can. You need to run.

—Cadi.

Check out the first chapter of the second installment in *The Last Year* on the next page.

Winter Omens is available Sept 25, 2012.

1.

I guess when we travel on our own we don't magically wake up tucked into our beds in clean pajamas. Instead, my filthy shoes grind Danbury dirt into the carpet of my Des Moines bedroom. The same wet, dirty clothes I've worn all day—or yesterday, whenever—cling to my clammy skin. The pride and novelty I felt at finally having control over hopping seasons fills me for a moment, and then vanish quickly as I remember the new note in my locket:

> *Althea—*
> *Lucas is safe. We will help in any way we can. You need to run.*
> *—Cadi*

Desperation over losing Lucas rushes over me as the memory of his dimpled smile, careless blond curls, and protective arms threatens to undo me. I shove it all into my center; giving up is the one way to ensure I'll never see him again.

Cadi says to run, but if I can't stay here with the Clarks, where can I go?

It doesn't matter. She and Ko have never led me astray.

The bag I packed to run away with Lucas is nowhere to be seen, so I fill a new one with the warmest clothes in the closet. Winter is settling in and this is Iowa; it must be freezing outside. Once that's done, I sneak across the beige carpet and crack open the bedroom door, greeted by a silent blackness. The door to the linen closet in the hallway creaks slightly, causing me to wince and freeze. Nothing stirs; not a sound comes from the Clarks' room downstairs. My winter family is asleep, like normal humans after midnight.

I grab three blankets, resisting the urge to take the whole stack, and reposition the rest so a glance won't show that some are missing. The longer no one realizes anything is amiss the better. It won't take them long. The Others are smart and there are only so many places to look.

Back in my room, I assess my options. I take a deep breath as my mother's disembodied voice bursts into my mind, pushing aside my own thoughts.

Run, Althea.

It urges haste, and after the events of the past months I'm not inclined to argue with her.

The blankets barely fit in the bag with the clothes, and after I add some toothpaste, a toothbrush, shampoo, and deodorant to the pile I have to sit on it to tug the zipper shut. Down in the kitchen, I prowl through the pantry and grab as much nonperishable food as I can find in the dark. My fingers race along the shelves, filching cans of vegetables, soup, and a couple bags of pasta. I dump the lot into a second bag and add six bottles of water to the top.

I slip through the empty living room, past photographs of me huddled with the Clarks on Outings to the local skating pond. I'm trussed up like a marshmallow in most of them, head and hands covered with thick woolen garments. They never provide enough warmth. Nothing does. Even though fire simmers inside me, and last autumn I even began to control it a little, I'm always cold. It's as though my center attracts the heat, sucking it inward and leaving my extremities constantly on ice.

My heavy winter coat hangs in the front closet as if I'd left it there after Cell, even though I haven't been back to Iowa for months. I slip it on, finding my hat and mittens in the pockets. My mother's voice grows impatient with my stalling, pressing harder and harder against my mind. The idea of stepping out of the warm house and into the bitter wind, not knowing when I'll find shelter again, fills me with dread.

I have to go, though. I know it deep in my bones. If I can find a place to hide outside the boundary before morning I might even have a chance. Not to escape forever—that's impossible—but to live another day. Maybe even get back to Lucas.

A blast of cold air nearly knocks me over as I crack open the door and my lungs constrict, trying to reject the frigid oxygen. Icy fingers squeeze my chest as I force myself to breathe deep through my nose. Pools of light from the streetlamps don't quite reach the rows of houses, leaving the porch bathed in darkness. The sidewalks are barren as I hustle down the quickest path to the park. Thoughts of Lucas bombard me, pushing tears down my cheeks where they freeze around my mouth and chin. The park reminds me of him, of what happened last night when we almost escaped together. The note says he's safe, but even if he were safe when it was written it doesn't mean he still is. He's going to be running, like me. Hunted. Alone.

The park is full of ominous shadows cast by the bare branches as they sway in the bitter wind. The frozen ground muffles my footsteps as I make my way to the boundary. I've got to get out of the city, but don't know how to accomplish the feat. There's not time to explore every inch of the fence the way Lucas and I did, hoping to find a gap in the electricity. We were able to climb over a dead section of the woven metal, but I found that spot by accident.

I study the electrified ten-foot boundary, at a loss.

Run, Althea. Now! My mother's voice shouts in my mind.

Shut up. I'm thinking. Better yet, go away.

Before last autumn, when I learned that my mother is Fire—an Element, one of the four most powerful Others—the encouraging voice in my mind soothed me. But the idea that she has access to my brain clangs warning bells through me despite the pull toward wanting to know her. Right now, getting out of Des Moines takes precedence over the confliction I feel about my dubious parentage. She's distracting me, and my frozen forehead crinkles as I try to focus on the problem at hand. The fences that border our cities are made of metal, so in theory it could melt, I guess. The high-temperature heat that flows through my body would be more than enough to set a pile of leaves on fire, or even one of my precious blankets. If it burned hot enough under the boundary it could soften a hole big enough to crawl through.

It would leave such an obvious trail, though, that I discard the idea. Damaging the fence isn't an option if I want my fraction of a head start to remain intact.

A memory pummels me, unbidden, accompanied by Lucas's heart-stopping smile:

" . . . *I saw you wandering by yourself near the boundary every day last week.*"

"*You saw me? How?*"

"*From the trees. You never look up, you know.*"

That's it.

Saying silent thanks and wishing he could hear me, I turn my eyes upward and peruse the tree line. Maybe a hundred yards away an ancient oak stands near the electric fence, its thick, leafless branches hovering over freedom, however temporary. I grimace at its height. I've never climbed a tree. In my sixteen-plus years on Earth I've never even *wanted* to climb a tree. But there's no time like the present to figure it out.

I stand underneath it and make an effort to calm the butterflies flapping in my belly. They're nowhere near as uncomfortable as the flock that attacks with Lucas's kisses, but they're annoying all the same. A deep breath helps. The guts to do this are in there. I injured an Other last night. I hid from the Wardens and saved Lucas from the Prime's son, the one they call Chief. I can climb a stupid tree.

A strong toss sends my bags sailing up and over the fence; they land with a dull thud on the opposite side. I turn back and face my new nemesis, stowing my mittens back in my pockets. Oak tree, meet Althea, daughter of Fire. I shall conquer you.

I swipe my red hair out of my face and pull myself up on some low-hanging branches. There are plenty of strong ones within reach, but even though the climb isn't difficult, my limbs shake violently, making it harder than it has to be. Still, the only major problem arises after I crawl out on a long branch to make my escape . . . when I look down.

The ground spins as my fingers clutch the tree, pointed pieces of bark jabbing the tender skin under my nails. I close my eyes and count to ten. When I open them, the world has stopped moving. My knees move inch by inch and, after what feels like hours, I reach the end. The boundary passed under me five feet back. I gauge the distance to the ground. At least twenty feet.

Maybe I didn't quite think this through.

Voices filter through the still night and freeze me in place. Men. Several, by the sound of it. I can't see their perfect faces or feel the stabbing pain that accompanies the sight of them, but their tones are melodious and sweet, oozing across my eardrums like globs of maple syrup.

Others.

Probably Wardens. A quick peek over my shoulder reveals weak flashlight beams penetrating the inkiness.

Their appearance makes up my mind, and I jump.

ACKNOWLEDGEMENTS

I've been incredibly lucky to be surrounded with a team of people far more insightful and detail-oriented than myself, and who helped make this book better than I ever could have on my own. Huge thanks to my editor, Danielle Poeisz, for all of your hard work. You went above and beyond the call of duty, and without your creativity and questions this story would not have blossomed into something better. Thank you for taking it on and for being excited. Also thanks to my sharp-eyed copy editor Lauren Hougen and Nathalia Suellen, who designed and crafted this beautiful cover.

I'd like to thank Wes Samson for being the first non-family member to read my writing and not laugh out loud, even though the piece you read deserved more than one derisive snort. If you *had* deemed my aspirations ridiculous, this book may never have come to fruition. Thank you for that, and for the reminder that no matter how brief a time a person spends in your life, they can still make a difference.

Thank you to my entire family—all of the Martins, Ziegenhorns, Heinrichs, Ingstads, Tylers, Wearns, and Dickinsons (and everyone else, too)—without a family like you holding a net of support and love, I'd never have had the courage to try. The possibility of failing didn't scare me because I'll always have you, and not everyone is so lucky.

To my fellow writers who critiqued for me on this, especially Eisley, Trieb, Ali, Bill, and Beth. Your feedback and encouragement (and yes, Trieb, even your acid tongue) were an invaluable contribution to this story. Rachel, Lissa, and Mom, your proofreading skills are magical and the perfect way to make sure I look as smart as possible.

All of the love to Denise Grover Swank, esteemed author, critique partner, paver of roads, cheerleader, wine connoisseur, and friend—not only would this book not be published without you, I would be rocking in the corner of a padded room shrieking nonsense. You've helped me improve my writing, understand this business, and retain my sanity. I cannot thank you enough.

I owe a great debt to the real Althea, who loaned my character not only her awesome name but her indomitable spirit. And to my teenage beta readers, Julia, Kerstin, and Anthony, for reading, for being so excited, and for attempting to keep me young and in touch.

Sumer, Alison, Brooke, and Karen—non-writer friends who laugh with me, push me out into the world, and stay friends with me even though I'm weird. I wouldn't be the girl who wrote this story without each of you in my life.

Andrea, my best friend for over twenty years. We've laughed, and cried, and seen each other at our ugliest, most vulnerable, and possibly insane moments. I take our friendship for granted sometimes, but I don't even want to think about the last twenty years, or the next fifty, without you in my life.

My Twitter friends, who have taught me, supported me, laughed with me, and encouraged me through this entire process—I never would have made it without you. In particular, thanks to Dan Krokos, Sean Ferrell, Bill Cameron, Gary Corby, Steve Ulfelder, and Jeff Somers, who have talked me down off ledges, lent humor when the situation called for it (and also when it didn't) and were some of the first people to make me realize that other writers were rooting for my success.

Last but certainly not least, to my parents and sister, who have grown many gray hairs watching me make the wrong decisions, start down wrong paths, too many times to count. I appreciate your love, your support, and your willingness to let me figure out life on my own terms more than I can ever say. I think we're finally on the right track.

ABOUT THE AUTHOR

Raised by a family of ex-farmers and/or almost rocks stars from Southeastern Iowa, Trisha Leigh has a film degree from Texas Christian University. She currently lives in Kansas City, MO. *Whispers in Autumn* is her first novel, and she's hard at work on the remainder of the series. Her spare time is spent reviewing television and movies, relaxing with her loud, loving family, reading, and being dragged into the fresh air by her dogs Yoda and Jilly.

To learn more about Trisha Leigh, please visit her at trishaleigh.com.

34238542R00233